THE SHADOW OVER PORTAGE & MAIN

The world inside these *Shadows* is a dangerous place to be. For one thing, it's terribly dark in there, and the darkness itself is horrible and unsettling. I urge you to take care. I suggest that you don't look up the photographs that will steal more than just your soul. And I wonder if it's wise to browse through this monstrous bookstore. And dear, if you think you're about to experience a peaceful morning in the country, I think you might be wrong. There are curious uses for corpses in this world. And some really, really bad healthcare that is not for the weak or easily distressed. If you are up to the unwholesome journey this book will take you on—I highly suggest you bundle up and keep a light handy. This darkness bleeds. And if it bleeds, I reads. You should too.

—SUSIE MOLONEY, author of *Things Withered*, stories, *The Thirteen*, *The Dwelling*, *A Dry Spell*, and *Bastion Falls*

THE SHADOW OVER PORTAGE & MAIN

Weird Fictions

edited by
Keith Cadieux and Dustin Geeraert

ENFIELD
&WIZENTY

Enfield & Wizenty
(an imprint of Great Plains Publications)
233 Garfield Street
Winnipeg, MB R3G 2M1
www.greatplains.mb.ca

Great Plains Publications gratefully acknowledges the financial support provided for its publishing program by the Government of Canada through the Canada Book Fund; the Canada Council for the Arts; the Province of Manitoba through the Book Publishing Tax Credit and the Book Publisher Marketing Assistance Program; and the Manitoba Arts Council.

Design & Typography by Relish New Brand Experience
Printed in Canada by Friesens

LIBRARY AND ARCHIVES CANADA CATALOGUING IN PUBLICATION

The shadow over Portage and Main / edited by Keith Cadieux and Dustin Geeraert.

ISBN 978-1-927855-36-2 (paperback)

1. Winnipeg (Man.)--Fiction. I. Cadieux, Keith, 1982-, editor
II. Geeraert, Dustin, 1983-, editor

PS8323.W56S53 2016   C813'.010806   C2015-908669-8

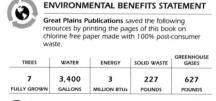

ENVIRONMENTAL BENEFITS STATEMENT

Great Plains Publications saved the following resources by printing the pages of this book on chlorine free paper made with 100% post-consumer waste.

TREES	WATER	ENERGY	SOLID WASTE	GREENHOUSE GASES
7	3,400	3	227	627
FULLY GROWN	GALLONS	MILLION BTUs	POUNDS	POUNDS

Environmental impact estimates were made using the Environmental Paper Network Paper Calculator 3.2. For more information visit www.papercalculator.org.

Canadä

FSC
www.fsc.org

MIX

Paper from
responsible sources

FSC® C016245

TABLE OF CONTENTS

THERE IS A THING THAT SHOULD NOT BE, SO WE MUST BE IN WINNIPEG

Jonathan Ball

"Why is Winnipeg so gothic and dark?"

This was not a question I had expected to answer, not something I prepared myself to answer, in the oral defense of my Master's thesis. I don't remember what I said. I had written a screenplay adaptation of E.T.A. Hoffmann's classic horror story, "Der Sandmann," as a creative thesis, and the question came from my external examiner, Cliff Eyland. Whatever I said satisfied him enough to move on to a different question, more on point. But now I didn't care about those other questions.

Now I wanted to know why Winnipeg was so gothic and dark.

———•·•———

Winnipeg is so gothic that people actually use the phrase "Winnipeg Gothic" to refer to, in Eyland's words, Winnipeg's "part of a much wider gothic-influenced scene, [which] shares Romantic, Freudian, and popular horror film and fiction influences with a much wider world of art." In an article on Jillian McDonald's video project REDRUM,[1] Eyland references a Gallery One One One exhibition, "The Gothic Unconscious," curated in 2003/04 (a year after my successful defense) by Sigrid Dahle.

Many of the artists Eyland lists as exemplifying or otherwise connecting to this haphazard aesthetic best described as "Winnipeg Gothic" also appear on my personal list of influences: Guy Maddin, Ivan Eyre, Diana Thorneycroft, Rob Kovitz, and the Royal Art Lodge. (I would add filmmakers Jeffrey Erbach and Solomon Nagler.) If "Winnipeg Gothic" means anything, it means that these artists with gothic sensibilities connect an atmosphere of threat, gloom, death, and despair to the urban environment of Winnipeg.

In *My Winnipeg*, for example, Guy Maddin spends a good deal of time talking about The Forks, that meeting place of two rivers, and claims that there are also two ghostly, subterranean rivers underneath them, which also happen to fork together in the same place. This makes Winnipeg, and The Forks, a dangerous place of magical, chthonic power. Since The Forks was traditionally considered a meeting place not just for the two rivers but also for the First Nations, Maddin's film plays into horror tropes about the dangers of constructing your home (in this case, a settler city) on top of an aboriginal burial ground.

Even discounting Maddinesque myth-making, Winnipeg seems ripe for horror. More than any other Canadian city, it conforms to the tropes of the horror story's "bad place." Winnipeg is Canada's "murder capital" (so-named for, most years, claiming the nation's

1 Cliff Eyland, "Here's Jillian," http://www.umanitoba.ca/schools/art/content/galleryoneoneone/mcdonald01.html

highest per-capita homicide rate) and thus a place of violence, both personal (murder) and systemic (at the time of writing, *Maclean's* stirred up national controversy by decreeing Winnipeg the "most racist city in Canada," citing alarming statistics).[2] Winnipeg's environment itself is deadly, monstrous even—as I write this, it's a balmy -31 degrees Celsius ... *before* the wind chill. (And it's morning now. While I slept, in the darkness, we reached -42. One colder day, almost a decade ago now, I went to unplug my car in the morning and the extension cord snapped like a twig.) Winnipeg is not just a place of cold, but a place of fire—with alarming arson rates—and a city that seems like a small town, with barely three degrees of separation between any two people, thus allowing it to play into both urban and small town horror tropes. Add to this Winnipeg's ruined landscape, gothic in its decaying architecture. A place famous for its ghosts, for bygone glory.

Most of all, its isolation. Winnipeg, the bad place that you can't escape. The perfect place to die.

———•—•———

I was once asked, for a documentary on the Winnipeg filmmaker John Paizs and his 1985 masterpiece *Crime Wave*, why Winnipeg seemed to breed so many strange, experimentally minded filmmakers. My response there seems to apply here: because Winnipeg is a city without hope.

Winnipeg is fate. It dooms its artists to obscurity, to failure, before they have begun. And so, ironically and paradoxically, it breeds artists who don't even bother to try to succeed, and thus don't water down their art to make it more marketable (it's impossible to

2 Macdonald, Nancy, "Welcome to Winnipeg: Where Canada's racism problem is at its worst," http://www.macleans.ca/news/canada/welcome-to-winnipeg-where-canadas-racism-problem-is-at-its-worst/

market, since it's from Winnipeg)—and can therefore succeed, in an artistic sense if not a commercial one.

Winnipeg the ruin, Winnipeg of the haunted past, Winnipeg of murder and flames. Winnipeg of cold and death, Winnipeg of the hopeless, Winnipeg the doomed. It seems significant that so many of the writers in this anthology, which proclaims to feature stories inspired by Winnipeg, don't bother to offer any actual indication within the stories that they are set in Winnipeg. Few of them mention Winnipeg, or mention any Winnipeg landmarks.

Why bother? It all goes without saying. Since there is horror here, and since the horror cannot be stopped, since hope is gone and the world is a nightmare of chaos, we must be in Winnipeg.

BODY WITHOUT ORGANS

David Annandale

Some ghosts are *very* old.

———•••———

Not that Trent knew from ghosts. They weren't something he thought about. He certainly wasn't thinking about them now. He was wondering what Geena was going to think about his day's work. He was waiting for her in the coffee shop, nursing a cup. It was a regular coffee, not gourmet, and black. It wasn't a strict preference. If someone offered him anything, he'd take it. But when he ordered coffee on his own, it never occurred to him to go for anything but the bare minimum.

Geena arrived just after five, her face stung red by Winnipeg's January winds. She ordered her coffee, then carried it over to the table. Trent peered at the cup while she slid out of her winter coat. The coffee was a greenish brown.

"What's that?" he asked.

"Sumatran." She sat down. "I don't have a lot of time. I'm meeting someone for dinner."

"Do I know her?"

"Him. No."

And there, he'd lost the match before it had even begun. Something bumped inside his chest, and it was very close to pain. He looked at her face, and her eyes reflected winter back at him. Well, what had he expected?

"I saved someone's job today," he said, going through the motions anyway, as he always did.

Geena sipped her coffee, saying nothing.

He forged on, getting it done. "Brenda Connelly. I don't think you ever met her. Dan wanted to let her go. He thinks Julia can handle accounts on her own. I talked him out of it."

"Why?"

"Brenda's a single mother. She doesn't make much as it is. It would be pretty hard—"

"No," Geena interrupted. "Why did *you* do it?"

"I don't know what you mean."

"Yes you do. Did you think what Dan was doing was wrong?"

Well, not really. It made business sense, and it was his business, after all. But Trent knew that wasn't the right answer, so he said nothing.

"Did you feel badly for Brenda?"

Don't answer that one either.

"So why did you do it? And why tell me?"

She wasn't asking any questions he could answer without making things worse.

"You can't have me back, you know."

Oh. So she knew anyway. "I know." He kept his eyes on his mug.

"No, I don't think you do. And what I don't understand is why you want me."

"I…" The words disappeared into the opaque fog in his heart.

"You don't love me. You never did." Her voice sounded gentle now, and Trent risked a look at her eyes. The frost was gone, but there was still no warmth for him there. Instead, now there was pity.

I want to love you. (What he would say if he could tell her the truth, if he could understand what was going on himself.) *I need to love you. I could learn.* (Oh, really? But that wasn't anywhere good enough, now was it?) Again, "I…" was all he could get out.

"Don't try to be something you're not," Geena said. "It's not going to do either of us any good. I'm not going to pretend that I understand why you think you want me back, but I suppose I'm flattered." She finished her coffee. "I have to go." She stood up and pulled on her coat. "I don't know what you were expecting, but…" She seemed slightly at a loss herself. "Do take care of yourself," she finally said. "And I'm glad you saved Brenda's job. Bye."

And with that, she was gone. Trent said nothing, but watched her go, his hands tightening around his mug of cold coffee. As she stepped out the door, Trent felt something rise in his chest. It wasn't sorrow or loss or desire or anger, but something that felt almost like panic. Panic that he *wasn't* feeling any of those things, and that he was seeing his last chance disappear into the snow.

But even that panic was something. It felt as if the fog inside him were coalescing, and if he followed the impulse, maybe things would go all the way, and he might even know tears. He jumped up, grabbed his parka and hurried outside.

He collided with an elderly man. "I'm sorry," he said, and distractedly helped the man up. He scanned the street for Geena. She was gone, swallowed by the evening.

The old man was still standing right beside him. Trent looked at him. The man was terrified. He was staring at Trent with deer-in-the-headlights eyes. After a moment, as if finally getting his body to obey, he backed away from Trent, trembling. Three steps, mouth open, lips trying to shape denial, and then the man turned and ran.

Trent blinked. He glanced at his reflection in the window of the café. Nothing wrong he could see. He looked back at the fleeing figure. His puzzlement dispersed whatever had been forming inside. Epiphany or emotion, it all dissolved back into the aimless fog. What chance he might have had to really, honestly *feel* something passed, putting him back into the calm limbo he had known all his life. Everything settled, except for the small, niggling claw-twitch of anxiety that had been growing all week.

Trent turned out all the lights so he could see the snow fall. He stood at his apartment window, twenty storeys above the Wellington Crescent drifts. He sipped a glass of wine and let his mind roll over the puzzles of the day while he watched the snow whirl, a shredded white aurora, through the orange glow streetlights of the bridge and down to the river. When the odd car still on the road at three in the morning crossed the bridge, it would catch the flakes in its beams, a vortex of fireflies.

Trent wasn't quite as calm as he had thought. He still felt restless. That wasn't much, but anything at all was very unusual, and it put him off his steady stride. He still didn't know what, if anything, he was feeling. It was too free-floating, a shapeless nudge that kept him awake but couldn't decide what it wanted to become. And what had all that been about at the coffee shop? It had been so out of character he hardly recognized himself. He wasn't sure what puzzled him more: his or the old man's behaviour.

Trent shrugged and raised his glass. The wine was almost finished, and as he tilted his glass to sip, he saw his snow scene fish-eyed and filtered red. It looked like a child's snow globe filled with blood.

In the first moment, he liked the effect. In the second, he found it a little unnerving. In the third, he wondered if it were really possible for him to be seeing so much detail. In the fourth, he lowered the glass and saw that the lights had gone out.

The entire city was blacked out. He couldn't see the snow anymore. He glanced down into the dark where his hand held the wine glass. He felt temptation but followed an instinct that knew better. He did not look through the red again. He bent down to put the drink on the floor. Then he straightened and stared out at the city.

His eyes adjusted. Other colours began to shade and shape the wall of black: the moon's light diffused by the clouds, the frozen river glowing blue with the nightshine of snow.

Power failures happened in the winter. He knew this. He'd experienced them. But he had never seen the grid go down across the entire city before. There was no light anywhere in Winnipeg. The orange that always smeared the night was gone.

Then the snow began to bother him. He still couldn't see it, but he felt it brush against the windows like invisible down. Its presence tickled him, and he couldn't scratch. After a minute, he backed a couple of steps away from the window. He didn't like the sense of being naked to the gaze of something coming down, touching the pane, dancing and twisting in ways he thought he knew but couldn't see.

The phone rang as he turned away from the window.

Trent stood still. He stared in the direction of the sound, eyes wide and useless. His phone should not ring. It was touch-tone and trilled. But it was ringing now. Torn between two instincts this time, he followed the one that feared ignorance. He felt his way toward the noise.

He picked up the receiver just before a ring. But then the phone rang again anyway. He held the receiver, letting himself be scared over and over by the ringing. *Ringing.* He lifted the receiver (weighing a ton) to his ear, and the ringing stopped with an inaudible, but felt, click.

"Hello?" He had to keep up some sort of pretence of the normal.

The line was dead. He was about to hang up when he began to hear static. It was barely perceptible at first, scattered faint crackles down a long black tunnel. Then it grew louder, until the crackles were snowflakes in a blizzard, thrown by the shouting wind. Trent's fist tightened on the receiver, which was becoming slippery with his sweat.

The static broke itself into words. There was no voice, but there were words. Slow words, hissing and buzzing, "Whisper me killing you."

Trent slammed the receiver down, but the air resisted and his hand moved with fatal slowness. When he at last let go of the stilled phone, he felt a despair and a fear. He despaired, because he *was* finally feeling something, and this was not what he had had in mind at all. And he feared, because it seemed that a transfer had been completed.

———•◦•———

It was almost one when Trent woke up. His head was pulsing, sending out flashes of pain. The ache made his mouth go dry. He lay in bed and tried to think through the pain.

He couldn't remember going to bed. He couldn't understand how he could have gone to sleep at all after being so frightened.

Ah, now that. He sat up slowly, wincing in the sunlight that speared him through his thin bedroom curtains. He rubbed his forehead. So what about last night, then? Memory or dream? The more he thought about it, the more it had all the earmarks of nightmare.

He was in bed. He had his water glass on his bedside table. He could see that his clothes were folded on a chair. This was all habit, all normal. If what he remembered were true, he would not be waking up like this.

Okay. Good. That settled it. He reached for his water to ease his closed and stinging throat.

There was no water glass.

Trent's hand floated over the bedside table. His fingers wavered, twitched. He jerked his hand back and held it close to his chest, protecting it. He was sure he'd seen—

Well no. Obviously he hadn't. He had expected to, had been so sure of the glass's presence that his mind had conjured a wrong sight. So there. *Get a grip.*

But that wasn't good enough. He showered and dressed, and couldn't do so quickly enough. He had to get to the office. It was Saturday today, and no one else would be there, but he had to leave his apartment. There was something wrong. He hoped it was just his headache. But it was as if an oily film had settled over the place. The air and the light were just slightly off-kilter. His sofa, his table, his chairs, his carpet—now they were *the* sofa, *the* table, *the* chairs, *the* carpet, no longer his. As if he had suddenly learned that a death had once occurred here, and everything was now covered by the slick of strange.

He left his building, stepping point-blank into thirty below. He blinked in sunlight hard and bright as broken glass. He took a deep breath, feeling the air rush in and hurt his lungs with ice crystals. It felt good. Cold and pure and scouring. Sterilizing. He smiled into a reality as hard as it was cold...

... and brittle. As he grew used to the cold, he detected a faint plastic aftertaste to the air. It wasn't much. He could almost ignore it. But it was enough to tighten his shoulder muscles again. *Just the headache,* he told himself. *This is called being under the weather.* He trudged over to the underground parking entrance to get his car.

It happened twice. Once just as he stepped into the garage, and once as he walked from his car to the office. And this is what happened: something blurred and moved in his peripheral vision. Dark fuzzy grey, a touch of something wrong with the picture. And both times that he jerked his head around to see, there was, of course, nothing there.

Collier & Associates was in one of the refurbished buildings in Winnipeg's Exchange District. He sat in his office, protected by fluorescence, and stared out at the warehouse across the way. His head had settled down from its pounding throb. The air in here tasted fine. The office furniture was slightly cold and foreign to his touch, but he could deal with it. *This is fine*, he thought. *This is great. But I can't stay here forever. How do I go home?* And all the while, a part of him marvelled at the wonder of experiencing fear.

Two hours later he was trying to get some work done, trying to lose himself in the tensions and fears of a world he understood. He leaned back and rubbed his eyes. When he looked down at the papers again, the light was flickering. Shadows were fluttering over the pages with the beat of moth wings. He looked up. The fluorescents overhead were vibrating grey. He braced himself, then swivelled his chair around.

The far offices had gone dark. The light failure was making its way up the corridor towards him. It took only a single coldsweat minute, and electricity was gone.

He forced himself to breathe, forced himself not to run screaming, at least until his eyes could see once more. Light came in from the window, but it wasn't enough, and the warehouse blocked out the sky. Inside the office, it was twilight. Silhouettes and shadows.

Trent stood up from his chair. *Do this carefully*, he thought. *Rush around and fall down and you'll be doing exactly what it wants.* It was the first time he had thought of an enemy, a sentient victimizer, a thing with desire. But he could no longer believe in the comfort of hallucinations, or in the perversions of Manitoba Hydro. No, the terrible magic he was living was the production of something's desire.

He took each step slowly, weaving his way around chairs and desks. He was not going to bump anything that would make the silhouettes and shadows move. He reached the coat rack, took his parka down (the stand did not wobble) and put it on, keeping to a minimum the whisperswish of nylon as his arms went through the sleeves.

He was stepping into the corridor when he heard something shift behind him. He looked back before he could stop himself. Even after all his care, one of the shadows was moving. It had no silhouette, but it held the potential for legion. It moved with dry grace, slow and vague, hard to make out but enough to send him running.

He knew it was a mistake, or the part of him that wasn't screaming did. He knew that panic was only going to speed everything up. He ran anyway, shoes sliding on marble, hands banging and holding banisters. He almost broke his neck clattering down the stairs to the street. He needed to be out; he needed to be where the shadows could not turn off the light.

But as soon as he was outside, Trent realized that he was wrong again. Night was when the sun was shut off, and this was January, and the dimmer switch was already well turned by this time of the afternoon.

He ran to his car. Just in time, he sensed its hostility, felt its desire, knew that it had been taken over, and stopped himself from touching it. He kept his eye on the car (*not his, gone over*), and took each backward step deliberately. He was not going to slip on the ice in the parking lot, and he was not going to turn his back on this vehicle. But the car's desire was not fully its own. The car was plugged into whatever was coming after him, and was conducting the desire. It had turned into a live electric cable.

Then he heard the shift behind him again, and he was running.

He slipped once. As he stumbled, his head jerked to one side, and he caught a glimpse of something. It was sticking to the shadows. It wasn't a soft, black, pulsing egg. It wasn't a shambling, ragged man. But it could have been either.

He ran three blocks at random. The streets were not empty, but the cold had most people indoors or in cars. The panhandlers walking the sidewalks were no comfort. In his fear, they were plugged in too.

He stopped to catch his breath. His lungs hurt, but he liked that the hyperventilation kept him from hearing any subtle scrapes of claws against cement. He was about to start running once more, still aimless, when he noticed a sign in a lit second-floor window of the building he was leaning against: PSYCHIC READINGS. Hand-lettered, yellowed and curling. The coincidence was right. Grasping the straw, he ran to the building's main door.

The corridor lights did not dim as he took the stairs two at a time. He'd built up a slight lead.

The door to the psychic's was open. Trent stumbled in, chest heaving. And there he was. Of course. The old man from yesterday. He was sitting at a card table near the window, a book at his elbow. There was another folding chair opposite him, a sofa in the middle of the room, but no other furniture. Nor could Trent see any beads, crystal balls or incense sticks.

"Hello," said the old man. His voice was soft and dry, almost chalky. He didn't appear to be frightened today. He sounded resigned.

"There's something after me," said Trent. The sentence was simple, true, and somehow made his terror all the worse for being so. No one, he thought, should ever have to say such a thing.

The old man nodded. "Come and sit down."

Trent did. As he sat, he saw the psychic turn a terrible pale. An old fear, unblunted by familiarity, was pushing the resignation aside. His eyes, pouched and haggard, seemed to pull away deeper into his face. "Why always me?" the old man whispered.

"What is it?" Trent asked. He felt ready to cry, but the tears would have been no achievement at all. Their time had passed.

"I don't want to tell you if I'm wrong," the psychic said.

"Is it bad?"

The psychic didn't answer at first, but Trent saw tears in his eyes, too. "I want you to think carefully about what I'm going to ask you. Answer honestly. All right?"

Trent nodded.

"Have you ever wanted anything?"

Trent blinked. "I beg your pardon?"

"Do you experience desire?"

"Well of course I—" *No. Tell the truth.* That was what yesterday had been about: not wanting Geena, but wanting to want her, wanting to want for the first time in his life, but the impulse was too little and too late. Of course he experienced desire now, when the deadline had passed. He desperately wanted the character he had never had.

He was honest. "No."

The old man sighed. "You're being haunted."

"Haunted or hunted?" He wasn't being clever. He had to know which it was, and which was worse.

"Haunted is both now," said the psychic.

"Is it a ghost?"

"Yes."

"But I haven't hurt anybody. I haven't killed anybody. My apartment is new and—"

The psychic was shaking his head. "This isn't that kind of ghost. It's much older. It's so old that it would have forgotten what it was before, only it never even had that. It haunts us all, but it can get at some of us more easily than others. It's been getting more and more people, lately."

"I don't understand."

The old man sighed. His fingers brushed the cover of the book. Its spine was cracked, its pages curling and folded. A *Thousand Plateaus*, the title read. "It isn't easy to explain. Imagine a body that isn't a body, that is only potential. It has never lived; it has never been marked by all the paths of existence. Unborn, unconceived." He folded his hands. "Now listen: all our desires, our ideas, everything we make, are machines that we plug into the body. We write on it. And though it hasn't lived, by changing it we kill it. But its past, its ghost, does live. Do you understand at all?"

Trent thought that he did. With his mind's eye, he saw a black, swirling mist of a memory rising up, created by the destruction of something that had never been. "Why is it after me?"

"You have no desire. You have only plugged in dead machines. It smells death, and it conducted itself along those cold lines to you. You have approached the original state. You have a shape, but you have no organs. Not really. It is going to take your shape from you."

The psychic sat back. Some fire had sparked in his eyes as he spoke, but now Trent saw him wither again. His speech had sounded odd, rehearsed. Old. As if it had been said so many times it had worn a groove in the man's mind and was now no more than a force of habit.

"How do you know all this?" Trent asked. He sensed he was just following the groove a bit further. His words tasted dusty.

"I don't know." The man's voice was drained melancholy, as if sadness were the only real emotion he had left. But when he spoke again, Trent heard a certain richness of terror. "I am given knowledge for my sins, whatever they might be. I keep trying to run too, you know. But you, people like you, keep finding me."

"What can I do?" Trent decided to trace the groove to the end.

The old man turned his face with its guttering eyes away. He watched the darkening outside as if it were a growing tomb. His cheek was wet. "Go home." He shrugged.

Light flickered.

—·•·—

Trent took the bus back to his apartment. The bus moved, was lit against the night, and was full of people. Still, by the time the bus reached Wellington Crescent, Trent could see something huddled at the back, nodding with the shadows that snuck in from outside. Trent tried not to panic, tried to be resigned, but it just wasn't right, and wasn't fair, and he ran anyway, all the way from the stop to an apartment that was no longer a home.

He didn't turn the lights on. He wanted to say goodbye to them, but he didn't think he could face seeing them stolen from him again. So he sat down in an armchair with its back against a wall, and waited.

He was exhausted. He didn't want to run anymore. He was ready to give up. But still, he shivered. Still, his heart beat the dance of his terror. Still, when something moved toward him, he moaned.

Outside, it was snowing again. He heard the wind pick up and press the snow against the window so it could see inside. He could not see out. His view was blocked by the ghost as it rose and reached for him with the flow of shadows.

"Will it hurt?" he sobbed. It had spoken once. Wouldn't it tell him this one thing?

No. Something dry brushed his face.

"Will it hurt?" he shrieked.

"*Will it hurt?*"

It did.

KEEP YOUR PANTS ON

John Stintzi

If he'd been asked to describe the feeling in his innards when he awoke with his brain painfully pulsing, he'd have said that it was the consistency of dead worms, as if he'd been eating refried beans but the chewed pieces leaked through the walls of his intestines instead of being digested.

She was lying beside him, facing away and curled toward the edge of the bed. His whole head pulsed, as though his heart had exiled itself there and was beating his brain against his skull, trying to make room. He was naked, and he hoped that she was too. He leaned slowly over to see if he'd made a terrible mistake. His brain screamed at the movement. He couldn't see her face very well, but from what he gathered, he hadn't done poorly. He'd done worse sober.

He slowly sat up in bed and instinctively put his head in his hands. He checked it all round, as he always did when hungover, to make sure that the horrible pain wasn't the result of some sort of trauma.

His mind, and his short brown hair, seemed to be in disorder. Yet his head was connected to his neck, and everything else seemed to follow. His brain felt like it belonged to someone else, someone bigger, though crammed in nonetheless and trying to escape.

The apartment was one small room with a bathroom, all hiding beneath a mess. It was a windowless studio apartment, which, as far as he knew, may have even been a dormitory. Was it underground? There were clothes scattered everywhere, from the chipped-paint burgundy door to the Formica kitchen cabinets. The fabric layer made the already small apartment seem not only tinier, but softer, as if he were waking up in a cluttered hamper. It smelled lightly of the muted body odour that clung to the dirty clothes. He tried to remember what he'd worn the night before, looking at the Technicolor coating of clothes, but he couldn't even remember his own name let alone recognize how he'd been dressed. There were so many possibilities, but his mind refused to focus itself on any in particular. His clamouring head relished its moment to be blurred.

He stumbled up, woozy. He grabbed hold of the bedpost through the cup of a slung brassiere and let his sluggish mind ascend back to his brain.

Slowly, he made his way to the bathroom. She stayed in the bed. He wanted Tylenol. He looked in the medicine cabinet and—among a selection of feminine things he didn't like seeing in his dizzy state— he found some. He popped two and bit a half off another, just to get a bit more. He stuck his face in the sink to guzzle up some water from the squat tap.

When he lifted his head up the girl was already hurling in the toilet.

"Good morning," he said, seeing her reflection in the mirror. The puke was purple. What had she been drinking?

"Morning," she said, wiping her mouth and resting her head against her arm, which sat on the lip of the toilet. She gave a pathetic smile. She wasn't bad at all. She wasn't gaunt, had enough flesh to emphasize her figure, and was well proportioned for a girl. Her hair was long, bright brown, natural. Some of it had trickled into the purple toilet water.

"Can I get you something? Some water? A piece of gum?" He chuckled a bit at the weariness of her and how she was trying to seem like everything had been worth it in the end. "Half a Tylenol?" he said, stretching his hand forward. She quickly went back to hurling. "A shotgun, maybe?"

After a bit, she stopped and looked up at him without turning her head.

"The latter would be fine," she said, one hand on her gut. "That, or some water and Tylenol."

"On it," he said, walking back out as she sat in her prayer stance above the purple holy water, back arching in sacrifice. He went slowly, cautious of his feet. No matter if you're a drinker or a sober saint, he thought, you must always look out for your feet.

He pushed his way through the layers of clothes. He grabbed a glass from the sink in the kitchenette and filled it up with water. He drank it down, kept it down, and then refilled one for her.

After another fit in the bathroom he heard her moan, "Oh god…"

"I'm on my way!" he said, trying to fill the apartment with enthusiasm, but the acoustics were terrible and it all dissolved into the soft clothing flood. He went to her very slowly. In his state, all his concentration was necessary to make sure he didn't topple the water onto the clothes, while at the same time keeping an eye out for his feet. They sank into the ground slowly, and he worried about what might be hidden.

Her hurling stopped just before he turned into the bathroom. She was reclining against the wall, watching him with a new pathetic look on her face. Her hand was still on her belly, but now beneath it was a slight bulge which, he thought, had not been there before. The rest of her almost appeared to be thinner.

"Help," she whimpered.

He hurried as much as he could to the Tylenol. His brain was abused and playing tricks and she was just sick. But he watched her belly and tried to think of the few things he knew about bellies, just in case. He thought maybe internal bleeding. He looked into the toilet and he saw that the water was still purple, but nearing the red end of the spectrum. Perhaps it was that.

"Jesus," he said, lowering himself beside her and handing her three Tylenol. "Does it hurt?"

"No," she said, looking down weakly. "Not exactly."

"Do you feel dizzy or anything?" He looked up from her belly and got a look that was downright slapping.

"Do you?" she said.

His eyes darted from hers. He, too, reddened. "That's a stupid question."

He handed her the water and she slowly took it down with the pills.

"What does it feel like?" he said, looking again at the belly. "Is it soft? Like… fat?"

"No," she said, moving her hand away from it. She expected him to touch it. He reached out with a finger and poked it quickly. It was tight like pumped muscle.

"Jesus."

"Word of the day," she said, chuckling and then pulling a face and weakly trying to get to the toilet. What came out splashed against the rim and spattered them both. It was only liquid, clear and purpley-red. He still felt bad for her.

"Shit," he said, standing up and wetting a facecloth. He went over to her and began to wipe her clean, starting with her legs.

"Help."

He said nothing, looking up to her face. Her head was tilted backwards and leaning against the wall as if all the muscles in her neck had weakened. Perhaps she was passing out, perhaps it was internal bleeding. He softly propped her head up so he could look her in the face. "What?"

"Help me," she said, panicking weakly. "Help me, please. Please help me."

His heart began to pound and his head hurt all the more. He cringed hard, grasping his head as if it were trying to burst open. When he opened his eyes, they were locked on the belly, which was larger than before, with thin blue veins running over the surface like rivers. He stared at it. She said something again, but he was too busy watching it to hear. He did not blink, and his brain bashed against its cell. The belly was getting bigger. He could see it.

"What the fuck," he said to himself, looking up at her. Her face was skin and skull and her eyes were shining brightly through him. There was a fire in her, and it was burning her down.

"Jesus," he said, painfully standing up and stumbling to the door, tripping on clothes. He looked back, her neck again drooping until her head hit the wall. "Jesus."

He turned and began to search through the clothes. He was crawling away, looking for his pants. He wanted the phone, yes, that's what he wanted. The phone. So that he could help her. Yes. He threw clothes everywhere, cursing. All women's clothes of various sizes. He heard her whimpering, like the mew of a destitute kit. He heard the sound of flesh rubbing against tile behind him. Where the fuck were his pants, where the fuck? Did he even bring them?

He quickly glanced behind him and saw the girl's hand pulling her along by the jamb of the door. He crawled, tripped, was caught up in the clothes, and lay atop them, watching her reach the doorway.

He began to pick through all the clothes around him, searching fervently. He didn't know what to do. He didn't know what was wrong with her. What was wrong with him? He didn't know what he would do when he got his pants, but his mind was mad for the pants. He was naked.

He looked back and she was in the doorway. He was backed up against the cabinets in the kitchenette, some twenty feet away. He had strewn a path there through the clothes and had bulldozed a pile between him and the cabinets that kept him a few feet from them. A few feet from the farthest he could go. From the optimum away. He did not find his pants. He did not have the phone, to help her. Yes.

He watched her try to say help again. She was now half-leaning out of the doorway. Yes, she had certainly gotten thinner earlier, because now she was skeletal besides the wrecking ball for a belly. It was consuming her. Her skin was tight to her muscles. He watched as she stood there, attempting to make words until the muscles in her face dissolved and her mouth fell open, dry and gaping. Her tongue was thin like a thirsty straw.

The belly was big, tight, and disturbingly round compared to the pointiness of the rest of her. The bellybutton poked out like a nose. It was as if she had achieved full gestation in five minutes. He couldn't help but think that. That she had gotten pregnant. She'd been made pregnant. Someone had impregnated her.

He was immobile, outside himself, a strapped-in spectator.

She leaned there, mouth gaping and eyes sinking into her head. He could picture them screaming at the descent, but it may have only been him. The arm muscles she used to prop herself up visibly snapped, and she slumped backwards so that nothing but the big outward belly button pointed at him from across the room. Before she fell, he had noticed the long hairs in her head slowly get sucked into her skin, one by one.

He was surrounded by clothes and didn't know whose was whose or which were made for him and people like him. It didn't really matter. He was too scared to stay and too scared to run past her and through that door into the apartment building. If this was happening here, what the fuck could be happening out there?

Instead, he began to pull the clothes around him. He covered himself in brassieres, panties, women's slacks, yoga pants, dresses, socks. Colours. He pulled them all around him like a cocoon. He heard her dry breathing harden and quicken into a seemingly steady suck as he buried himself. He didn't breathe; he just wanted to be under.

When he was finally hunkered into his little pile of clothes, in an immobile darkness, she grew silent and the whole room seemed to stop breathing. He heard his heart beating at his ribs and his brain was throwing itself at the locked doors of his skull. He sat there and waited, and it was silent and it was dark. But the darkness and the outer silence only made it worse. There were too many possibilities in absence.

So he took his trembling finger and slowly burrowed a passage to the light. He looked out. His eyes adjusted, focused. She was now nearly nothing but the ball of her belly. He watched her legs getting sucked into its perfectly round form, noted the long thin red line dragging itself slowly along the horizontal line of her bulb, like a zipper, and felt that soon the sphere would begin to slowly open itself up like the mouth of a Venus flytrap, or a great blood-red eye after a long, long sleep. His eyes would not close. Hers was about to open up and gaze at him.

STUCK

Keith Cadieux

There were two photographic portraits taken of young Henry James Mitchell during his short life. This, at a time when the chemical processes were new and expensive enough that very few had the means or opportunity to pose for even one. The first was taken when he was still quite young, no longer a toddler, though not yet school age. It was an extravagance upon which his father had absolutely insisted: a photograph of the young heir to his promising business fortune.

Long afterward, Henry remembered vividly the day it was taken. His dress clothes itched and were ill fitting, though admittedly he did look rather smart. Everything was set up in the first-floor sitting room of the large Mitchell house. Henry's mother sat in a tall, wingback chair. Once she was settled, Mr. Mitchell approached with a length of thick yellow drapery and spread it over her, making sure that she wasn't at all visible to the camera. Then he lifted little Henry and perched the boy neatly atop her covered-over lap. Even through the heavy fabric, Henry felt her bony knees and the strong grip of her fingers.

There was a stranger in the house, a thin man who had set up a little tray next to the camera on its high stand and covered it with odd instruments. The man came over to Henry and stooped, hands on knees. He said, "It's not so bad, sport. It's only mid-morning yet, and if you keep quiet and mind me, like a good lad, we'll be all finished up by this afternoon."

Henry felt a long sigh escape from his be-draped mother. The man stood to his full height and talked straight past Henry, through the yellow fabric. "You might be a little stiff and you'll feel like you need to scratch"—his eyes shifted back to Henry—"but your mother will help you keep still and I know you'll do fine. Right, boy?" The stranger walked over to the camera, fiddled with something, and sat down beside it.

It had barely been a quarter of an hour when Henry's father grew bored and restless. He paced and circled about the room. He went out into the hall several times, eventually wandering back in after a few moments, the boy and his mother keeping still all the while. Henry did not yet have a mind for tracking the passage of minutes and hours, but he did know that it had been a dreadfully long time.

At first, all his effort was devoted to holding on to stillness. Soon though, it began to feel just the opposite: that if he did not try to move, he would forever lose the ability and the stillness would take over.

The picture in a photograph works through a special kind of chemistry, his father had once explained to him. But Henry thought the stranger's tiny vials and odd instruments looked more like the tools of a potion maker or an alchemist, like in a fairy story. He imagined a tincture that could turn a living boy to stone, or something very close to that. Through this special craft, the photographer was using a slow, creeping kind of transmogrification to make Henry into the static image that would appear on the finished film. Holding still was helping that process along.

And the process wasn't being carried out on just him, but on his mother as well. The heavy drape provided no protection and she became hard and rigid. Sitting on her spare and jagged lap was growing more difficult. Henry's thighs and tailbone started to hurt. If he strained, he could just hear her soft breathing: slow little pants sucked through the fabric. His stare was fixed forward where he could see the photographer sitting and leafing through the pages of something, while his father kept pacing. And then, as time wore on, try as he might, he found he couldn't hear her breathe at all. The spell had finished with her, though it was still working its way through him. No longer did he feel just the simple compulsion to fuss and fidget shared by all children; if he did not move now, he would never again be able to.

He was decided, resolved. He would move, even if only a touch. But before the signal had fully fired in his brain and rippled through his limbs, his mother's grip tightened and a hiss came through the weave of the fabric.

"Don't you dare move now, Hal, or we'll have to start this whole bloody business over again." He nearly screamed, so shocked was he to discover that there was still life in her.

He did hold still and the photograph came out pretty well. Sadly, this experience would become one of Henry's only memories of his living mother, as all his thoughts of her became dominated by the second photograph for which they had posed together. She is not covered up in that one. Instead, both mother and son sit side by side on the long chesterfield in the sitting room. They are holding hands. It was taken six days after she died.

———•◆•———

After hearing of his mother's death through a brief telegram handed to him by the school's principal, Henry made the trip home by train, alone, as he had done only a few times before. Such a trek was usually reserved for Christmas or other very special holidays, though at his parents' behest he had spent the most recent Christmas and New Year's in his dormitory. For this journey, his headmaster had warned him to prepare for a long stay at home and given Henry his condolences.

Henry didn't mind riding the train by himself. At first, he'd assumed this trip would feel different, given the circumstance. But it felt quite ordinary, and he didn't think much about his mother the whole way. He saw other children his age but none riding alone.

Once the train pulled into the station, he stepped off the platform, tugging his heavy suitcase behind him, and was greeted by a familiar middle-aged woman with auburn hair and an unfortunately toothed smile.

"Hello, Henry," she said, holding her arms out to him. "Do you remember me? It's Jenny. Mr. Mitchell sent me to fetch you home."

"Of course I remember, Jenny," he said and hugged her tight. It was her hugs he thought of when he got down to thinking about home. "How could you believe I might forget? I think the cheese has finally slipped off your cracker."

She laughed in one loud burst. "Look at the wit on you," she said. Quite a few people turned to look at them but she didn't seem to notice, and soon Henry saw everyone lose interest and return to their own business.

"With you staying at school all last year, it seems ages since I last saw you. It must be nearly two full years now," she said.

"It couldn't be that long," Henry said. But she was probably right.

"Well, you look sprightly and fresh. Surely you won't mind a bit of a stroll. The hansoms have become so expensive lately, I'm afraid we'll have to walk to your house." She smiled hard but soon the expression softened, as though it were inappropriate to smile at such a time. "May I carry your bag, Henry?"

"No, I can manage it," he said. "You'll see."

Henry did his best to carry it the whole way to the house but it was very tiring. After the better part of an hour, he set it down on the sidewalk and sat on top of it. Jenny didn't notice and kept walking, so he had to shout, "How about we rest a minute?"

She looked back and returned to him. "We're almost there, now, remember? Don't tell me you've forgotten your way about town." She laughed again, but Henry kept his eyes on the sidewalk. "Just a little bit farther," she said. "I'm sure you can manage it."

Henry felt helpless, a useless a little boy. He took a deep breath and stood. Before he could say anything Jenny had reached under him and taken hold of the suitcase.

"You've already brought it most of the way, Henry. That's a great favour to me. Your father won't be happy to see you come up to the house carrying your own bag, now will he?" She winked at him as she swung the bag up with ease and laid a large, soft hand on the boy's shoulder, nudging him back to walking.

"It feels good to do things for you again, Henry. It's been months since I proper worked for Mr. Mitchell, with wages and all," she said.

"Well, surely with wages, Jenny. My father wouldn't have anyone work for him without wages." Henry chortled and her expression changed. "He still pays you wages, Jenny. Doesn't he?"

The older woman blushed. She snuck quick looks at Henry while she spoke but wouldn't meet his eye. "Listen to me, nattering on about things that aren't my business to tell you. No need to worry, little Henry. Your father will fill you in on everything once we get you home. He'll straighten out what I've managed to muck up just now," she said. There was a pause. "He's just so excited to see you." They were both quiet the rest of the way.

Once through the front door, Henry heard his father's booming voice, but what was being said, and to whom, was out of place with what he remembered of home.

"At this time, Mr. Weir," his father said, "I am prepared to negotiate a price for the furniture in the sitting room only. If you'd like to pay me a compliment, I'd prefer it didn't come with a monetary value."

"Begging your pardon, sir," said the smaller gentleman Henry did not recognize, who seemed undeterred by the tone in Mr. Mitchell's voice. "I can't help but notice the stunning woodwork, and I see that you have at least two rooms sealed up already and assumed—"

"I do not need to tear down my house in order to sell the pieces," responded Mr. Mitchell. "Now, are you prepared to accept the amount I've negotiated for the furniture or not?"

There was a long hush as both men looked each other up and down before shaking hands. The stranger flipped open a leather-bound ledger with large, shining rings inside that held a great many documents. He scribbled something into it and then tore out a small strip of paper, which he passed to Mr. Mitchell, who folded it into his breast pocket.

"I'll send word when you can expect my men to pick everything up."

"Very good," said Mr. Mitchell. "And thank you."

He followed the stranger to the door, an arm outstretched to block any sudden move to come back in, and closed it firmly once the man was safely outside. There was a loud click from the tongue of the lock, and only after a moment of quiet and re-collected calm did Mr. Mitchell take notice of his son.

"Here's my Henry," he said as he scooped the boy into his arms. Henry held his back straight, his limbs rigid. A hug from his father was not unheard of, and it had been a long while since the two were in the same room, he supposed, but there was an immediacy that Henry didn't associate with familial affection. He couldn't have broken away from that hold, even if he'd wanted to. He had never known his father to seek that kind of contact before. Soon, though, the awkwardness passed and he gave into the happy feeling of being nestled in his father's strong, tweed-coated arms.

"Welcome home, Hal," Mr. Mitchell said. It was out of place for his father to use the nickname. He squared the boy's shoulders with his heavy hands then stood to his full height. His stare landed on Jenny and he seemed to become embarrassed. "Would you be so good as to take Henry's bag up to his room? I'm sure he remembers where it is, but the Mitchell gentlemen need to discuss family business," he said through a strained smile.

"Certainly," she whispered. There was more uncomfortable quiet until Jenny, most of the way up the stairs, turned and said, "It feels like better days, having the younger Mitchell back home, doesn't it?"

"Yes, it does," said Mr. Mitchell, not taking his eyes off his boy.

Henry could think of nothing to say and felt ungainly looking up at his father's face. There wasn't a word spoken by either of them. He looked around at the house, which felt empty even with all three of them inside. The doorway to the family's library was covered over with boards and a tarp, as was the door to the dining room. Sealed off, if the stranger were to be believed.

"Come upstairs and see your mother," said Mr. Mitchell. He took a hand from his pocket, rested it on Henry's shoulder and led the boy towards the stairs.

"What do you mean?" Henry said. His father didn't answer, just kept coaxing him up the steps. At the top of the stairway, Henry looked to his right, to the far corner of the hall where he remembered his bedroom door to be. He hoped Jenny might offer some interruption, to show him where she'd laid out his things, or insist he change his clothes, or bring him back downstairs to the kitchen for a snack. The door was ajar and he saw his suitcase on top of the fresh-made bed, but no Jenny. There didn't seem to be anyone upstairs but he and his father, who tugged him in the opposite direction.

The door to Mrs. Mitchell's room was also ajar. Mr. Mitchell led the boy inside, pausing to ensure that Henry entered first. It was tidy, still, and smelled overpoweringly of flowers. The bed was made and Henry's mother had been laid stiff atop it. There was no pillow under her head, leaving her flat. There was a sheet pulled up to her waist and her hands were set on its edges, one crossed over the other. A cluster of flowers sat close enough to graze the edges of her fingers. There were flowers on the night tables, a wreath hanging over the headboard and more tied to the bedposts: lilacs, gardenias, lilies, posies, little nosegays.

Henry's father led him right beside his prostrate mother. The flower smell was no longer pleasant this far into the room. He could see that her eyes and mouth were pressed closed. Her chin was sunken, as though lying in this state had caused her jawbone to sink to the back of her neck.

"It will still be a few days yet, before the photographer arrives to do the portrait," Mr. Mitchell said. "I tried to press him but he claims he's travelling as fast as possible. He suggested she be laid out in the cold cellar until he arrives." His voice grew quiet, lacking the booming confidence that Henry remembered. "Imagine," his father whispered. When he spoke again, his voice had regained its powerful timbre. "It was Jenny, collected all the flowers. Her suggestion, actually." He looked about the room, everything around hushed again for a moment. "They are lovely," he said.

"Why are you keeping her in the house?" Henry asked. He pressed the end of his nose with his palm. "I don't like being in here, like this," he said.

"Nonsense, now," said Mr. Mitchell. "This is her home. Once the portrait is taken, we'll have a burial and it will all be done. But in the meantime, she'll be comfortable here. And look," he said, pushing the boy closer to the bed, "isn't she peaceful?"

There was another interval of paralyzed calm. Henry heard the fluttering of one or two loose flower petals falling to the floor. "Jenny said she hasn't been working at the house," he said.

Mr. Mitchell sighed. "Yes, that's the case for now, Hal."

Henry had never cared for the short form of his name and it was only his mother who had ever used it. His father must have thought it a kind of tribute to her.

"I've managed to arrange for Jenny to be here to help you readjust to life at home. But soon she'll have to leave again and you and I will be on our own." He took a breath. "But that won't be for long," he went on. "The same goes for these troubles I'm having with your school. You'll stay home with me for now, but in time we'll have you back there and we'll have Jenny working back here."

Henry felt inertia all around him, the room and everything in it held in place by quiet.

"Everything will go back the way it was," said Mr. Mitchell, "just how you and I remember it. And then everything will stay that way. I promise." Mr. Mitchell took one of Henry's hands and placed it on his mother's dead ones, her skin like cold paper. The house was silent with expectation for a long while before Mr. Mitchell spoke again. "You best give her a kiss now, Hal. It's your last chance."

Henry didn't want to, but worried his father would be disappointed. Whatever discomfort he felt in the presence of his mother's corpse was not shared by the elder Mitchell, who seemed weirdly comforted by it.

Henry steeled himself and, with slow deliberation, leaned over and whisked his lips against his dead mother's forehead. It was cold, the skin very soft.

"Let's see Jenny about something for supper, then," said Mr. Mitchell, moving aside so that he no longer blocked Henry's path to the door. It took all the boy's willpower to stay calm, to walk out of the room with respect and deference, instead of charging out at a dead run.

———•—•———

The next few days were dull and drawn out, mostly because Henry had a hard time sleeping. During the day, Jenny helped to keep him busy. She showed him how to wash his own clothes and the proper way to sweep the hallway floors so that he ended up at the front door and could swoop the dross out into the road. She showed him how to make hot water for tea and why you should always spread jam with a spoon instead of a knife.

In the evenings, Henry read or kept himself occupied with some of the writing and grammar lessons his principal had sent home with him. While he worked quietly, he could hear Jenny and his father in the kitchen. Mr. Mitchell asked a great many questions and sometimes swore aloud, while Jenny showed him how he best run a kitchen if he hoped to keep his son fed.

At night, Henry lay in bed with his eyes open, trying not to glance over at the bedroom down the hall where he knew his mother was. Mr. Mitchell liked to leave the door to her room open, and Henry had a clear view out the doorframe of his room, down the hall, to the foot of her bed. The smell of flowers, now also dead and starting to turn, grew worse at night as the house released the heat it had absorbed during the day. Henry couldn't help but watch her doorway, convinced she was on the verge of getting up and walking about, though all the while he prayed that no such thing could happen. He tried closing the door, to shut her out of his mind, but not being able to see into her room, to not be absolutely sure that she wasn't out of the bed, was even worse.

So the door stayed open and Henry stayed awake. There was nothing to see, but he couldn't stop himself from visualizing a faint shift of the blankets, movements in the shadows. He would see that his mother was now most of the way down the hall, though he hadn't seen her rise up. She'd be inside his doorway, flowers jutting out of her dress and hair, reaching over to his side of the bed, and then he would jolt himself awake. The house was still and there was no one in his room, no one in the doorway, no one in the hall; his mother was undisturbed and in just the same place. These dream-dozes were all the sleep he had for almost a week.

Then one morning there was a knock on the door during breakfast. Jenny answered it and came back into the kitchen. "The photograph man is getting his things ready in the sitting room," she said, then went back out to tend to the guest.

"We'll be doing the portrait this morning and afternoon, Hal, so get yourself dressed," said Mr. Mitchell.

Henry's vest and trousers were pressed—Jenny had shown him how—and he slipped them on one at a time. Then his tie and his uncomfortable shoes. Once dressed, he sat on the edge of the bed and waited. He could hear things being moved around in the sitting room underneath him, the soft murmurings of his father and the photographer exchanging pleasantries. After a moment of quiet, the sound of footsteps moved to the stairwell and the voices were no longer muffled.

"How many days has it been?" said the other voice.

"Six," said his father's voice.

They plodded, making slow progress up to the second floor.

"She won't be stiff anymore." The footsteps stopped. "Forgive my bluntness, Mr. Mitchell. It may be difficult to keep her propped up, is what I'm driving at. I'm prepared for it, though. I've something of a stand."

After a pause, the steps resumed. Henry watched his father and the other man reach the top of the stairs. Mr. Mitchell directed the photographer into Mrs. Mitchell's bedroom, then crossed the hall over to Henry's room.

"Hurry on into the sitting room, Hal," he said. "This has taken too long already."

Henry watched his father disappear through his mother's doorway, then he got off his bed and made his way downstairs.

The sitting room was rearranged, the chesterfield dragged to the middle of the floor, the camera on its stand just opposite. One end table was covered with the photographer's things, a chair taken from the kitchen sat nearby. Behind the chesterfield was the bookcase, which hadn't been moved. Henry walked over to it, finding the photograph of himself on his mother's lap, her body covered in thick drapery. He remembered that the fabric had been a sickly yellow, though everything in the picture now had a tinge of brown to it. His own face was a pale cream colour, the details of his features blurred and dull. He could make out every facet of his mother's shape, even through the covering: the cocked angle of her neck, exactly where her fingers dug into his thighs, the outline of her knees.

He again heard the sound of shuffling about, but from overhead this time. Soon after, he heard the sharp, short breaths of his father and the photographer as they came clumsily down the stairs, hissing instructions of where to step and when to lift. They carried the body of Henry's mother into the sitting room, his father holding her by the armpits. The two men laid her across the chesterfield with a flop that shook down her spine, quivered through her legs. They each took a breath then propped her into a sitting position just off the centre of the sofa.

Mr. Mitchell leaned on the far arm of the chesterfield, panting, and gestured to his son. "Come and sit now, Hal," he said between breaths. Henry didn't move. Mr. Mitchell came over, took the boy by the hand and led him to his place next to the sitting corpse. His father shoved him closer to his mother, so close their hips almost touched, then he took Henry's sweaty hand and wrapped it inside her cold one, closing the fingers one by one. She smelled of the dead flowers from upstairs.

"Your father tells me you've sat for a photograph before," the other man said. He stooped at the knees, coming very close to Henry's face. "You just remember to hold as still as you can and you'll be done late this afternoon, early in the evening at the very latest." The man stood.

"Her eyes don't look right," said Mr. Mitchell. He came closer, bringing his face within inches of the dead body's. "They're uneven. This one is nearly closed," he said, pointing.

"Easily mended," said the other man. He went to the table covered with his things, the alchemical tools of his trade, and took up a tiny bottle. He unscrewed the top, under which was a dainty little paintbrush that reached down to the bottom of the vial. Henry's nostrils filled with a bitter, chemical smell that soon overpowered all traces of the rotten flowers. It tingled unpleasantly, like vinegar mixed with the alcohol that's rubbed into skinned knees. He made a face. The photographer painted a thin line under Mrs. Mitchell's eyebrow, another line across her lashes, and thumbed the lid upward, holding it there for a few seconds. Then he did the same with the other eye.

The man stood behind the camera and said, "Mr. Mitchell, would you stand behind there and point her head toward me?" Mr. Mitchell did. "A touch to my left," the man said. "All right, boy, look right into the camera. And stay still, now."

Right away Henry felt an urge to move, as though it were the only thing that might keep him alive. He tensed and held rigid, trying not to touch the inside of his dead mother's hand. She was horribly still. However indirectly, the transmogrification that Henry had felt beginning years ago had managed to claim her first.

He felt her grip tightening, even though he knew that was impossible. He stayed fixed on the camera but started to think that she was ever so slightly turning her head, bringing her stuck-open eyes around to stare into his. He looked at the photographer, then his father, who stayed in the room this time. Surely they would be reacting if she were moving. Or perhaps she was moving too slowly for them to notice, so imperceptibly that only Henry could tell. The smell of glue grew worse. His muscles and joints were sore from the effort of holding still. He wasn't sure if he'd be able to move now, even if the opportunity should arise. He had become petrified, like his mother.

But her head did turn. It lolled heavily towards Henry and the weight and momentum pulled her shoulders down into a slouch, inching her closer to him. He shrieked and jumped off the sofa, but his hand was still gripped in hers. He shook and pulled, only wrenching his hand free after he'd dragged her off the chesterfield.

There was shouting from both Mr. Mitchell and the photographer as they hurried to gather Mrs. Mitchell up out of the heap she had become on the floor. Her face pressed hard into the carpet, the glued-open eyes staring forward, brushed by the dusty fibres. Henry stared, waiting for the eyes to dart around, to seek him out. But soon Mr. Mitchell and the other man had her propped back on the couch, just as before, staring lazily forward. They could no longer keep her body from slumping to the side.

"I'll need a moment," the photographer said, shuffling through the large case of things he hadn't yet unpacked. "Lift her head and hold her just like that," he said to Mr. Mitchell, who obliged. The other man brought over what looked like a metal post. At the top was a joint, then an arm that reached outward, ending in a clamp. The two prongs were rounded like the backs of spoons. After turning wing nuts to adjust the height and angle of the protruding arm, he set the prongs on either side of Mrs. Mitchell's head and then turned another wing nut to hold her in place.

"Come on now, Hal. We have to get this done," said Mr. Mitchell.

Henry stood behind the camera and didn't move.

"It's all right, Henry. I won't be upset, just so long as we manage to finish."

"We'll have to hurry along, Mr. Mitchell," the photographer said. "We have to restart the exposure and if it's not done before we lose the daylight, the film won't come out properly. It will be ruined."

"Come now, Henry. You heard him."

Mr. Mitchell walked over to Henry, took him by the shoulders and marched him back to the chesterfield, sitting him down like before. Once again, he set Mrs. Mitchell's stiff hand around the small boy's fingers. But instead of looking toward the camera, Henry turned hard to the side, looking straight at his mother's head, now clamped in place. He stayed motionless, put all his effort into willing her to hold still.

"Henry, we don't have time for this," his father said.

Henry didn't respond.

"Damn it, boy," his father shouted.

Henry jumped a little at the noise but didn't turn his head.

After a minute or so of quiet, the photographer spoke up. "You know, he doesn't look bad like that," he said. "It's not so out of place. Has a kind of reverence, I think. It looks ..."

"Spare me," started Mr. Mitchell.

"Devotional. It looks devotional. Shall I carry on, then?" the photographer asked.

"Yes, I suppose it will do," his father said with a sigh.

—————•◦•—————

After his mother's corpse was removed from the house and buried, Henry's sleeping improved for a short time. One morning, though, he was awoken by shouting coming from his mother's bedroom.

"How dare you disturb this place, Jenny?" his father bellowed. "I thought you'd more sense than that."

"These flowers have all turned to rot, Mr. Mitchell," Jenny answered. "They're stinking up the whole house. Once they're cleared out, then you can get this room closed up as well."

Henry trembled with anxious nerves but he didn't detect any such quality in Jenny's voice.

"I will not close up this room. This is her home. For you to make such a suggestion." The volume of his father's voice went up just as he seemed to run out of words.

"She'll get no use out of the place now. It isn't good for Henry, you behaving like this. With respect, sir. His mother died and he needs to have a full grasp of what that means." Henry could hear her gathering things up, the crumple of dried and disintegrating petals and stems. "Sealing the room may be too much but at least leave me to clear these flowers away." The ensuing quiet and resigned footsteps of his father going down the stairs told Henry that was the end of it.

A few mornings after that he woke up on his own, much more pleasantly, and went down to the kitchen where he found his father spooning hot porridge into bowls.

"Where's Jenny?" Henry asked.

"It's just the two Mitchell men for now, lord help us," his father replied. Henry knew it was hard news to give and pretended not to be affected. His father smiled and passed a dish of honey closer to Henry's place setting.

They were most of the way through a quiet but comfortable breakfast when Henry could no longer hold back his question. "Why aren't you leaving for work this morning?"

"I'm doing work at the house all day," Mr. Mitchell said. "First, a short appointment here this morning, which means we best get on with breakfast." He shovelled in his last two bites. "After that, I could use some help. Do you have some free time today?" He winked.

Henry smiled wide and was about to answer when there came a loud knock at the front door.

"That'll be them now," said Mr. Mitchell. "Just wait here a bit, Hal."

It was soon obvious that there were actually quite a few people at the door. He heard his father lead them into the sitting room and then the sounds became harder to follow: scuffling boots, scrapings on the floor, barked orders. His father briefly snuck into the kitchen with the photograph of a much younger Henry perched on the lap of his drape-covered mother and set it down on the edge of the counter. Over the course of an hour or so, the troop of heavy boots made several trips back and forth between the sitting room and the front door, and Henry did as he was bid and waited at the table.

He heard the front door close and everything grew quiet, but Mr. Mitchell did not come back into the kitchen. Henry waited a while longer, then pushed his chair back and headed into the hall. From there he could see his father standing in the doorway to the sitting room, casting a dark silhouette. Past the shadow, Henry could see that the whole room had been emptied and left bare. There was dirt in odd patterns along the floorboards, dusty footprints leading out to the front step. Nothing else. Mr. Mitchell stood with his hands at his sides, looking around at the emptied space. He breathed slowly.

"Is something the matter?" Henry asked as he moved to stand next to his father.

Mr. Mitchell seemed awoken from a nap. "Of course not, Hal. Just making sure they got everything." He patted Henry on the shoulder and looked around one more time. "Nothing for it but to close it up like the other rooms. You're going to help me, aren't you?"

"Of course. What should I do?"

Mr. Mitchell gestured at Henry to wait, then bounded up the stairs to the hall closet, and then came back down with his arms full of tools.

First, Henry swept out the room, banishing the sweepings out through the front door as Jenny had shown him, while his father nailed boards over the room's two windows. He pounded the nails very gingerly to avoid breaking the glass.

"Fetch us the lamp from the kitchen, would you?" his father said. Henry did.

Under lamplight now, they measured out a length of thick canvas and covered the boarded windows.

"This will keep the drafts out," Mr. Mitchell said. There was no longer any way for wind or daylight to find their way in.

Henry and his father went out into the hall, bringing the lamp and closing the door tight behind them. Mr. Mitchell drove one nail at an angle through both the door and the frame. He tugged on the head and when it didn't budge, he gave the hammer to Henry. He showed the boy how to hold the nail in place and knock it just enough that it could stand on its own.

"Now hit that bugger," his father said, "but make sure to leave it sticking out some. After all, one day we'll be opening up this room again. Everything just as it was."

The door now held shut, they measured out a much larger piece of canvas and covered the whole doorway. Mr. Mitchell hammered the nails at the top, leaving the tarp to drape loosely. He let his son hammer in the rest, securing the tarp around the edges of the doorframe. Henry found himself feeling rather practical and accomplished, as though he had managed to complete a real, grownup task. But the look on his father's face reminded him that nothing about this day was to be celebrated.

"That's done earlier than I expected," said Mr. Mitchell after checking his watch. "Maybe it's best that I do head into town and do a little business, not lose the whole day. What do you say, Hal?"

The small, satisfied smile on Henry's face fell. "I suppose," he said, not wanting to hinder his father.

"There's bread and jam in the pantry, if you get hungry. But we'll have a proper supper once I get back, so don't have too much."

"I promise," Henry said, but he didn't feel much like eating anyway.

———•◦•———

Over the next weeks, the two remaining Mitchells established a dull but steady routine. The only rooms open to their uses now were the kitchen, the hallways, and the three bedrooms: Henry's, Mr. Mitchell's and Mrs. Mitchell's.

Though Henry was alone quite a bit, he and his father always managed to eat breakfast and supper together. Admittedly, their evening meal was often quite late since its preparation had to wait until Mr. Mitchell returned home for the day, and sometimes it required a second attempt. Nonetheless, Henry grew fond of the routine.

After everything had become cozy and comfortable, the printed photograph of Henry and his dead mother arrived by post.

"He could have at least brought it by himself," his father mumbled once he realized what the package contained. "Come have a look, Hal. You look like a proper gent," he said, laying the stiff paper in his son's hands.

Henry hardly noticed what he looked like. He couldn't look away from his mother. Her dead stare transfixed him, her eyes open so very wide, almost comically so. The detail was remarkable, every line and shape in sharp focus. And though her gaze fell only clumsily in the direction of the camera, Henry could feel it looking straight through the paper and into him.

"Come on, bring it upstairs with you," Mr. Mitchell said as he bounded up the steps. The picture emitted a faint chemical smell and Henry held the thing away from his nose. He also turned it to face away from him.

His father met him at the top of the stairs with a small, wooden picture frame. He stepped into Henry's bedroom and motioned for his son to follow him. "We only have the one, of course, but I want you to keep it in here," he said, smiling. He opened the back of the frame, then took the photograph from Henry and slipped it inside. "We can set it right on your night table, facing the bed. She'll be able to watch over you while you sleep, just as she'd have wanted to." His father positively beamed.

Henry felt an urge to get away from the picture; either he or it needed to be outside and away from the house. But he didn't want to disappoint his father, who obviously thought that putting it here next to the bed was an act of great generosity.

"Don't you want to look at it?" was all Henry managed to say.

"I'll see it often enough. It's more important for you to see her, to remember her as she was." Mr. Mitchell picked up the frame and looked at it intently. "I'm glad it's you sitting next to her and not me. I'd have just uglied the thing up, I'm afraid." He held the frame out to Henry, who could think of nothing to do but take it. The thing felt hard and wretched in his hands. His image looked blurry, much the same as the old photograph of him. Perhaps he was a little clearer but his mother, she looked perfectly focused. Henry's nostrils prickled, the chemical stink like glue growing stronger.

"Is anything the matter, Hal?" Mr. Mitchell asked.

"I was just—" Henry paused, still staring into her eyes. "I was only looking at her," he said.

Mr. Mitchell patted the boy on the shoulder, as though immensely proud. He turned the boy's face up to his. "How about some sausage or blood pudding with supper tonight, or maybe something with beef? I'll pick it up on my way. Your colour is off, Hal. You could use some iron," he said and then went downstairs.

Once his father was gone Henry set the photograph down on the night table and shuffled out of the bedroom backwards, never taking his eyes off of it, sure that it was about to do something awful.

———•—•———

As his father had predicted, Henry's mother did watch over him. That was the worst part. Every night was now much the same as those few nights when her body lay in the bedroom down the hall, except now she was only inches from his head. He began losing sleep again. Try as he might, he couldn't keep his eyes closed. He was always looking to make sure that the picture hadn't moved, or rather that she hadn't moved it. And no matter how dark the nights became he could always make out her stuck-open stare.

Then one night, after getting into bed, he reached across the table and spun the photograph so that it faced the wall. Sometime later he heard his father making his way to his own bed, Henry not yet asleep himself. Mr. Mitchell snuck a quick peek into his son's room and, seeing the photograph turned, stepped inside and spun it back round. His heavy slippers made a good deal of noise but Henry pretended to sleep through it. He lay awake a long while, well after the sound of Mr. Mitchell's snores started rumbling through the upper floor of the house. Though he was facing away from the photograph, Henry could still feel its stare on him. He stayed that way all night, and in the morning he was quietly relieved to see that at least the photograph hadn't moved since his father had fussed with it.

Despite the foiling of that first attempt, Henry kept turning the photograph away every time he climbed into bed. But every morning it was spun back around to face him, even though he hadn't been roused by his father's heavy footfalls in the room.

During the day, Henry welcomed as many distractions as possible. Without Jenny or anyone else to keep house, many tasks fell to him. While his father was out all day tending to business, Henry swept out the staircase and the hallways. He dusted the surfaces in the kitchen, in the hallways, and in his father's and mother's bedrooms. Mrs. Mitchell's room was much more pleasant without her or the prickly scent of the dead flowers. The one room he repeatedly neglected to clean and tidy was his own, because the photograph was in there. Once he was up and dressed, he would go all day without going back in there.

Occasionally, every week or so, Mr. Mitchell would leave behind a few coins and a short list of food items that the pair needed. These were Henry's favourite days, and he could make a trip into town for bread and milk last a whole afternoon. Inevitably, though, he would have to return home and eventually up to his room to bed, where the picture was always already waiting, turned back to look over the spot where he was meant to sleep. He began sneaking handkerchiefs from the top drawer of his father's dresser, and before sliding under the bedcovers, he spun the frame around and draped the cloth over it. But each morning the handkerchiefs were gone and the photograph looked at him from the edge of the night table. Mr. Mitchell remarked that many of his handkerchiefs and some of the tea towels were missing so Henry had to stop pilfering them. It seemed that no matter what Henry tried he was going to wake up staring into his mother's dead eyes. It became terribly normal.

———•——

"What if we hung the picture over here?" Henry asked, holding it up against the wall in the kitchen. "It looks nice in the light."

"Why did you bring it outside your room, Hal?" his father said as he came around the corner. "Make sure to be extra careful if you're carrying that around." He looked quickly from the boy to the photograph pressed tight against the wall. "I don't think that's a very good place for it," he said.

Henry brought it down, trying not to spend too long looking into her eyes. He shuffled slowly out into the hallway. Near the staircase was a cherrywood table that his father used to pile mail and other papers. Henry set the frame down on it. "It looks good over here," he cried.

"What's this nonsense about, Hal?" Mr. Mitchell walked into the hallway and stood over Henry for a moment before letting out a long sigh as he sat on the bottom step. "We put the photograph in your room so that your mother could watch over you."

"What about you?" Henry said. "It's not right that I should have it all to myself."

"That's very considerate of you, Hal. But this portrait is meant to be something special for you. It's what your mother would want, as well. You go put it back in your bedroom, just where it was, and don't feel guilty about having it anymore," his father said. "And be careful with it."

Henry did bring it upstairs, but he spun it around and pressed it flat against the wall.

That night Henry roused from a light doze, still unable to fall into a normal sleep. The photograph faced him, pushed right to the edge of the night table. It was late enough that his father must have been in bed as well, though he hadn't heard the usual parade of slippered footsteps.

Just turning the picture away wasn't working; it was only avoidance. Henry grabbed hold of the thing and got out of bed. He slunk quietly through the hall, down the steps, all the way to the front door. With tiny, minute movements, he turned the knob and felt a soft click as the latch came open. He stood in the open doorway, looking out toward the street, though he couldn't see much of anything in the dark. Could it be as easy as tossing the photograph out? What would he say to his father? What plausible scenario could there be, other than Henry had thrown it away? His father wouldn't forgive such a thing.

It was too dark to see past the front step but Henry could still see his mother's eyes peering at him, assuring him that he would never be rid of her.

He closed the door, turning the knob just as carefully as before, and set the frame down on the cherrywood table in the hallway. He went back upstairs to lie in bed awake for the few hours left before morning.

————•————

Henry got out of bed once he heard the noise of his father making breakfast downstairs. He found the photograph once again sitting on his night table, unobstructed, turned to face him. He grabbed it and, with a shout, flung the thing hard against the farthest wall. The glass cracked and the frame broke apart at the corners as it hit the floor. There was a hurried sound of footsteps as his father bounded up the stairs.

"What's happened?" he said as he came through the door.

Henry stayed in bed, half under the covers, not answering. His father looked at the broken frame on the floor.

"Henry, what have you done?" he demanded. Shouted it. He stepped closer to the wreckage, glass crunching under his slippers. "Why must I keep putting up with this? You've no respect." He stooped and carefully lifted out the photograph, minding not to tear or scratch it, and left the room.

Henry breathed a great sigh. Perhaps his father wouldn't trust him with the photograph anymore. He stepped to the hall closet, took the broom, and began to clear up the mess he'd made.

After a few minutes, his father came back, the bare photograph pressed to his chest. He pulled aside the covers and sat, tugging Henry down beside him.

"Henry," he said, then paused. He was choosing his words carefully, breathing loudly through his nose. "Hal, I know it has been hard to come home at a time when everything is turned on its head. To leave school, adjust to running the house, just you and me. It's not the life I pictured for you. And I know this is no substitute for your mother actually being here." He thumbed the corner of the thick paper and Henry looked at the blank side, hoping his father wouldn't turn it around.

"I know how frustrating it must be, to have only a photograph to take her place. But you must try to be grateful that we do have it. It's more than just a piece of heavy paper with a picture on it. Don't you see that?"

Henry blinked.

"It's one of the few fortunes left to us," his father went on. "Sometime soon I will have everything set right and things will go back to normal. Just as they were. But until that day, this is our reminder." He took the picture from his chest, laid it in his lap, and pulled the boy closer. Mr. Mitchell inhaled and rubbed his hand on Henry's shoulder. "Your mother, in this picture," he sighed, "she looks just as I remember her." He kissed the boy on the head and finished gathering up the broken pieces of frame Henry had started sweeping. "Get dressed and come down for breakfast," he said.

Henry dressed slowly. He heard his father moving about the kitchen, pulling a chair to the table, and eventually he heard the front door open and close when Mr. Mitchell left for the day. Only after that did Henry start down the stairs.

In the kitchen, he found that his father had laid out some bread and jam and left the last apple for him. Also on the table was the photograph. The corners of the frame were pressed back together but there was no longer any glass in it. A hint of something chemical cut through the regular kitchen smells. Henry opened up one of the highest cupboards, cleared some space and gingerly placed the frame face down inside. He closed the cupboard door quietly, hoping maybe the picture wouldn't realize that he had hidden it away. On the counter were a few coins and a short list of sundries, both of which he pocketed. He took the bread and the apple with him and ate alone in his room.

—·•·—

Henry ambled through town, enjoying the time away from the house and all the things he was unable to avoid there.

"Why if it isn't the younger Mr. Mitchell," he heard shouted from across the street. He turned to see Jenny waving excitedly and making her way over to him.

"Hello, Jenny," he cried.

"Henry out doing his own errands. So grown up," she said, stopping to give him a gentle little hug. Henry hugged her back.

"Oh, excuse me, Henry," she said, standing up, recalling her proper manners. "I was just so happy to see you."

"I'm glad to see you, too, Jenny. The place is so different with just me and my father and—" Henry almost said "her" but caught himself just in time. There was a pause as Jenny looked him over.

"Henry, you look awful. You've almost no colour at all. You look like faded paper," she said, placing a hand against the boy's forehead. She brushed his cheek. "Isn't your father feeding you well?"

"Yes, of course," Henry said. "He's actually not such a bad cook now."

"Well, you should be at home resting if you're not feeling well. You wouldn't find me letting you out of bed looking so ghastly. You'll catch cold out here. Let's find somewhere to sit," she said.

They went through an open, waist-high gate to a little garden with a bench and sat down. Jenny set her things on the ground and Henry held his small bundle on his lap. They sat silently for a good while, both contented with the fresh air and each other's company.

"When are you coming back, Jenny? It seems like it's been an awfully long time that you've been gone." He thought of the closed-up rooms, how often his father was away from home. And he thought of his mother's stare. "I'd like it very much for you to come back," he said softly. "I'd like for everything to go back the way it was."

Jenny's smile never left her face but the happiness seeped right out of it. "Now, Henry," she said, setting her hand on top of the little boy's, "I love your family very much. And I have tremendous respect for your father, too. But let me explain something that he wouldn't like me to." She waited a moment to let Henry realize how serious their talk had become. "I won't be coming back," she said.

"But he promised. He said everything would go back the way it was."

"I know, love. And I wish that things could work out like that. But there's my wellbeing to think of, too. I can't wait until your father regains enough money to pay me a wage, if that day ever comes. I've a new house to look after now."

Henry started to look away. Jenny reached out and, with just the tips of her fingers, turned him back to face her.

"Your father is clinging to the notion of things being just the same. But the world doesn't work that way. Things won't ever be just the same and if you never let go of that idea, then you'll find things moving on without you." She took her hand back but held Henry's stare. "Life isn't meant to stay still," she said.

After a moment she stood and said, "Surely the rest of your errands can wait until you've put some colour back in your cheeks. I'll walk you home." She took his hand again, then waited for him to get to his feet and join her.

They walked back to the Mitchell house and hugged again when they reached the door. Henry held her tight for a long time.

"Now don't worry too much about your father," Jenny said. "He just needs you to talk a little sense into him. While you're at it, you best tell him you don't like the name Hal or he'll never stop calling you that." She smiled at the look of surprise on the boy's face, then leaned down and kissed him on the cheek. "Goodbye, Henry," she said. And then she left.

———————

After Jenny had gone, Henry let himself into the house and brought the small bundle into the kitchen. From the front door, he walked down the hallway, past the sealed doors of the library and the dining room, and into the kitchen, where he saw the pile of breakfast dishes he'd left out.

On the edge of the counter, in its new customary place since the sitting room had been closed up, sat the older photograph of him on his mother's lap, her covered over. It had been a long time since he'd even thought of it. Henry was a little surprised in himself that he didn't feel the same dread as he did for the other image.

He still remembered how it had felt to hold so still that first time. He looked at the details of the room captured in the picture and realized that they were now all gone: the armchair he and his mother sat on had been sold, the clothes he wore were now far too small, the sitting room where they'd posed was sealed up, and of course his mother was dead. Jenny was right, he thought. Things were moving forward without him.

He could see the shape of one of his mother's hands through the heavy drape, clenched tightly around his hip. It was easy to make out her posture. The shape of her under the fabric was familiar, her head tilted to one side.

He could even make out the intricate pattern on the drape itself. He remembered that the cloth had been yellow, though he hadn't seen it since. It was a horrid, ugly pattern. Arabesque was the word for it, he thought. It was made of shapes that drooped and lolled and curved without seeming to repeat. He chose one point and tried to follow the pattern to an end, tracing his eyes along the lines, over folds and creases, looking for it to come back over itself. The detail was remarkably clear, he thought. How still his mother must have stayed that whole time. He followed the pattern up to the spot where the fabric was laid over her head. Here the shapes became decidedly round and bulbous. He stared at two prominent orbs in the deepest part of the cloth and after a long, quiet moment, they blinked open. His mother's dead, frozen eyes stared back at him through the pattern of the drapery, through the photograph, through him.

He managed to keep from screaming but he did run out of the kitchen. He went straight up the stairs, toward his bedroom. But he stopped in the doorway when he saw the photograph of him and his dead mother in its accustomed place on his night table, the broken frame pressed together at the corners, missing the glass plate.

Henry stood there a long time. There was nowhere to go. The thing had gone from the kitchen cupboard downstairs back to his room. He headed for the hall closet, where there were tools. He came back with a hammer and one long nail. He moved fast and went right to the photograph, half-expecting it to jump out at him or rush away from his grasp as he approached, but it didn't move at all. He picked it up, placed the face of the frame flat against the wall and carefully tapped the nail into the back. Once it was deep enough to hold on its own he swung the hammer with both hands, driving until the head of the nail was flush against the back of the frame. Then he returned the hammer to its proper place.

He paced up and down the hallway, poking his head into his bedroom every now and then to make sure the thing was still nailed to the wall. After a while, he decided he could safely move about the house. He went downstairs and felt up to the task of boiling water for tea. He had a generous helping of bread and jam along with it, eating until he was full. For a fleeting moment, he felt as though he had accomplished something worthwhile, something grown up. But soon worries about his father's reaction began to creep into his thoughts.

He brushed the crumbs from his plate and placed it back in the cupboard. He slurped the last of his tea and wiped the inside of the cup. It was already quite late, moments away from sunset. Mr. Mitchell was later than usual. If he was late enough, Henry might already be in bed when his father came home. If the door were closed, he would surely let the boy sleep and then there wouldn't be an opportunity to the see the photograph until the next morning.

Henry returned to his room, elated that the picture frame was still nailed to the wall, facing away, just as he'd left it. He sat on his bed and waited for his father. For a short while there was enough light by which to read, but he found it hard to concentrate. As it grew darker, he didn't get up from his spot on the bed, not even to pull the curtains or light the lamps. He just let it get dark. And the photograph stayed stuck to the wall, shadows creeping in a slow circle around the frame until all was black.

After some time, he heard the sound of keys and footsteps. Then he efficiently, but without hurrying, closed the door to his room, climbed under the covers and pretended to be asleep.

Mr. Mitchell came into the house noisily but didn't call out. Henry heard his footsteps as he checked first the kitchen, then trudged up the stairs. The door handle clicked when his father turned it and the hinges creaked open just wide enough for his father to step into the room. Henry stayed still, facing away from the door, waiting. But his father kept standing there. Henry tried hard not to reveal that he wasn't sleeping. He fought a desperate compulsion to move.

His father, on the other hand, remained quite calm, standing in the doorway. The floorboards creaked as he rocked his weight between his heels and the balls of his feet. He let out a great long sigh that, to Henry, sounded rather sad. He lingered a moment longer then, softly, left the room. He made almost no noise at all.

Henry lay for a minute or so and then took a relieved gasp of air. He had forgotten to breathe. The room felt safe and warm, which it hadn't for a long while. The sound of his father moving about in the other parts of the house, the sense of motion, was comforting. And though Henry was accustomed to lying in bed awake most of the night, he fell asleep.

When Henry awoke in the morning his mother's dead eyes were the first sight to greet him. The photograph was once again in its customary place at the end of the night table. There was a hole punched through it, near the top, and the long nail Henry had used was lying next to the frame.

He didn't throw the picture, or even reach out to touch it. He recoiled, scrambling across the bed until his back was against the wall. He turned away and clamped his eyes shut. He wriggled as deep into the corner between the wall and the bed as he could. The smooth plaster was cold on his nose and forehead.

Try as he might, his eyes didn't stay shut. He used all his effort, his strength, his will to hold them closed, but he felt his eyelids peeled upward and then held open. He didn't see the plaster of his bedroom wall, though he could still feel it pressed against his face. He didn't see any part of his bedroom. Instead, he was inside the sitting room, seated on the chesterfield, the heavy woven yellow rug underneath his feet. He couldn't see across the room to the opposite wall, as though his sight didn't reach that far. Past the chesterfield all seemed to drift away into a white nothingness. A blank.

He couldn't move but he could feel his itchy clothes, the lumpy sofa cushions under him, the snugness of his shoes. One of his hands was held by something cold. There was an overwhelming chemical taint in the air, like the smell of glue. The thing clamped on his hand squeezed tighter. It started to hurt. Henry could only move his head, and even then, only in one direction. He turned and saw his dead mother sitting beside him, her hand clasped deathly tight around his. And her head started to turn as well. Her neck lolled, her face drooped down towards Henry, who fought in vain to look away. Her enormous, stuck-open eyes grabbed onto his with tremendous force, and in a slow, draining blink the only thing left in all the world for him to do was to stare back at her forever.

TAPESTRIES

Joanna Graham

If Penny's older sister were here, the two of them would pretend the abandoned basement hallway was a secret tunnel to an enchanted world. But Penny stands alone in the silent space. Yellow light creeps into the shadows from the storage fridge behind her and pale light pokes through cracks in the rotting wooden doors at the end of the hallway, illuminating hovering particles of dust. Penny squints to determine how far the hallway extends and walks towards the darkness.

Feathers rustle ahead of her and goosebumps raise the hairs on her arms and neck. A bird propels itself over her head towards the doors. Penny turns and follows its flight path. Shadows flutter in front of the outside light before the small body smacks against the wood and thuds to the ground.

Penny winces, then waits for the bird to make more noise.

Denise killed a robin when Penny was seven. After spending the spring watching blue eggs transform into noisy chicks, the sisters saw one bird fall out of the nest onto their mother's rock garden. The bird landed on its back, legs stuck straight up, crippled wings flapping, beak opening and closing without making sounds.

Penny cried as she watched it, so Denise bent down and whacked the bird with a trowel. Its ribs crunched and blood squirted from its chest. Penny stopped crying, stunned by the sudden quiet and fascinated by the body resting among the flowers and stones. The feathers surrounding the caved-in chest looked soft and warm, even redder because of the blood rising out of its broken body. They decided to bury it but, as Denise finished digging a hole beneath the creeping jenny, their father came outside. Penny reached towards the corpse as he walked over to them, but he saw what they were doing and hurried them inside. Denise left to wash her hands as ordered, but Penny stayed to watch their father as he picked the chick up, wrapped it in a plastic bag and dropped it in the garbage bin.

In the hallway, Penny crouches to study the crumpled ball of feathers at her feet. She wants to describe the body to Denise—still vibrant red-feathered chest, outstretched wings, black eyes flickering up and down—but Denise has been dead for seventy-one days. She died in a car crash, swerved off the road into a tree, dead on impact. But looking at the robin, Penny imagines that Denise's eyes kept seeing and moving until they were glued shut.

Penny wipes tears from her eyes and notices crumbs scattered below the robin. They extend in a line down the hallway.

"Is it dead?" a low voice behind her asks.

Penny's heart jumps. She stands and spins around but can't see the speaker. "Excuse me? Where are you?"

Penny watches a silhouette walk forward and stop in front of her. She sees individual, delicate features in the dappled light—a high forehead, sharp cheekbones and a wide, full mouth—but the overall composition of the face remains hidden, so for a moment Penny imagines her sister's face in the shadows.

Blood pounds in her ears and tears well in her eyes, but Penny doesn't let herself blink. She reaches towards the shape. The figure recoils and Penny drops her hand.

"I'm sorry," she says. Heat creeps up her neck and she steps backwards until she bumps against the wall.

"That's all right." The voice is too low for a woman, and, as the figure moves forward again, Penny sees short hair and a long nose. She starts shaking.

"I didn't know if I should pick it up or leave it. I don't think it will live," Penny says as she glances towards the open fridge door.

"No. Best not to touch it. It looks delicate, but it's still vermin," he says, and then hunches over the bird and scoops it up with his bare hands.

Penny clenches her fists as he walks towards her, the robin held in front of him like an offering. She looks behind her. Ten steps and she will be back in the florist's basement. Twenty and she will be upstairs in the bright, public store.

"I should introduce myself. My name is Hadrian, with an "H.""

"Penny," she blurts out. Her nails dig into her palms as she looks down at the robin resting in his hands. Blood drips from its neck and slides between his fingers.

"You should get rid of it," Penny says. "You're supposed to bury it."

Hadrian folds his arms against his torso, cradling the bird. "I'm not going to waste it," he answers. "Excuse me." Penny hears his footsteps get quieter, then there is a creak and a thud before the hallway is silent again.

Penny darts back to the storage fridge. She slams the door and dashes into the basement. Halfway up the stairs she stops with her hand on the railing. What was he going to do with the dead bird? Maybe he would try to eat it.

Penny climbs the rest of the stairs and walks into the store. Her heart rate slows. Daylight pours through the windows and fluorescent light spills out of the display fridges. She picks up the store's phone and dials her co-worker's number. No answer. She leaves a message, crosses her arms and leans against the wall, glancing towards the basement steps. She picks up the phone again and calls the police. The officer who answers keeps asking if the man threatened her. He suggests an alarm and tells her to keep her cell on her. Penny hangs up.

For a few moments, she stands with her arms crossed and gazes at the space: display fridges encase pre-made arrangements and cut flowers, a table with thin metal legs supports potted azaleas and chrysanthemums, a window display showcases white wedding arrangements to the few pedestrians on the street, and warped metal vines hang down from the ceiling. The vines are pastel green, but the paint has flaked away in some places, forming dark spots that spread like mould over the dated decorations.

She wishes it was the weekend and someone was working with her. She crosses the store and puts the "back in fifteen minutes" sign away, hoping some of the pedestrians turn into customers. When no one comes in, she drifts back to the phone, picks it up a third time and dials the number she's always called for advice. It rings three times before a cheery voice asks her to leave a message at the beep.

"Hey, I'm just at work and I finally went into that weird passage I told you about, and … and—" Penny slams the receiver down. She presses her fists and forehead against the wall, clenching her teeth against the familiar agony of suppressed grief.

———◦•◦———

Penny chews at her bottom lip, peeling off thin layers of skin as she shuffles down the deserted street on her way to work. She feels like she's deteriorating. Her lower back aches and the persistent blisters on her ankles, heels, and toes throb as her sneakers scrape against the sidewalk.

She passes ten concrete steps leading down to her building's warped delivery doors and watches a stray cat stalk around the space at the foot of the stairs. It ignores abandoned coffee cups and fast food bags to hunt scattered brown feathers shifting in the breeze.

Penny rounds a corner and walks up four eroded steps to Ed's Flowers. She pauses and, as she digs in her purse for keys, stares at the window display. The roses, calla lilies, hydrangeas, daisies and baby's breath filling the space are dead, their shrivelled petals and leaves scattered over worn velvet fabric.

Penny puts her things away. There's a voicemail from her boss with a list of things to do. She scribbles the list on the back of an old receipt. The last thing is cleaning the basement fridge. Penny underlines the task with her nail.

After she sweeps, Penny cleans up the arrangements. Last week she spent an entire shift cutting flowers, placing them between grids of clear tape, and adjusting their stems and greenery so they looked beautiful in their vases. Making arrangements is the best way to keep her mind off Denise because it keeps her hands and mind busy. When she'd first started working shifts alone she'd practised making corsages. She tried different combinations of flowers and greenery, but for her favourite she'd pinched together a red rosebud and purple cup flower, along with some tree fern and wound green tape around the stems. But she'd been scolded for wasting stock when her boss found out.

Penny pulls out a rose, calla lily and piece of baby's breath from the old arrangements. She puts them together and uses a stray hair caught in her sweater to tie the stems together. She tries to adjust her fragile creation, but the hair snaps and flowers fall off the baby's breath. She tosses it in the garbage. Then she grabs the rest of the old plants and does the same thing. Her creations land in the dust she swept off the floor and she knows they will be buried throughout the day under dead petals, ripped leaves, cardboard, receipts and cellophane.

She restocks the display fridges, waters the potted plants and then leans against the counter, waiting for customers and debating cleaning the fridge. She picks at a line of dirt under her fingernail. Once it's gone she keeps picking until a line of blood appears instead. She uses the sharp pain to counteract the soporific effect that the humming of the display fridges, the circulation of dry air, and general lack of customers have on her.

Despite the pain, Penny's thoughts wander. The ground over Denise's grave finally thawed two weeks ago, and Penny and her mother planted purple irises in front of her tombstone. Row after row of white, grey, and black slabs stretched in every direction as they worked. She hadn't seen any other plants in the ground, only cut flowers resting in built-in vases at the base of polished tombstones. The stems sat submersed in stagnant water, so instead of blossoms, dead, brittle twigs marked the graves, waiting for a strong wind to separate their particles into dust.

Penny wonders what's happening to Denise now. Has her coffin started eroding? Has dirt trickled in through the sides, or is the ground still frozen six feet under the surface? Would there be water in her coffin when it melted? How long are her nails? What stage of decomposition has she reached? Are centipedes crawling over her skin? Does it tickle? Does it hurt?

Penny shudders and paces the store. She passes the list resting on the counter, then locks the door and hangs up the "back in fifteen minutes" sign. She grabs a small blue bin, a garbage bag and a box-cutting knife and heads downstairs. Her keychain hangs from a coiled wristband and clinks as she walks. She pulls open the storage fridge's white wooden door and flicks the light on. Moisture curls in slow spirals through the warm, humid air.

She glances around the small, concrete space. She covers her mouth with her hands, dropping the recycling bin with an echoing clatter. In the middle of the floor, the dead robin perches on a nest of twigs and flowers; its neck is bent at a severe angle, so she knows it's the one from yesterday. It's as if it found its way back to its nest.

Penny smiles behind her hands and lowers herself onto her knees. She creeps towards the sculpture. Plants twist up out of the intricate nest between the feathers and into the robin's body. Its open, unblinking black eyes move up and down. She waves her hand in front of its face and its eyes follow it. She strokes the red breast with the back of her knuckle. She touches the tip of its beak. She lifts its wing and a blue fly rushes upwards.

Penny drops the wing. The fly circles the fridge, lands on the floor, crawls towards the hallway's door and disappears under the wood. Two muffled knocks echo through the room. Penny stares at the door in the wall. It looks out of place, a second, smaller door in the room, like the mysterious portals she and Denise read about years ago.

Hadrian knocks again. She stands, but before she answers, she picks up the box-cutting knife and pushes it into her back pocket. Then she picks up her gift and opens the door a crack.

Hadrian retreats from the light.

"What's this?" she asks.

"One piece of a collection," he answers. "Do you like it?"

"Is it alive?"

"No."

Penny glances down at the robin's liquid black eyes. "Its yes move."

"Sometimes, when the roots grow into the body, they touch nerves or muscles. They can squeeze joints until they bend," Hadrian explains.

"They grow that fast?"

Hadrian shrugs.

Penny weighs the sculpture in her hands. "How big is your collection?"

Hadrian doesn't answer and Penny opens the door wider so more light spills into the hallway. He steps further back, shielding his eyes with his right arm. "You've blinded me."

"Sorry," Penny says. She grabs an old box and uses it to prop open the door. "Are there more?"

"That depends," he answers. "What do you think of it?"

"It reminds me of my sister, which makes me sad, but in sort of a nice way because it's making me think about her," Penny answers. Hadrian's silence compels her to say more. She shifts her weight from foot to foot as she thinks. "It's like this robin is safe in its nest and nothing can take it away." She pauses. "This place actually reminds me of Denise too. We'd always explore weird places, go through staff-only doors and see what was there."

"When did your sister die?" he asks, standing completely still.

"Seventy-two days ago."

"Still frozen," Hadrian murmurs.

"What did you say?"

"I'm very sorry." Hadrian reaches out and takes the sculpture from her. He looks down at it, smiles and then snaps his head up. "Would you like to see my tapestries?" he asks with sudden excitement. Penny nods. Hadrian seizes her hand and pulls her down the hallway. His firm grip and cool fingers make it easy for her to follow him. Denise used to hold on tight to Penny's hand as she pulled her towards another game.

Penny fumbles for the small flashlight on her keychain. She flicks the thin beam of light to get a closer look at Hadrian's face as he twists his head back to smile. The light doesn't reach his eyes, but shines on his open mouth and chin. Flashes of light glint off his tongue, teeth, and lips. Then she focuses the beam on the uneven floor so she won't trip. Penny's thumb hurts from pressing down on the flashlight's button so she lets the light sputter out.

Her eyes adjust to the light coming in through the doors behind them as they reach the trapdoor at the opposite end of the hallway. Hadrian wrenches it open and Penny shines her flashlight into the opening. A metal ladder clings to the left edge and its rungs disappear into shadows that her feeble flashlight can't illuminate.

Hadrian swings himself down and descends. Penny's heart beats faster. She counters her fear of climbing down into a dark pit after a strange man by reminding herself that this is her idea. She asked to see his artwork, she has a knife in her back pocket, she can run right now, but she's choosing to follow him.

She fumbles her way onto the ladder and counts nine rungs as she goes down. She places her feet on the floor, but something slips beneath her and she stumbles to her knees. She throws out her hands and her palms scrape over slick, uneven stone. Tiny legs crawl over her fingers and up to her wrists. She snatches her hands back, scratches her skin and shakes her hair to get rid of all the curious insects.

Hadrian doesn't move, speak, or offer any assistance; he just stands in the dark, waiting.

Penny gets up and points her flashlight at the ground. A moving carpet of rotting stems, leaves, and flowers covers the floor. Her fall disturbed centipedes, beetles, ants, silverfish, and other insects that are now scurrying over and under the leaves to find new resting places.

"Welcome to my hall," Hadrian says.

Penny breathes clean, damp air. It's refreshing compared to the dry, re-circulated air that pumps through the store. She shines her flashlight down the hallway in both directions. The circle of light dashes up walls of dirt and mud, which are supported by columns of stone. Roots grow out of the walls and into the air like stray hairs twitching in a quiet breeze. Denise might see something like this once her coffin breaks down: roots and worms squirming through the ceiling of earth to dab at the surface of her face, searching her delicate features for a place with perfect access to the nutrients in her corpse.

"Do you live here?"

"For now," Hadrian answers. "It's not a traditional home, but it will do for the time being."

"How long have you been here?" Penny asks, still shaken from her fall.

"I returned about three months ago."

Penny's chest twinges. She looks at the open trapdoor above her. One mad dash and she'll be back on familiar ground. "How did you get down here?" She shines the flashlight on Hadrian's face. He bends his head down so the light hits his forehead and creates black hollows in his eye sockets.

"Please don't do that, my eyes are sensitive. It's why I like it down here: I can see perfectly."

Penny lowers the beam to his feet.

"And to clarify I didn't get down here, I got up here."

Hadrian points to his right. Penny looks down the hall and realizes she's staring beyond the structure of the building. The flashlight beam should strike a wall, but it continues, showing stems stretching from the decay into the warm air.

"Where does it go?" Penny asks, leaning towards the tunnel.

"I can give you a full tour," Hadrian says, "but I want to show you my tapestries first."

He grabs her hand and squeezes. Penny flinches but lets him hold on. His long fingers coil around her wrist, pressing down against her pulse. He jerks her forward.

"Look at the wall. I created it," he says.

Displayed at different levels, animal corpses fill crevices all over the wall. Bird bodies hang near the ceiling and rodents float near the floor.

Hadrian walks backwards with his arm towards the wall like a guide in an art gallery. The corpses become more decayed as she walks on, and the plants become thicker. Some bird skeletons have vines twisted entirely around their bones, growing through the tiny holes in their skulls and the delicate joints in their wings. Penny bends down to examine a rodent skeleton. Vines weave in and out of its tiny ribcage. Roots twist around its spine and then back into the wall. It has no skin or tissue left. No ants or flies swarm over its carcass. Buds poke out between its ribs and one purple orchid blooms in its eye socket. Penny smiles at the peaceful bones.

"How do you do this?" she asks.

"I can demonstrate," Hadrian offers and leads her back towards the ladder. He takes the robin from under his arm and hands it back to Penny. Hadrian digs a crevice at eye level and shapes it into a horizontal rectangle. Roots fall into the chamber from all sides. The crevice is above a larger, vertical rectangle. Penny thinks it might fit a raccoon or a cat. Hadrian takes the robin and yanks it out of the nest. Vines trail out of it like loose threads. He positions it in the crevice, facing forwards.

"Now you tie the roots to hold it in place."

Penny starts pulling long roots towards her. She holds thin branches between her fingers and weaves them between the feathers around the wings. She twists and ties knots over the joints until the robin is suspended.

"Does your sister look like you?" Hadrian asks while she works.

"People always asked if we were twins," Penny answers. The robin feels soft and light and stiff in her hands. A film clings to her fingers when she's done.

"The last step is encouraging the roots to grow properly. Bird bones are hollow, so if you're lucky they can grow straight through the bones sometimes. May I please use your knife?" He holds out his hand and Penny places the box cutter in it. He uses the tip to puncture the robin's chest under its feathers and then pockets the knife. He pulls one root and threads it into the wound. "Would you like to try?"

Penny takes a vine and copies Hadrian's movements. She pushes it under the feathers and struggles to balance the amount of force necessary to push it into the body against the amount of force that will snap it. More blood rolls over the vine and makes her fingers slippery, but eventually the vine holds. She steps away and smiles. Their work has created a new artery and vein that grow out of the robin's chest.

The robin hangs with its wings spread. The roots bend its feathers in all directions. The outstretched legs make it look like the bird is about to seize something out of the air. In the vacant rectangle below it, Penny imagines a cat stretched on its hind legs, hanging in mid leap to pounce on the descending bird.

"This will be the centre," Hadrian declares and spreads his arms as wide as he can. "The rest of the tapestry will extend in mirror images around it. What do you think?"

"It sounds beautiful. But all the sculptures kind of get lost unless you're right next to them." Penny answers.

"Yes, so far I've only got vermin, and flying vermin, so scale is an issue," Hadrian says. "But the birds are getting bigger; I even have a crow. I'm going to unseal those doors so maybe some larger creatures will creep down to visit."

Penny looks back at him, her eyes shine with excitement. "I saw a cat near the doors this morning, maybe it'll come back. I think a cat would look perfect by the robin."

"I was thinking of a human," he answers and turns to her.

Penny freezes.

"Did your sister like art too?" he asks.

Penny imagines Hadrian standing over Denise and cutting her chest open. Penny shudders. "You can't get to Denise; she's in a sealed coffin. She's buried."

"It'll be difficult," Hadrian answers and moves towards her. "It would be much better if I could use someone closer to start with." He stands in front of her, waiting.

Adrenaline rushes through Penny's body. Her vision sharpens. She hears her breathing and the hum of flies in the air. Her eyes flick back and forth. He still has her knife.

"Nora, my co-worker, is upstairs," Penny lies. "She'll come down looking for me. I could bring her into the hallway; we could get her down here." Penny's voice shakes.

Hadrian doesn't answer, but he steps back and gestures towards the ladder, making way for Penny to climb up first.

"After you," Penny says. Hadrian bows and starts climbing. He moves fast and disappears through the trap door as she climbs up after him. Penny's fingers grip the edge of the hallway's concrete floor. As she starts pulling herself up, the trap door slams onto her knuckles.

Penny screams and loses her grip. Her feet bash against the rungs as she falls backwards. The concrete slams into her back and kicks the air out of her lungs. She splutters and coughs. Hadrian jumps down after her, lands on all fours, straightens and begins to circle her.

Penny watches his movements but can't initiate her own. Her fingers twitch and her legs throb. "Me," she mouths, "not Denise."

He looms over her. He doesn't look familiar any more. Blue and purple veins twist up his neck and stretch over his forehead, creating marble-like patterns on his skin. His eyes stretch open too wide, as if the skin is being pulled away from them. They sink inside his head and he doesn't blink. Dark spots spread around his jaw and hairline like mould. The sunken eyes and pale skin remind Penny of an unpainted mask.

"The tapestry must be balanced," he says with his face over hers. "Forgive me if I didn't explain it properly. English is my ..." He moves his hands in front of him and touches his thumb to the tips of his fingers multiple times. "It's not my first language."

Penny tries to move again, but all she feels is pain. Her hands are wet and warm. Blood rushes to her head, as if she stood up too fast, but at the same time, she feels like she's falling, the way she feels right before waking up, but nothing is changing. Insects scurry over her arm, crawl over her forehead and into her hair. It tickles. She wants to wipe them away, but she can't move.

Hadrian lifts her chin with his left hand and takes her box-cutting knife out of his pocket with his right. Penny watches his eyes loom over her face. Her heart beats stronger than it has before. Hadrian drags the stinging blade across her throat and blood gurgles out. Her fingers and toes tingle as dark spots spread across her eyes.

Penny feels cold. A wall of earth appears in front of her. It's familiar, but it takes Penny a moment to realize she's in the crevice below the robin. Something is tight around her neck. She feels tendrils threading into her open wound. They sting as they grow inside her skin. She can't move, her arms are limp at her sides and she can't feel her legs. Hadrian packs dirt around her and layers roots over her stomach and chest. He raises her arms. He weaves vines around her wrists and broken fingers so her bloody hands open towards the robin. He has to pay careful attention to her fingers so they don't curl inwards. It's slow work.

Penny looks down. Between her arms, she sees a thick root with a vine twisted around it coming out of her chest, just below her ribs. They create a constant pressure under her skin; it feels like they are reaching up, pushing other parts of her out of the way and making her chest tight.

"The eyes must stay open," Hadrian says as he reaches his hand down to pinch her right eyelid and feed tendrils into her socket. They spread against the inside of her skin and take hold, hooking her eyelid open. He does the same with her left eye.

Penny wants to blink, to grab the roots and yank them out of her, but she's stuck. Her skin tingles and the back of her head aches. She's afraid, but her body doesn't react. She feels like she would before cringing or squirming, but she can't withdraw. All she can do is watch and feel what's happening.

Hadrian digs in front of her and creates an opening to the robin's crevice and one into the wall beyond. The robin's chest is bright and its right eye glitters. Penny stares forward as Hadrian creates a second chair-like shape across from her. He steps back and surveys his work, becoming an obscure shape in her periphery. As he stares, she sees his vision too: a robin in the centre of his tapestry, hanging between two seated figures, and all of nature's bones stretching out behind them. Hadrian claps his hands together before turning and marching into the darkness.

Penny looks at the holes in the robin's body. They seem to get bigger as she watches them, their edges curling away from the roots in a slow disintegration. She wonders how long Hadrian's creations will last. When Hadrian returns with his stolen corpse, Penny will sit across from her sister, like they used to at their parents' table, but now she'll watch Denise decay before her eyes; her wounds growing larger and deeper until Penny sees muscles, organs and bones exposed, a process mirrored in her own body. The robin will watch too, a corpse reflected in each flickering eye until the earth decays them all.

WAITING ROOM

Richard Crow

Nothing. He woke to nothing, the boredom of the waiting room. And pain, in his neck and left knee. Hair hung in his face, stabbed his eyes, and he raised his right hand to move it away.

He looked at the hand for a moment then, watched the air move around it, with the sudden sensation that he'd looked at a stranger's hand. Too old to be his. Only in his mid-thirties, but the hand of an old man. A thick club of tree bark. The fingers twisted inward at rest. Had the world been so hard to his hands?

He caught himself looking and put the hand away. Then moved his gaze around the room. Across from him, a slim woman shivered. Veins spilled down her arms like blue ink. Beside her, a thick man in glasses with a *Reader's Digest*. The cover of the magazine mentioned bears.

He didn't know what was happening. He didn't know the woman with the veins or the man in the glasses. He didn't know this sick, yellowed room. Before his eyes nothing in this clean, pale world he knew.

He twisted to look over his shoulder and a vice crushed his neck. The pain clasped him like a father and he knew now where he was.

He closed his eyes against the pain and when he opened them looked at his hand again. It sat in his lap now, laid over the other, and he turned both palms upward. Then turned his eyes away. But no matter where else in the room he tried to look, his gaze kept shifting back to his hands, as if they held gravity.

His too-old hands. What must Sarah think when they touched her, how must she feel?

Sarah.

He wanted Sarah. He didn't see her and couldn't remember why. Head cloudy, immersed in fog. He drew a long breath and held it to dissipate the fog. Then he remembered and the breath went out of him.

He rose, clenched his teeth. Saw a receptionist set into the wall twenty feet away and moved to her in limping strides. A short line queued before her, but he walked past it to the front where a giant man bent to argue with the woman in the wall. The giant didn't have the proper form. The woman in the wall tried to explain this. He stepped forward and the giant stopped talking. Pushing past the tall man, he put his hand down on the counter, hard.

"Where's my wife?"

The woman in the wall looked past him and he knew that security was coming, fast.

"I want my wife. After the accident—"

"Sir, you're going to have to wait." She continued to glance past him and he knew security was almost there, would arrive before he had another sentence out. "If you'll just—"

"I won't—" and a hand clasped his shoulder. The pain in his neck incredible, a knife below his brainstem. He shrieked and almost collapsed and the hand pulled away.

"I barely touched him," the guard said to the woman in the wall, his witness.

"Sir. You need to wait. The doctor will see you soon, but you have to wait for now. Please take a seat."

"I don't want a seat. I want my wife."

"You will have to take a seat for now. The doctor will see you soon."

His resistance pointless. All alike. Functionaries that refused everything. He didn't move. The guard hovered. "Just tell me where she is, right now. Is she still in the operating room?"

"Only the doctor can tell you. You have to wait for the doctor. Please."

If only, he thought, with sudden aggression. *If only you'd beg.* But it was an order, that *please*, not a request. He turned back to the yellowed expanse of the waiting room. In the turning his knee bit into him. He thought to ask for something for the pain but knew the answer. He'd have to see the doctor—if he wanted anything with power, anyway. He'd have to wait.

He limped back to his seat. The guard hovered. The woman in the wall turned back to her giant.

Sarah in surgery, and him here. How long had he slept? Sarah laid out on a table and them cutting into her. He gagged at the thought and swept the room for something to focus on, something to push the nightmares from his head.

The dark-veined girl scratched her jeans with worried languor. The thick man held the *Reader's Digest* close to his face, engrossed in some nonsense. Maybe Sarah's article? No, he remembered, her article would not be published. They'd cancelled it, still owed her the kill fee she'd negotiated. Her kill fee.

He wanted to sleep again. He hated the waking world. The floor blue and the walls yellow and he hated them both. He claimed this hate and would care for it always.

Were they cutting into Sarah now, or still sharpening their knives? How long had he waited? What time was it now? He searched the walls for a clock but could not find one, then heard someone call his name.

The voice called. He listened but did not respond and did not know why. The voice called again. From somewhere else, behind him—and still he did not respond and did not know why. Something in the voice closed his throat and made him want to hide. The voice called a third time. A line from one of Sarah's favourite poems rose in him, unbidden. *What I tell you three times is true.*

Why didn't he respond if it was true, if this was his true name? A nurse moved to stand beside him. She looked him over, a question in her eyes. He stood as if standing was an answer.

"Follow me, please."

He followed. Feeling dull, a worn pencil, the ragged edge of its wood housing about to tear the paper. The thought of Sarah being opened came to him again, so to push it away he thought back to the poem. In it, a man forgot his own name. He wondered what that must be like, and if Sarah felt strange to see her name in print—her new name, the last part his.

He still had not confirmed who he was to this nurse, although he supposed that following her meant confirmation. Yet though she knew now who he was, he felt he could not speak his name. That he needed to keep it from anybody listening. Thinking this way made him tired again, and he lapsed into an injured half-sleep. And followed the nurse, thoughtless, down halls of half-light that smelled of old blood.

The nurse led him down one hallway, then another, and another hallway then, the halls brightening as they went. Of these halls there seemed no end. He lost track of where they were in relation to the rooms he knew and he wondered where Sarah might have woken to find herself in this cathedral of clean, well-lighted halls.

The nurse turned down another hallway, this one lined with wheeled beds, shoved tight against the right-hand wall. The halls grew narrow and the beds cut them in half. Clean and white, the beds; clean and white like the halls. *Clean, well-lighted,* these words came back to him, words he'd heard before somewhere. They caught in his head like some torturous song.

Clean, well-lighted. Something Sarah read to him no doubt. She read aloud while they drove, hated the radio. As a consequence, he knew many things and had read much more than he'd ever cared to read or know. To Sarah words meant something wonderful, but to him they were just rocks, things to be picked up and looked under and put down, or crushed beneath.

The nurse turned again, down another hall, and he thought *we are turning left,* and in an instant those words replaced the others, *we are turning left.* Crowding his mind, this idiot thought. And he remembered that left was the way you kept turning if you wanted to get to the centre of a labyrinth.

Another hallway, more empty beds. The halls narrowed, and the metal rails of the beds chilled his arms when he brushed them. As they went, the beds became ragged in their placements, as if thrown aside in haste, and he thought it good to notice this. They turned again but instead of another hallway met a door of scratched grey metal framing a window of clouded glass.

A battered lock. A ring of keys appeared, one unlocked the door, and then they disappeared again, into the pockets of the nurse. She held the door for him and he strode forth. She followed, clicking the door shut, and he found himself in another waiting room.

Of course. This room smaller and white and white again and empty but for a line of red plastic chairs and he and the nurse. He looked down at the nurse's nametag, but the nametag just read *Nurse*. A cost-cutting measure? Somewhere a bureaucrat that didn't understand the purpose of nametags? Nurse, then.

"Nurse. I'm sick of waiting. Where's my wife?"

"Please have a seat. The doctor will see you soon and discuss the conditions with you."

The plural frightened him. How many things were wrong with her? He moved forward in a panic and she pulled back. "What conditions? What's wrong?" His hands balled, their nails chewed his palms.

Nurse's red hair was wound in a tight bun, and she raised a hand to check its tightness. "Please sir. Wait here." Satisfied with the bun, she lowered her hand.

Then stood there, awkward and silent. Her eyes moved aimless, avoiding his—pretty eyes, green flecked with grey. He realized he blocked her path and she was trapped in the furrow of the door. He thought about asking more questions, pressuring her, then moved aside. She was just the nurse, just Nurse.

Then she swept past him, a breeze blowing into the next room, and clicked that locked door shut as well.

———•◦•———

Bright fluorescents glared off the blank white walls to scour the white floor clean. The line of thin, red chairs provided the only colour, a bright cut on the wall's pale wrist.

The ideal waiting room, in its pure and perfect essence. He counted the chairs, eight. He sat on the fifth and grew conscious of there being no middle chair. This made him an intruder, the despoiler of the room's symmetry.

He looked for a clock, but there was none. His own watch had shattered in the crash. At the thought of the crash, a bolt of pain clattered into his head, rising from his leg to his neck and into the bloody mist of his memory.

He was aware of the world as a temporary thing. Wrapping paper wound tight around a pulsing nightmare. Torn away with the least effort, by mere accidents, or when the pulsing thing happened to expand.

He must have slept again, because he awoke. And stared at the room's nothing, the inkblot test of the day.

"Doctor will see you now." The words were a shell and exploded in his head.

Nurse led him down a small hall into the next room, an office, where Doctor already sat, a pleasant change from the usual routine. He'd begun to think of the man as *Doctor* and, sure enough, the nameplate on his desk announced the same.

Doctor did not rise, did not even glance up. His eyes fixed to some papers on his desk. The office itself shone in oaken splendour.

Sarah had once interviewed the CEO of some IT company for an article in their corporate newsletter. The office as she'd described it was all hardwood and sunlight. Rare books against the walls, a complete set of first-edition Faulkners, signed. Unread. The sole concession to the CEO's role in the company a small laptop on her large oaken desk.

Doctor's office mirrored that CEO's office—minus windows, sun, and laptop. The light here, even and cold, was provided by the same fluorescents he'd seen elsewhere in the hospital. The desk buoyed a scattering of papers and detritus but no computer. Two silver pens jutted from a black stone mount. Doctor selected one pen without moving his eyes from his papers and began to click it against the desk.

Doctor didn't care to look at him and now, before Doctor, all his aggressive questioning after Sarah dissolved. The last thing he wanted was for Doctor to tell him about Sarah. He wondered if he could leave and live with himself. Walk away and put everything from his mind forever. But this was not that world.

Instead, he waited for Doctor to address him and looked around the office. The books on the shelves were ancient, elegant editions. He spied *On Sphere-Making* by Archimedes and *Porisms* by Euclid, alongside Molière's translation of *De Rerum Natura* by Lucretius. Some people had too much money. An occasional concession to literature, including a two-book set of Aristotle, *The Poetics of Tragedy* and *The Poetics of Comedy*, that occupied a small stand beside the large, musty bookcases. None of the usual equipment or charts. The office less a medical doctor's than that of a psychoanalyst in a Hollywood film. A low red chair sat before the large desk, the same blood-dark plastic as the chairs in Doctor's waiting room. He lowered himself into its chilled scoop.

Doctor clicked his silver pen and did not look up from the papers. A louder click behind him and he turned to see that Nurse had closed the office door, though she remained inside, beside the now-closed door, shifting on her feet. Awkward, awaiting instruction.

The clicking stopped and Doctor twined the silver pen in his yellowed fingers. The hands fell atop a closed file folder, also red. Doctor turned thick head and dark eyes to him and tapped the pen on the folder. Then used the pen to tip the folder open and began to read aloud from the papers inside.

The words meant nothing to him, medical jargon and legal gibberish. The word *patient* surged and resurged. Was he discussing Sarah's surgery?

Doctor buzzed on, meaningless. "Options are varied but non-negotiable. Particulars left to Doctor's discretion. Two main options, non-compatible, present themselves."

"What are you talking about?" The pain from his neck and his leg grew with each word that Doctor spoke, writhed to converge in his stomach. The smell of rotting books coiled there too, curdling. "I want to know how the surgery went. In plain English."

Doctor looked up from his papers as if at a dog not learning its tricks. "The surgery continues, although it has been stilled for the moment, whilst we deliberate."

He tried to make sense of this while Doctor returned to his script. "Option one entails, barring abnormalities, the operation's failure and the consequent death of the patient. There are no conditions attached and no obligations attendant on any party."

The operation's failure. The rope of pain that connected his neck and leg knotted in his gut. Its frayed ends brushed the inside of his skull. He focused on it to keep these words away. But they sing-songed through his head like the words he'd fixated on earlier. He turned to the floor but the whorls of the hardwood made him dizzy, made him want to vomit.

He turned instead to the second silver pen, still in the heavy black mount. Beside it grew another empty sheath, the first silver pen still in Doctor's hands. Those hands twin spiders, tarantulas, curling down on either side of the medical file, backs sprawling with coarse brown hair.

Doctor continued. "The alternative option entails the patient's replacement and insertion into a new reality, as commencement of training, with death transferred to the patient's spouse."

The spider hands scuttled out to click out the pen's ballpoint. Its tip hovered over the papers in the file.

It struck him that Doctor was waiting for his response to this nonsense. These doctors all the same, just like Sarah at her worst—always trying to make you feel stupid or make you into something with their words. "Enough of this shit. I want to see my wife."

"That isn't one of the options. Look."

Doctor moved the papers forward so he could examine them for himself. Instead, he swept the folder and its papers onto the floor in a single, violent motion.

Doctor bit his lip in controlled rage and leaned back into his chair. A slow exhale. Then spoke, calm yet furious. "You gain nothing by this."

"Take me to Sarah." He stood. "If she's okay, maybe I won't need to get my lawyer involved."

"There is nothing your lawyer can do to me."

"He'll find something."

"Sit down." Doctor stood and grabbed his shoulder, squeezed. The pain cut like nothing could. He swore and swung his good arm to slap the hand away.

Doctor pulled back, raising his slapped hand, examining it as if he'd never been touched before. The pain in his shoulder and neck remained sharp, as if Doctor still held him, and he staggered to the side of the room, bumping the bookcase. That gave him an idea, and he began to pull the rare books from the wall.

As the books hit the floor, Doctor flinched. "Those cannot be replaced!"

"Take me to Sarah." *The Worm of Midnight* by Edgar Allan Poe crashed to the floor and its worn binding cracked.

Doctor clenched his jaw, spoke through his teeth. "Nurse."

And in a flash, she stood beside him, grasping his arm, her fingernails biting. A long needle flashed and sunk into his neck.

—————

He yelped, and Nurse withdrew the needle, clean and quick, as he shoved her off. She hit the bookcase hard, jarring a few more volumes onto the floor. They burst like rotten fruit, spines tearing, spilling mould.

He knew he should run but whatever was in the needle prevented him. Instead, he slumped against the bookshelf beside Nurse and dropped to the floor in stages. His eyes felt too large for his head and he pulled back his eyelids hoping to make more room for them.

While Nurse recovered herself, Doctor stooped to lift him off the ground and back into the red chair. Doctor lifted him like he was a pillow. He wanted to grab Doctor's tarantula hands and snap their legs off one by one but he just let Doctor guide him back to the chair, resisting only the urge to blink his too-large eyes.

Doctor returned to his chair and to clicking the silver pen, while Nurse collected the papers from the floor and set them back upon the desk. Doctor held the pen up just below his lips, as if the pen's clicking would focus attention on his mouth, and it did. He stopped clicking the pen and began to wiggle it instead. When Doctor spoke, it seemed as if the words were being written by the pen, visible in the air rushing out of his red maw.

"I will repeat the dilemma in layman's terms." The silver pen swayed, mesmerized. "You were in a car accident. You and Sarah. She sits in the waiting room now, while they operate on you."

Senseless ghosts, the words from the swaying silver pen.

"I stilled the operation, the reality of the operation, at the insistence of my superiors." Doctor offered a cold, sardonic smile at the word *superiors*, as if there could be no such thing. "They have taken an interest in you," he continued. "They believe you could become a Doctor yourself one day." His tone made it clear that this was impossible.

He's insane. Drugged, he thought this the way he would think the chair red—a plain fact that aroused no interest or emotion.

"So I present you with two options, as directed by those others. You may return to your life and the operation. Most likely you will not survive. Although of course, miracles happen, as the ignorant say. I can't guarantee your death with true certainty. I simply don't care to investigate the extent of your injuries enough to form a professional opinion, which is why I've inserted that wording about *abnormalities*. But at a glance"—he closed his eyes, as if he could see another world when they were closed—"things aren't looking good for you."

He smiled, eyes still closed. Relishing whatever he saw. Then opened them. "Of course, there is your second option." He paused, and his face soured. It was clear which option Doctor preferred. "You may elect to have the reality altered."

He felt that he was coming back to himself, just a tiny bit, and tried not to show it. Focusing on Doctor's words as if there were nothing else in the world.

"There are limited alterations. Some I am not capable of performing. Most I am not willing to perform. In this instance, I offer to transfer the injuries to your wife—you will survive and be assessed and trained in a modified reality. Perhaps you will be offered some position at a later date—whether Doctor or Nurse or something else, I cannot say. My work is elsewhere. Although, from time to time, I am forced to abandon those duties and attend to insignificant, bureaucratic nonsense."

Doctor clicked the pen. "So." And set it down on the desk, breaking whatever spell.

His head hurt worse than ever—a side effect of the drug? It had worn off for the most part, he felt sure, though he was still afraid to move, to show this. Doctor leafed through the papers and then pulled out a form. He could see that most fields were already filled in. "You have a decision to make."

He was stunned to hear it all so plain. So this was the nightmare world. A chaos with monsters like men, who just wanted you to fill out the proper forms.

Nurse had moved back toward the door to give them what passed for privacy here. He tried not to show himself noticing this. But it was hard to hold these things inside. "I want Sarah." He almost cried from the choice and the pain.

"Is that an answer? I require a clear answer. If you simply want to see her, that is not a viable option."

Doctor enjoyed this, he could tell. The torture. Needles and forms. Enough. He reached for the second silver pen, the one still in its mount. His head had cleared, and Nurse's needle had taken the edge off his pain. Small mercies.

He brought the pen to the form, clicked out its point. Doctor stared, expectant. He slid his eyes around the page and moved as if to write something, then stabbed the silver pen into Doctor's left eye.

———

For a moment he did not know what he'd done. Doctor fell back and off his chair, bleeding and holding his face, fingers splayed around the pen. But did not scream.

He looked down at his hands again. Whose hands were these? Nurse came at him, slashing with the needle, but though she cut a red line down his left shoulder, he managed to twist behind her and slam her head against the thick desk. The syringe in her hands jittered as she reached back towards him, trying to rise, and he let her up a little but then slammed her face against the desk again. The syringe and her nails scratched at the desk as she scrambled and clawed, but he slammed her head again and began to tear through her pockets for the key ring he'd seen earlier.

Doctor had slumped onto the floor, but his body jerked upright so that his back slapped against the wall. He didn't move after that, though his remaining eye watched as Nurse's face smashed into the desk, again and again. Except for her scratching and clawing, and the noise that her head made as it hit the desk—a wet thunk with no constancy—the scene played out in a jarring silence.

He found the keys and slammed Nurse's one more time, harder, then pushed her against the nearest bookshelf. More books burst, like stars or fruit, spilling brittle pages onto her spastic, bloodied form. He stepped away in a loping run and his injured leg began to buckle. He teetered but recovered himself, refused to fall.

He rushed through the office door and down the thin hallway to the waiting room. The stillness followed him, punctured by his heavy steps and quickthick breathing, but otherwise all swam in a soupy silence.

Endless were the things he kept expecting to hear, and he thought, Is the world so quiet? And he marvelled at the things he had just done.

----·•·----

The waiting room remained empty but seemed filled with the silence now. He searched the keys as he rushed across it. He'd seen Nurse use a key on the door, but which key? Which key? Though he couldn't hear them he knew they must be behind him, they were somewhere behind him, it could not be this easy, they must be behind him, their bloodied faces. Which key? But when he reached the door there was no door.

There was no door. Just a blank wall, white and gleaming. His face reflected in its shining tile.

He dropped the keys. Stopped. Footsteps behind him and he turned to face those footsteps. There was no door and nothing else to do.

Doctor strode towards him, and Nurse followed. Doctor hadn't pulled the pen from his eye, and blood ran down in tears, the pen jarring more blood with each quick step. It seemed that Doctor *wanted* the pen there. To show off, to worry the wound. That he *liked* it.

They stopped before him, bleeding onto the clean white floor. Where the blood fell in crimson drops, the floor sucked it in, drank it down, absorbed it like a sponge, so that it disappeared and did not mar the gleaming tile. He wondered what here was the monster. Did the waiting room feed this way? Had it orchestrated everything just so it might have its blood?

Then his time to wonder ceased. Doctor watched him fall back against the wall, legs buckling. Watched him slump to the floor. Doctor turned his head so that the dead eye with its silver pen faced him as he sobbed in a new silence. Nurse hung back, obedient, nose broken, lips split in a half-grin, some of her teeth shattered. Blood dripped from both faces to the hungry floor.

"Leave me alone." He huddled into his knees, a lost child.

"I need an answer." Doctor looked away with his good eye, scanned the bare walls, bored, though his dead eye stayed fixed forward, as if it saw. "Is that an answer?"

They wouldn't stop. They would never stop. They would bleed out rivers before they stopped. Doctor looked down and clicked out his pen.

All of a sudden, the terror left him. Doctor ridiculous. Another functionary. Pen poised. He almost laughed, but a new horror arrived, to choke the laughter.

There was something else. Something beyond. Before which even Doctor would slump, terrified. Something that required these forms.

Before he knew it, he had answered. "Yes."

Doctor made a mark on the form.

Then knelt down, to eye level, to mock him. "There. It's over. Was that so hard?"

———•◦•———

He expected more, but they walked back to the office, their business concluded. The pain burned his bones now. He knew that it would never leave him. The wall felt colder against his back, metal, and he twisted to see that the door had returned. Nurse hadn't bothered to retrieve her keys, and after many failed attempts, he unlocked the cold door.

He walked the halls and tried to think of nothing but the walking. He found himself amazed at this walking, how his feet moved with such precision, at the slightest senseless thought.

He walked from one hall to another, always turning right, until he found himself back in the first waiting room. After hours that could not be counted or regained. As he entered the waiting room, he heard a nurse call his name.

He did not respond. The nurse called his name again and he waited. This was the waiting room, after all. He waited for something to happen, for her to call on someone else, for a new name.

If he understood Doctor, this was not his world. Something similar but stranger. But it didn't matter. He didn't care.

What mattered was the thing inside him. The thing that made something, somewhere, think he'd make a fine Doctor one day.

He turned his head when the nurse called a third time, turned away. In the turning, his neck flared. The pain clasped him like a father. He knew now who he was.

LIKE FALTERING, LISPING TONGUES

Brock Peters

A forest stood silently at the edge of town. Small houses sat tucked in between the trees like eggs in a nest, as though they weren't so much foreign bodies but just an extension of the wilderness. Many were made with wood from those same trees, sitting upon stones cleared diligently from the golden ocean of farmers' fields that stretched endlessly outwards from the other side of the highway.

By five in the morning, some of the farmers had begun to stir on the fringes of town, preparing to face a hard day. The only person moving inside the town proper at that hour was a young man in his kitchen, preparing coffee with a press. His house was perched on the cusp of the forest. The back door exited out onto a small deck that offered a perfect view of the tree line, where the thickening of the trees was so subtle that it was hard to tell where exactly the forest began. Compared to some of the farmers and shopkeepers whose families had lived and died in this very town for generations, Albert was still an outsider.

He poured his coffee into an old white mug that haunted an otherwise empty cupboard and added fresh cream bought from a kind lady across town. Sometimes it seemed like the farm animals wandered through town more or less at will, and the crowing of the roosters and gentle exclamations of the cows, as though surprised, made it hard for Albert to find sleep.

Pulling on his jacket, he went outside into the chilly early morning. Two old wicker chairs sat on the deck at either side of a careworn wooden table. He wiped dew from both chairs with his cuff before sitting, and the wicker creaked loudly. The air was absolutely still. Occasionally a rooster called tentatively, as though hesitant to break the silence. Given another hour, they would have no such qualms.

Albert let his coffee cool before taking a sip. He felt nearly calm, almost peaceful, but he did not feel happy. His emotions were detached from the serenity around him. He wore a weary expression.

From a pocket in his jacket, Albert produced a chocolate bar of fine quality, the work of a chocolatier who lived nearby and whose products were highly sought after. The fading hand-painted sign on the highway that advertised his craft was hardly necessary, as many travellers would make a special trip just to peruse the shelves of treats hand-wrapped in gold and silver foil. Albert carefully placed the chocolate on the other side of the table and then leaned back to wait, drinking his coffee.

It always began with the whispers. They flitted through the air like hummingbirds, incomprehensible and echoing. Once, he shocked himself by stumbling upon the notion that the whispers amounted to all of the sounds—at least the human ones—that had ever passed through that place, working their way through the ages. Eventually, he thought, they must cycle back to the beginning, and the very same whispers would be heard again. Listening to the whispers was like trying to have a conversation beside a waterfall. Every morning he attempted to catch snippets of language, just a word or two, without success. Sometimes he dreamed about what the whispers could mean, what it seemed the voices were saying, though the chances that they were even in English were slight indeed. Throughout the new morning, the whispers would persist without becoming any louder or softer.

Next, Albert would notice things moving through the trees, almost like flares of light filtered between the leaves. At first, months ago, he'd tried to focus on these elusive forms, just like the whispers, to make out a shape or an outline. But now he sat back and watched as though it were a show, the flitting shadows and the voices creating a dreamlike performance and he, on the deck with his coffee and the untouched chocolate bar, was the lone member of the audience. He knew, however, that he could not have been the only one to ever sit here, and so counted himself among an audience that spanned time rather than space, a faceless congregation of the bewildered who gathered here at nature's altar to delight in the stillness and the wonder.

There were mornings when that was the extent of it. The extent of it, Albert thought, as though such an experience could be belittled. On these mornings he would sit and watch and listen, and eventually break the spell by glancing at his watch before picking up the uneaten chocolate bar and going back inside. If he came back out, even after only a few minutes, the air would be silent but for the crowing of roosters, and the trees would be still. One such fruitless morning as he stood to leave, Albert was seized by frustration. He tore his watch from his wrist and threw it against the deck, smashing it and spreading its little pieces all over the ground.

Today, though, he could feel the urgency in the whispers and the speed of the moving spirits, and he knew that it would not be a disappointing morning. His heart began to beat quickly. There was a spot near the fence where two pear trees stood side by side, with just enough room for a person to walk between them, and it was here that Albert rested his gaze in anxious anticipation.

The branches of the pear trees began to rustle and Albert permitted himself a tired smile. One way or another his desire would be satisfied. From between the trees stepped a tall figure standing upright on long, impossibly thin legs. Its torso was grey and its ribs poked through the skin; the only clothing the figure wore was a brown loincloth. Its head was elongated, and it had large, curious eyes and thin wisps of transparent hair. It met Albert's gaze before walking toward the deck, slowly and resolutely, as if it had to carefully ponder each step. Albert had a strong suspicion that if it hadn't wanted to, it need not have walked at all.

He'd seen this spirit before. Upon its first manifestation, its appearance had alarmed him; others of the spirits tended at least to resemble familiar beings, while this one was a truly unique creation of nature. It was kind, though: benevolent and inquisitive. It didn't judge his iniquities as harshly as some. This spirit, Albert knew, did not speak English, and as such, he'd never learned its name.

The spirit slowly climbed the stairs to the top of the deck and sat in the chair opposite Albert. The chair made no sound, as if its occupant was somehow unsubstantial. The spirit twisted its thin mouth into a peculiar smile and opened its enormous eyes even wider.

"Good morning," Albert said.

In a deep, smooth voice, the spirit intoned something that Albert could only assume to have a similar meaning, though like the whispers he couldn't identify words within the sounds. A few of the spirits spoke a lyric, archaic form of English, like they'd learned the language by reading ancient books, and communicating with them was nearly as difficult as with those who spoke no English at all.

"Well," said Albert, "I did it again yesterday." The spirit looked up, and even with its past gentleness in mind, Albert hoped that its inscrutable new expression was one of sympathy. Some of the spirits responded with rage. Hesitating, Albert finally continued, "I drove west off the highway, and I found a field and waited there with my bag and some bait, and I caught one. The little guy never knew what hit it. There has to be a better way than this, don't you think? It just makes me feel so desperate." As Albert spoke, the spirit unwrapped the chocolate bar deliberately, pausing before peeling away each corner. It adopted a thoughtful expression as it ate, as though taking care to ensure that Albert realized how intently it was listening to what he had to say. "I took it to that little shack by the service road and woke it up and did away with it. The sounds it made, my God, the sounds were terrific. Just wonderful. I hear them when I'm trying to sleep, the squeals and the screams, and it's so soothing. It almost helps."

There was a pause as Albert finished speaking, and the spirit turned its large eyes up to the sky and leaned back soundlessly in its chair. It seemed to be appealing to something in the cosmos. Then it bent forward, reached across the table, and embraced him with its long arms. Finally, the spirit regarded him with transparent sympathy and began to talk.

Listening to a spirit talk was like listening to music, music that you understood intimately and intuitively. Each change in inflection and tone had meaning, and without being able to put it into words, Albert could somehow understand what the spirit was trying to say. Its arms traced slow circles in the air, accentuating the steady rhythm of its speech. It became a dramatically gesticulating orator from the woods who was telling a story, the literal meaning of which was utterly lost to Albert, though its sonorous essence remained.

It spoke this way interminably, never once pausing for breath, lulling him into a deep trance. As always, he felt his eyes become heavy. His head bent forwards and darkness fell over him, and suddenly he bolted upright as though having been shocked, eyes open wide. The other chair was empty, and the spirit was gone.

Albert picked up his coffee cup and the silver wrapper from the chocolate bar and scanned the tree line once or twice. He was comforted. He knew that talking to the spirits was nothing but a respite, that he would end up again in the same place with the screams and the euphoria and the gentle trickle of blood. But not today. He wondered whether the spirits might eventually tire of him and resolve that he wasn't worth the effort, that he was beyond redemption. Slowly, Albert walked back inside the house, closing the screen door firmly behind him, and went back to bed.

A WINTER'S TALE

Daria Patrie

I detest my husband. He is a bastard.

The girl is terrified. When she rushed in the room and slammed the door shut behind her, the music stopped and all the dancers turned and looked. She panted wild-eyed while they stared at her, dispassionate as my not-so-darling husband's pet flung itself repeatedly against the other side. Her hair damp with sweat from running, her partially torn nightgown no doubt a testament to claws just-missed and teeth almost but not quite close enough to take their prey. She is lucky to have gotten this far, really. Most monsters have one head. That one has three. She is lucky, too, that the door she has pressed herself up against latches, although that, like her escape, is far less likely actual luck than it is elaborate orchestration.

Her chest heaves, pulling the white bodice of her thin shift tight with each breath. Her beauty is stunning, though I would expect no less. Her long black hair spills over her shoulders in waves of tousled shadow as she glances around the room, seeing it for the first time, seeing the panelled walls with their tapestries, the chandeliers, the dancers. She does not see me.

For a few moments she and the dancers stare unblinking at each other, then the concertmaster claps his hands, the music strikes up, and the masque continues on as though the outburst had never happened, as though there were no young pretty running for her life, or as though such activities were completely normal, which they are. In a daze, she slowly steps away from the door, confused at the shift in scenery and the false implication that she has escaped what was threatening her.

The dancers look much like a room full of dolls, their movements forced and wooden. That is on purpose. They could appear more natural if he wished. They will appear any way that he wishes. My husband adores detail. Each velvet fold trimmed in lace, each silken slipper, each ruffle has been replicated in minute detail from something he found amusing at some point. I wonder if the brilliant plumage would even separate from their faces if she tried to remove one of the masks. The shiny, gaudy, glittery figures whirl in perfect time to the waltz. Like flightless birds they sway: pirouetting in pairs, their steps in three-quarter time. The pageantry is mirrored in the gleam of the dark marble floor, the gleam from each facet of the chandeliers. He adores lush expensive décor, my husband, and lush exquisite playthings.

Mechanically ignored, the young girl moves away from them. She does not try to stop any of them as they prance. Does she sense the horror that would await her should she attempt to tear off one of the masks? Or does she feel a natural aversion to anything so grossly re-animated? Does she know why she unconsciously shuns this pantomime of gaiety? I do not know. I do not know and do not care, and yet I do care and follow her without her knowing I am doing so.

She walks past the dancers, past the pillars and the swirling skirts and the lights, past the feathers and the black and the gold filigree. She reaches the side of the ballroom and begins ascending the spiral stairs closest to me and I follow. I follow and watch the ragged tears in the skirt of her nightgown flutter around her legs and thighs, her skin pink with exertion in contrast to the white of her garment. Her feet are bare, with polite toes unused to fending for themselves without footwear. She has slender, delicate ankles.

As she climbs, a look of urgency crosses her face, as though someone were calling her. But of course! Someone is. So crafty my husband—drawing the prey nearer as it thinks it is running away. Up, up, above the puppet show. I muted my ears to his voice long ago, preferring silence to his lies.

He is there, of course, on the landing. His hair frames his current face in handsome black ringlets. His eyes are smiling with the pretense of kindness as he leans back against the balcony rail in a sensual poet's shirt and dark pants. Predictably, she falls into his arms, sobbing, begging him to help her. Ah, fool! Beg the devil to lead you out of hell. He loves it when they trust him. It adds depth and meaning to his games.

A thumb and one finger under her chin, he lifts her tear-streaked face. His lips slightly pouting, saying soothing words to his frightened "guest." There is possessiveness in his eyes, and artifice, but it is hard to see unless one knows what to look for. She hugs him tightly in response, unaware her existence has been confiscated by the wretched beautiful demon that is holding her, soothing her. No, she does not see it. She drinks in his smile. I cannot hear what else he says to her—no matter. At this point, I know it off by heart. He will take her under his care, keep her safe, be her guardian and she his ward, if she will but offer this one thing to him, this one tiny thing for which she doesn't even have a use any more.

Her fluid body solidifies into a statue and she rigidly pulls away from the arms around her. Oh my sweet creature! You are a fighter! This is both beautiful and terrible, and I cannot look away. A frown is on his sensuous lips, but his eyes... his eyes are laughing. He is delighted by her rejection. It bores him when they give in too quickly. I wonder if he deliberately mis-worded his trap or if she was smart enough to figure it out on her own? Now I want to hear. What is she saying to him? She is shaking. He leans back against the railing, his long hair sweeping back behind perfect cheekbones and elfish ears, and he laughs out loud.

She scrambles like a cat on a freshly polished floor, pulling herself away from him in a panic and slipping, her bare foot catching on the blood-red carpet. She falls, frantic as he laughs at her, pulling at anything around her to place it between my husband and herself. And then she is up again and running along the balcony overhanging the dance floor. She tries first one door and then another while his laughter chases her. Eventually a handle turns, and she darts into a new hallway and slams the door behind her, as though that could somehow keep her safe from what is about to happen.

I know where she is going. All upper hallways lead there. I, too, am enchanted by her beauty and her spirit. I cannot help but follow, and my vile husband watches as I trail after his prey, his dancing eyes following me as I melt into the wall. I am more tenuous than air and I waft through the cracks until I hover above the water of the river that runs below the bridge she is going to run across. Large arches support the footpath. Moonlight refracts off cold wet stone.

I hear footsteps. She approaches.

The wind raises a fine spray of water and buffets my insubstantial hair. I feel it shifting in my amorphous clothing, making my dress swirl, creating diaphanous ribbons of mist and smoke. I hover and rise almost to the level of the bridge, but I stay low. Low enough to ensure that she will understand. When she turns, I will myself visible, and she gasps as she sees me.

The wind presses her clothing to her body, one moment outlining her pear-shaped breasts, another her crescent buttocks, shifting her dress no matter which way she turns. The moist air is heavy as she stands on the bridge, breathing deeply, taking stock of her surroundings, no longer sobbing. She is determined, independent, not yet certain of her doom but certain she will choose her path. She is the most beautiful creature in the world to me now. In that moment as I see her and she sees me, I love her.

I do not speak but I plead to her with my eyes. The waves smash against the stone walls on either side of the bridge, raising water that splashes down into itself in waves of white and black in the silver moonlight. I reach out to her and beg her silently to join me.

She leans against the railing, and her black hair drips over the edge of the teetering bridge. Lean over to be with me, my love. Rimona. I can see it in her face, beautiful red-rimmed eyes. Her name is Rimona. She reaches out her hand, and her fingertips almost touch mine. I mouth my name to her. She feels the connection between us and she leans forward, but then she catches herself and looks down. The sharp rocks below glisten; they are large black diamonds in the moonlight, the teeth of a welcoming maw.

Startled, she looks at me, questioning. I nod my answer. Yes, my love. I bring you death. But death that is free of him. It is an escape through cold water and sharp stone. Take it, my love. Take my hand. Melt into me. Breathe me in as your last breath.

A tear makes its way down her cheek. I have lost her. The wind catches my sigh and brings it to her lips but she will not take my gift.

There is a bone-wrenching howl, and then another, and a third, shattering our communion. A heavy body flings itself against the door she came through. I give her a tearful smile. Run, my love. Run. It will tear you apart when it finds you. You will scream for hours and I will be grateful that I can no longer hear. Run. If you will not take my quick, clean gift, then run.

I blow a kiss to her as she flies across the bridge. The wind tears it from my mouth and runs it through her hair, beside her ear, down her chest and between her legs. That bastard. Damn him and his dogs and his music and his wind. I can feel him laughing as the wind rustles Rimona's nightgown around her legs, whipping it up, from below to cover her face, tearing it a little more, revealing more of her skin. She doesn't realize each gust is his breath, each wind-whipped splash of water his fingers caressing her body through her clothes. Ah, delicate prey, you are so fierce, so beautiful, so doomed. The outcome will break my heart, yet I must watch to the end.

Damn him for making me love her. Damn him for letting her believe she has a chance.

I will watch her to the end. Not for him. Not for myself, but to honour her. There should be a witness to her strength of spirit, even if she is to fall, and fail, and die trying so hard to escape, to live. I will watch.

And so again I fade, slipping through the cracks, a discarnate vapour sliding across and between and through the cold stones. Up, through the rock. Up, through the wooden floorboards, through the lush carpet. And I hover behind her, invisible.

Rimona stands before the doors to the upper chambers of the tower. They are immense and intricately carved. A hermit on a mountain is fed by a raven in the top left. Another panel shows a cup—the mark of death upon it—handed to a man by his brother. Next to it, a similar panel of the cup glowing with the grace of God (etched in gold leaf) as the saint blesses it and removes the poison. Another carved image speaks to people gathered in wonder. There is an image of a city, shining (etched in silver leaf) while enemies are turned away by the man in front, praying to God. My favourite, at the bottom of the right door, has the saint converting witches, casting Satan out of a grove of trees and sanctifying a pagan altar which had previously been dedicated to the goddess of the dead. The outer edges of the doors are adorned with bells, broken cups, and ravens. In the middle, his face whole with both doors closed, stands the saint— a rod in one hand, a book in the other, stepping on a snake, protecting the innocent from poison, witchcraft, and all evil.

Rimona touches the carved foot, the one that is crushing the snake, and looks back, through me, to the end of the hallway she came through. Oh, fool! Do not enter the doorway. The saint is false. He will not protect you from the snake. That door was carved by a man who thought he was creating beauty to glorify God. He died within sight of his masterpiece, screaming while three hungry mouths fought over who could pull out more of his entrails.

A howl echoes down the hallway. The beast is coming. Biting her lip, Rimona pushes open the door, splitting the saint in half. I cannot keep from following behind.

And there they are, all of them, in the chapel. The dancers from below: neatly ordered, no longer flamboyant, no longer moving, but sombre, restful as the bride enters. They all turn to look at her, and I am invisible behind her. Their eyes are hollow in their hollow-eyed masks. Near the front, my false husband stands, the loving groom, his hand outstretched to take her.

Rimona spins and pulls at the door, but the saint has betrayed her and will not open. Beside her, I become visible. She sobs and reaches out to touch me. Her hand passes through mine, and I shake my head in sorrow. I cannot help you, child. I can only bear witness and offer you my cold comfort. Go now to him. There is nowhere else to go.

She is drawn past the porcelain faces and the wooden pews. Halfway to the front, she turns to one side and begs one of the dancers for assistance. His clay face cracks and half his head slips off his shoulders to shatter on the floor. Rimona pulls away, crying as I come behind her. Oh, to hold her and comfort her, even for a moment. I will not look at my husband. I will not see the cruel glee in his face at this display of my weakness.

The air is heavy. Thick jasmine overpowers the senses. We all move as though we are moving through water. At the altar, there is no priest, but a casket: a pretty box with a glass lid, the kind a fine lady would place her jewels in, but larger. Rimona backs away from it, through me, until her shoulders brush against a giant bouquet of lily of the valley taller than she is. They caress her, the blossoms flattening against her neck and face as she sobs between deep gasping breaths, turning this way and that, a helpless lamb caught in a thicket.

Pandora does not want to open her box.

My husband, the dark angel, tilts his head, and a thin tendril of hair slips down in front of his face as he smiles.

The predator raises his right hand. The lid of the box opens. The little lamb screams.

There lies Rimona in the box, a twin of the screaming girl just a few feet away. Little worms crawl through little worm tunnels just beneath her skin. A cockroach suckles at the corner of one milky eye. The expression of pure terror can still be made out on her decomposing face.

Rimona's screams continue, ragged, with brief interruptions for breaths of air to fill her lungs to scream once more.

My husband's cold green eyes send their bitter laughing glances through wisps of his black hair. She thinks he is laughing at her, but he is looking at me, the bastard. The wretched, manipulative, bastard.

She tears at the lilies while they twine even tighter round her wrists, her ankles, her neck, her waist. She writhes as they lift her and bring her towards the box.

All this time, I thought she was the focus of the game. That the corruption of the innocent dove was purely a diversion from boredom for my wretched husband. He laughs as understanding overtakes my face. The screaming young thing is lowered into the casket, brought closer and closer to its rotting twin, and that is when I know.

He never meant to let his pet eat her. He never even meant to take her soul. He meant all along for me to love her, but not so I could be sad when she dies. She will not get to die. He will make me watch as he drives her mad and destroys the fire that has so entranced me. His torture of her will not end.

When I was taken from my mother to this place, I made a vow. It has been the only thing that keeps me separate from him. It has always irked him that I would not stoop to his level. That I would not touch, not partake of the physicality of his detestable existence. I have always remained fey, intangible. And so he makes me choose.

And I choose the only choice that I can bear.

I materialize and become flesh. I rip the lilies from the terrorized child and I hold her. My husband crows his triumph. I pull the lamb close, her breasts pressing up against mine, and I pull her into a deep kiss. For a moment, Rimona struggles, but then she realizes that it is I and I think—I hope—she understands. Relaxing, she breathes her last breaths into my mouth, down my throat. My lungs expand. Hers contract. Six times. Her lungs do not expand again.

I kneel and lay the child down gently. My husband wills the marionettes to applaud. I stiffen as his hands caress my now damned neck. The little lamb has been sacrificed. My mouth is filled with tart red blood. I have given her freedom through murder. And for that, I have paid a price that is far, far too high.

"Persephone, my love," his voice coos in my ear, "so good of you to join us."

KNOWN OF OLD AND LONG FAMILIAR

Géza A. G. Reilly

There's always been something about bookstores that I've adored. I thought they were special places. Some of my best memories were of them, and my favourite pastime was to wander up and down the long, stately rows of bookcases containing treasure after treasure. It was those treasures I was after, those gems of narratives and ideas that could fill my head and my hours, connecting me with the world around me, with the grand narrative of humanity that had preceded me. Each book was, to me, a monument, a memorial, an eternal reminder of all that we could be.

It had always been that way. When I was a little kid, my father would take me to a strip mall close to our house whenever I needed a haircut. There was a cheap and friendly barber there who was good with children; he was an old guy who moved slowly but had very sure hands and a gentle tone of voice. I think my father liked him because he reminded my dad of his father. The key to keeping me still in the chair, my father discovered, was in the second-hand store next door to the barbershop.

We stopped in there one day, to pick up a replacement for some household item or other, and I was immediately entranced by the place. The dust, the rickety shelves, the unabashed used-ness of all the items on display—I was instantly in love. What really hooked me was a big old cardboard box that the owners of the store had put up front and stuffed full of battered comic books. I gravitated to that thing like it had me in a tractor beam and immediately pawed through every issue. Most of them were romance comics, which I dismissed as girly, but some of them were superhero comics. That first trip, I found a huge, oversized one-shot issue of a famous strongman character fighting an even more famous boxer and begged my father to buy it for me.

I didn't know it at the time, but a life-long passion had been born.

Every time my father took me to get a haircut, we had to stop at the second-hand store. And every time we stopped at the second-hand store, I had to go diving through box after box of texts—first comics and then, eventually, full-on books—to try to find some rejected gold. It quickly became an addiction, one which I lived with for years and years.

After that, I couldn't walk past a bookstore without at least spending a few minutes inside. No matter how meagre their stock, I was always dazzled by the potential sources of knowledge and enrichment they held. To anyone else, they were just brick-and-mortar buildings, but to me they were temples. What they held was holy. They were blessed, possessed of a numinous quality that I couldn't find anywhere else.

"Why d'you think it is that so many horror stories are set in bookstores?" Will asked.

He leaned forward on the battered wooden-topped counter, elbows between the ancient cash register and a stack of ratty old romances that he hadn't gotten around to shelving yet. As he put his weight on his arms, Will's tattoo of Frankenstein's Monster on his forearm bulged and distended. He had been a hard-edged punk in his youth, but unlike most of his peers, Will hadn't been able to give up on—or at least adapt—the style as he began hurtling towards middle age. As his chin had disappeared into his neck and his close-cropped hair began to grey, his style began to look more like a farce than a statement of rejection. None of Will's tattoos had held up to years of angry living. The worst was his Skinny Puppy VIVISECTVI tattoo, worn at the nape of his neck; it had been Will's first, and he was proudest of it, despite the fact that it had faded and run into the rolls of fat that had cropped up over the years.

Still, Will's sneer, always bitter but now seeming more desperate than threatening, belied a fierce intelligence that I had to respect. And it wasn't like I was aging any better than him.

"I don't know," I said. "Never really thought about it."

I ran a thumb down the edge of a gently used copy of Robert Anton Wilson's *The Illuminati Papers*. It was in good shape, but I already had an earlier oversized edition at home. Falling Leaves Books was the best bookstore in Steephill. Not that there was much competition; Steephill mostly hosted chain stores that cropped up like latte-serving boils bolted onto the sides of shopping malls. I'd been coming to the store for years, even before Will had taken over the day-to-day management from the owner of the shop. The racks and shelves of books crowded close in the five rooms, leading from the glass front door, covered on the inside by an old paper shade, straight back into the depths of the building. Everything smelled slightly of dust and old paper, and it was always warm inside, the rubber runners laid squarely over every bare patch of floor soft underfoot.

"I dunno, man. Seems like not everyone's into bookstores."

"Ah," Will said, holding up a finger, "but everyone knows books. And what are bookstores except extensions of books? It's like they're support systems."

"Shells around the snail," I said, picking up on Will's vibe.

"I was gonna say crab, but whatever."

The exterior of Falling Leaves was a series of old-style display cases with glass fronts facing the street outside. I could see through the windows crowded with special offers and eye-catching hardcovers that night had fallen already. It was wintertime and sunset always came on fast and hard this far north. Night brought with it blustery flurries of snow and harsh, sharp winds racing down from the escarpments surrounding Steephill. I had seen some of the city's few homeless out on the streets, soaking up what little late afternoon sunshine they could, on my way to the store. I hoped that they had gotten to shelter before the night came on fully, especially the one that I had seen on the corner near Falling Leaves, sniffing at the air with her head—I presumed she was a woman—tilted back like a hound. Assuming that she was suffering from one affliction or another, I had given her a wide berth, a bit unnerved by the way that her yellowed eyes had widened, nostrils flaring, as I passed by. There was something unusual about her, but I hadn't gotten a close enough look to be sure what it was and I was glad when I made it indoors.

I wasn't much of a customer that day. Falling Leaves lay on the main bus route I used to get between work on the outskirts of Steephill's urban centre and my cramped bachelor apartment in the middle of what passed for slums hereabouts, so I'd often stop in to kill time and browse the stacks I'd picked over hundreds of times before.

Being in love with books was a vicious cycle, I always said. If I wasn't wasting time, and risking wasting money I couldn't afford, I was selling books to get back money I needed for food or rent.

I sighed, sweating slightly under my heavy winter coat in the hot air of the store. My stomach rumbled and I looked out again, past the display cases into the cold, dark night barely visible through the front windows. I was hungry—Hell, I hadn't eaten since breakfast—but I couldn't give up on the shop just yet, even though it was just past closing time. Maybe Will would put up with me thumbing my way through the science fiction section again. It'd been about a month since I'd last picked over those sorry bones.

Trusting Will to ignore me unless he was really annoyed, I strode through the empty doorframe that lead from the larger counter area back to the first room of the stacks proper. The music was muted back here, speakers hidden behind the tall bookshelves that stood floor-to-ceiling on every wall, sticking out here and there to break the room up into smaller, more compact areas. The wooden floors of the old building creaked underneath the rubber runners as I walked through. These first two rooms were crowded with more popular books, romances and murder mysteries in the first space, so-called literary fiction in the second. Falling Leaves' owner had set up the system, and, since it seemed to work, Will propagated it; most of the customers wanted something more mainstream, so it was best to give them what they wanted up front rather than make them dig for it.

Only hard-core collectors—or, more honestly—genre nerds like me, had to go to the back to find what they lusted after. I couldn't have stayed out of there if I had wanted to, in all honesty. Bookstores were, after all, a refuge for me; they were a safe haven in what was otherwise a fairly dreary life. I don't think three consecutive days had ever gone by where I didn't stop into one bookstore or another. There was nothing better, I thought, than finding a bookstore, any bookstore, and just wandering the rigid lines of its shelves, the crazy geography of its piles.

Not just any bookstore, though. I mean, I could put up with the chain places in a pinch, if I had to. But what really made my blood sing were the little shops. The hole-in-the-wall bookstores where the selection was small but deep and the staff always kept a few surprises in reserve. That's why I kept coming back to Falling Leaves: out of all the dingy, tiny, barely-keeping-the-lights-on bookstores that I had ever been to, it was the best. It was like the paragon of bookstores, the Platonic ideal of everything I wanted in a shop. Even when I was hard up for cash, even when I'd already bought past my allotment of books for the month, I would still come to Falling Leaves.

Whenever I walked into the back of the store and submitted myself to the quiet, warm, and close, suffocating air, my eyes lit up. My heart skipped when I saw the battered, faded covers of all those phenomenal stories, lives bound between boards or soft covers. The thrill of discovering something new filled me and left me desperate to comb the shelves, hoping against hope that I'd find something—anything—that would spark my sense of wonder in a meaningful way.

It didn't happen all the time, or even often. But it did happen.

My exploration that day, however, was like it was on most visits. I scanned the shelves, unable to stop myself from trailing a finger along spine after spine as my eyes roved over titles and authors' names, even though nothing leaped out at me. It was the same as it ever was: whole blocks of shelves taken up with selections from long-running series, with scores of single-volume works from four decades ago in-between. There were a few recent titles, mostly in hardcover, but none of them caught my eye or captured my interest. I walked back and forth, growing more discouraged as a wave of exhaustion came and enveloped me.

I paused as I came to the end of the science fiction section to straighten my tired back. With my hands on my hips, I leaned as far back as I could, joints popping, and groaned. I looked up into the recessed lights above, eyes momentarily dazzled, before looking over to one corner of the room where a hidden speaker was located. Will must have been playing around with the music: his usual litany of punk rock classics had become louder, angrier, as he undoubtedly got the store ready to close.

Squinting up to the tops of the bookcases, near the ceiling, I could see that the profoundly irregular bass of the music was making something move. Dust and particles of dirt were jumping up and down, clouding the almost clinical whiteness of the light housing. Something up there shivered or slithered towards the edge of the bookcase, threatening to fall. I took a step back, unsure of what could possibly be up there, and then, all at once, it fell.

It was a book. Or, at least, it was shaped like a book. It was a thin hardcover of some kind, its boards covered from end to end in a cream-coloured finish. The covers flew open as it fell and I could see that the pages inside were all loose rather than attached to a binding. They came out in a thin flurry, some of them getting caught by the book's covers as it hit the hardwood floor. Surprised, I hurried over to take a look.

The book was shockingly heavy for its small size. I gathered up the loose sheets—there must have been at least a hundred—as best as I could, trying to put them back in between the covers uniformly. On the inside of the cover was an inscription in bold typeface: THE CANCER OF SUPERSTITION. Beneath that were a series of initials stacked one on top of another: H. H., followed by H. P. L., and then finally C. M. E. J. I assumed that some of these were publisher marks, maybe, while the others were authorial initials. Or maybe one— or all—of them were an abbreviation for some esoteric slogan.

I ran my hand over the cover. It must have been up there for some time, judging by the amount of dust and dirt accumulated on the front. The pages were in good repair, however; a few were slightly brittle with age, but there were no signs of mould or water damage. Not even any sun fading. I held the book up under the light and leaned against one of the slim bookcases of the horror section, flipping at random through the pages. Most of them seemed to be handwritten, with several lines crossed out per page, each with corrections written underneath. The corrections seemed to be written in another hand, but neither was particularly clear. I squinted, trying to make heads or tails of the spidery script, which occasionally ran off the line and changed direction into the margins. One passage jumped out at me:

> Superstitions have a later growth, among ignorant and irrational people, along the exact lines followed in primitive times, because the elements involved are the same—uninformed and unreasoning minds confronted by natural phenomena which they fear, do not understand, and wish to influence.

Reading the cramped, florid script brought on the threat of a headache. My initial assumption of a hundred pages between the boards of the book now seemed like a gross under-approximation. Many of the pages were as fine as onion skin, suggesting that there could be at least double my initial figure, maybe more. I couldn't have taken in more than a few ink-blurred handwritten paragraphs at a time without sprouting a migraine. Riffling through the contents of the book, I found that a few pages were typewritten. Not computer-printed script—they were obviously composed on a mechanical typewriter of some sort, possibly an antique. Whether these pages were authored by the same person as the script pages was impossible to tell; for all I knew they could have been written by the corrector, or maybe even some unknown third author. Picking one at random, I read:

And at the same time, man's imagination and poetic faculty are expanding. He not only sees new details in the workings of natural phenomena, but invents details and principles which do not exist—based on fancied analogies. Imperfect repetition as the tales are handed down gives rise to omissions, amplifications, distortions, and sometimes parallel versions, this haphazard process usually creating special features (often highly irrational and even contradictory) which eventually become more or less standardized as popular folklore. This folklore can be highly personal in tenor; whereas architecture and art are the links which give a civilized society its only sense of real tradition, that same drive can, in the heart of the individual, become twisted into a superstitious belief in that which does not exist. Here Freud, with his theories of the *unheimlich*, has caused much damage to the progress of civilization: it is not the place which adopts non-material qualities; it is the superstitious beliefs of primitive men which projects them.

The typewritten text broke off halfway down the current page, with the rest occupied by a heavily corrected series of handwritten lines. These appeared to be on the same topic as the typewritten text, although it was difficult to tell. The author, or authors, went on at length about places and superstitions, and how best to destroy erroneous beliefs about locales, since such ideas had negatively impacted the rise of civilization through the ages. Much time was spent on haunted houses and the like, but I was surprised to find that an almost equal amount was spent on investitures of belief on places that lack overt supernatural qualities, such as the house one is born in, or the great buildings of government. One sentence in particular stood out:

For a building, location, or space is just that: nothing more than a thing-in-the-world. It does not do for a person of learning and civilization to hold with the superstitious belief that buildings can possess non-material qualities; they are objects, nothing more, and whatever we find within them is nothing but a projection of our own hopes for life.

From what little I could surmise, this was a treatise with a singular purpose: to describe superstition in all of its forms and to pull it out from the human condition, excising it as one would rot from the centre of a diseased lung. To be honest, I found the text fascinating, though the small sections I read at random were less than persuasive on their own merits. The authors, whoever they were, were strident in their convictions but wholly lacking in evidentiary support, and there seemed to be something intuitively wrong with their axioms. I thought it impossible to believe that all superstitions were negative in their effects, even if they did happen to be untrue. Besides, the authors had lumped more positive superstitions in with overtly dreadful ones, which I didn't think appropriate. There must be ground for the sweeter beliefs, I thought. The beliefs, anti-scientific as they may be, that do not teach us to be afraid, but instead lift us up.

Clasping *The Cancer of Superstition* tightly with one hand, I looked around me with more than a tinge of sadness clouding my vision. The thought of being without bookstores—my special places—haunted me. I feared the day when all the filthy, run-down little remnants of past values like Fallen Leaves dried up and blew away like the dust from an overripe plum. Too many of my days and nights had been spent in between rows of bookcases, lost in worlds I had never been alive enough to create for myself. Without them, without the thrill of discovering them, I would have been like the boards of *The Cancer of Superstition* without the sheets between them: devoid of substance.

I pushed aside those morose thoughts, knowing that I needed to add my find to my collection if at all possible. Only once had I stumbled across a book as odd as this: a first edition hardcover of *Brave New World*, autographed by Huxley to its owner, who bizarrely happened to be Harpo Marx, forgotten in a pile in a cluttered shop in Vancouver. When I had taken my find up to the dingy teacher's desk that served as the store counter, the owner named a preposterous four-figure price. I'd scoffed, and, as I later regretted, left the book behind. If *The Cancer of Superstition* was as unusual as I thought it was, it was rarer even than that copy of Huxley's masterpiece; there was no way I would leave another unique opportunity behind.

I made my way through the twisting warren of bookcases, through Military History and past the decorated shelves of Women's Studies, resting precariously above the single shelf-and-chair arrangement that was Falling Leaves' Poetry section. Rounding a corner surrounded by shelves of cookbooks and dog-eared Aboriginal Fiction, I came out past True Crime and stopped in front of the counter with my back to the one case devoted to rows of battered CDs and DVDs.

"How come you didn't tell me you had this?" I asked Will.

He looked at me with tired eyes, well beyond caring about the oblique comments of customers—even those who were, roughly speaking, friends.

"I don't know, man," he said. "What is it?"

"It was up on top of a bookcase, by one of the speakers."

Coming to a quick realization, I opened the covers and looked for the numbers that should have been written on the inside in dull pencil.

"There's no price," I said. "Maybe somebody left it here?"

"Wouldn't surprise me." Will shrugged. "People leave crazy stuff here all the time. Like, once we had in a really nice small-press deluxe printing of *The Sound and the Fury*. Fucking thing hadn't been up on the shelves a week before somebody brought it to the desk to complain; turned out some asshole had spread shit all along the inside of the slipcase."

"What, like human shit?"

Will looked at me like I was an idiot.

"Does it matter?" he asked.

I nodded, looking down at the work in my hands.

"Well... How much for this, then?" I asked.

"No idea."

Will moved a heavy stack of textbooks from one corner of the counter to the other.

"Look," he said. "It's past closing time, and I don't want to have to fight the weather."

I looked out the front windows, shocked to see that a storm had whipped up since I had gotten off the bus from the factory where I worked. Snow snapped and wailed past the store, wind rattling the old front door in its cheap frame. Not even the curb outside was visible; if this kept up we would soon be in whiteout conditions.

"Why don't you watch the store for me while I run and make the night deposit now? That way I can get home before everything goes to hell out there."

"And in return you'll let me have it?" I asked, hopeful.

I must have sounded too hopeful, since Will wasn't exactly a shrewd businessman.

"We'll call it five bucks," he said.

He had me over a barrel, and he knew it. Even five dollars was too expensive—I'd have to eat rice and chicken for a few days to deal with the unimagined expense. But I just couldn't let it go.

"It's a deal," I pronounced. "What do I do?"

"Just stand behind the counter, man." Will sneered. "It's not exactly rocket science. Besides, we're not hopping with customers here."

The wind howled outside and the building rattled slightly, as though it were hungry for bodies and agreeing with Will's sad assessment.

"All right," I said with a sigh.

Will pulled on his parka, an old military surplus number, grey and green and covered with badges that he'd sewn on over the years. He shoved the proceeds from the register into a large zippered cloth envelope, which he then placed in a deep external pocket of the parka. I slid around to the staff side as Will went out the door into the roiling snow. Alone, I breathed deeply, closing my eyes to enjoy the solitude. There was an old steel stool with a cork seat behind the counter; I slid it up to the battered counter and sat down with *The Cancer of Superstition* propped up on a pile of outdated magazines.

My eyelids grew heavy; it was still hot in the store and my thick winter jacket sat heavily on my shoulders. I turned the pages of *The Cancer of Superstition* at random, looking for something to keep me awake until Will came back and I could plumb the book's depths at home. The authors seemed to have spent a lot of space drawing lines between groups of persons, especially the "civilized" or "modern" man and the "primitive" man. Such a distinction raised my hackles, mostly due to my punk rock roots, and I wondered if the authors were fascists or not. I couldn't tell that much about the book without a more energized examination—not even how old the book was, since I couldn't find any copyright page to speak of. Thumbing my way through, I found the same section I had been reading before. Picking a spot at random, I continued on:

> As we have seen at length, the beliefs of common men are more akin to those of savages than they are to the materialist thoughts of civilized persons. Where modern science and philosophy insist on the pure material, they cling to

abstract notions that fill them with fear rather than enlightenment. Where the civilized man sees architecture as the living, instantiated heart of tradition, they see only a darkened frame filled with haunting ghosts and lurking monsters. And where the civilized man finds bold horizons to explore with the full might of his intellectual capability, they find only the menacing vale of night driving them back into their complacent havens.

Even more, it is these havens themselves that draw the line of distinction between the rational man of civilization and the superstitious man of atavistic inclination. The belief that the locations known and treasured possess a quality setting them apart from those unknown and potentially filled with peril is a superstitious one, and is most vexing to any man possessing the powers of his heritage. For the rational man does not delude himself into thinking that one place is inherently special for any reason other than the quality of its design, nor does the rational man allow himself to think that any site is protected by powers divine or otherwise. Indeed, the civilized man, when faced with a place that he is tempted to think of as special, magical, or otherwise worthy of veneration, recoils from this superstitious perspective and girds himself with the knowledge that it is no different from any other place. And, therefore, it is not to be treasured any more or less than an old, dilapidated mansion is to be feared.

Indeed, the civilized man, divorced from the superstitions of his savage precursors, knows full well that there can be no bulwark against the threats of the world. No fire-lit and bless'd circle to keep away the threats of the *naturae gloriam.* More pernicious even than the superstitious belief in the *locus malum* of Virgil, then, is the belief in the protected place of sanctification. To divest himself of the unsupportable, immaterial superstitions of his ignoble ancestors must be the first goal of anyone truly at home in this modern age.

I found all of this quite puzzling. It seemed absurd to me that one person, and possibly more, had banded together to write a book all about the importance of destroying superstition. Still, the author or authors had a profoundly engaging style, if a bit on the antiquated side. Even though disagreements ran back and forth in my mind, I nevertheless found myself turning the pages with increasing interest.

Suddenly, the front door banged open. I could hear the howl of the wind outside combining with the tinkle of the bells hanging from the doorframe to create an eerily merry sound. Looking up, I could see a figure scuttling through the door, keeping the gap between the frame and the jamb as narrow as possible. At first I thought it was Will, since the parka was off-grey and old, but it was far rattier than his was. The figure was shorter, too, now that I took a closer look, and the hood was up.

"Can I help you?" I said, levering myself up from the stool.

The figure didn't respond. He or she held their hands out to either side, their back to me, and I could see that they weren't wearing any gloves. Their skin was mottled, with either filth or liver spots, and their nails were abnormally long, sections raggedly torn off. They ducked forwards, pressing themselves up against the display cases at the front of the store. Reaching down, I turned off the stereo, feeling a bit rattled.

"Hello?" I asked, raising my voice and standing straight up so that they could see me easily. "Anything I can help you with?"

The figure spun around with the speed of a hunting animal, then slid a few steps towards the counter. I recognized her: it was the homeless woman I'd seen on the street corner earlier. But she was like no woman I had ever seen before. The skin on her face was pebbled like a reptile's. Perhaps they were scars, or evidence of being burnt by a fire a long time ago—I couldn't tell. It was hideous, however, and her lipless, oddly seamless face disturbed me greatly despite my instinctive urge to be sympathetic. Her eyes were huge orbs, the black irises filling them almost to the edges, where they ran unhealthily into her yellowed whites. She raised one hand slowly, almost mechanically, then snatched back the hood of her parka with a darting motion.

Snow fell all around her in dilapidated clumps, and her hair burst free in a wild, tangled spray. She stepped towards the counter, her feet moving assuredly while her upper body remained perfectly still. I recalled how her thrown-back head had reminded me of a hound before, and I shivered as I realized that she seemed even more animalistic now.

"Help me," she said.

"I, ah, what do you need?" I stammered.

It—she, I told myself—stared at me in the same way that a normal person would stare at a featureless expanse of stone. There was no recognition in her eyes, no point of reference that told me that she understood that she was looking at a being like herself. I swallowed reflexively and gripped the edge of the countertop; the foot-and-a-half of wood and glass was all the protection I had between her and me. Seconds that felt like minutes passed before I realized that she wasn't blinking.

A low groan or hiss came from her mouth even though the bumped and puffed lines that should have been her lips were held perfectly steady, slightly parted. She sidled along the length of the counter like a crab, then spun around and pressed herself up against one of the nearby bookcases. Her head shot up, canted farther back than was reasonable, making it look like she was studying the ceiling more than she was searching the shelves for a particular title.

My mouth was suddenly dusty. "Are—are you looking for something?"

She hissed again, the exhalation rising at the end this time to turn into something like a grunt. She shivered for a few moments and I felt myself recoil. Then, quick as a cockroach, she swivelled and made off towards the back of the shop. I hesitated, as I think most people would, and silently pledged to myself that Will could be damned—I would never watch the store for him again. I made my way around the counter, every bone in my body yelling at me to stay where I was.

A loud thump echoed from one of the twisting corners of cases, where Westerns bled into Religion, followed by a loud screech. I snatched up the copy of *The Cancer of Superstition* without thinking, holding it to my chest as though it were a babe in my arms. I made my way, doubting each step, towards the back of the shop. The cases seemed threatening, towering over me, leaning in at the tops and capable of collapse at any moment. The air felt thick, stifling, claustrophobic. The lights hanging from the ceiling were either too piercingly bright or cast shadows of malign significance in my peripheral vision.

Being in the shop with the woman—if she was a woman—terrified me. It was like looking up and realizing that, somehow, you had become trapped in a cage with a feral predator. Some part of me knew that, in all likelihood, she was just some down-on-her-luck homeless person, mind burned away from years of trauma and addiction. But there was some quality to her that I hadn't ever seen before and that was what I was stuck dwelling on. Whatever hardships

I had endured, they'd never come close to turning me into something like her. Whatever she was, whatever she had gone through, I couldn't help but think it hadn't left her as human as she was when it found her.

Cursing the way my snow boots creaked on the runner, I crept into the spot where the romance section aligned with the home repairs section. From there, I had a perfect line of sight to see the junction of Westerns and Religion, where I thought she might be. Steeling myself, I peered around one of the freestanding bookcases—she was in plain view and apparently preoccupied, crouched down, resting on the balls of her feet. Absurdly, I noticed that she had on classic All Star running shoes. Her shoulders were hunched forward, arms drawn inwards towards her and shivering or spasming in a way that I found instinctively loathsome. Her hair sprayed backwards in a fan, its crusted length leading down to seemingly pointed ends. The mane of it was bunched up at the nape of her neck, above the hood of her coat, bulging obscenely as though it concealed some sort of tumorous mass.

At first, I thought I could hear her talking to herself in some secret language, meaningless to anyone but her. I quickly realized that what I was hearing wasn't speech, however. It was the sound of rending paper. Of crumpling. And, most horrifying, of chewing.

With some idea of what she was doing, my resolve became strong. I had to at least make an effort. After all, this wasn't some monster. It—she—was just a person.

"Look, lady," I ventured, rounding the corner to the aisle that joined the sections in this area of the shop, "you've got to get out of here, or I'll call the cops."

She turned then, spinning around fluidly at the waist to such a degree that I would have thought she'd fractured her spine. Her elbows were drawn towards her stomach and her clawed hands were up close to her jaw, mantis-like. The shredded remains of a paperback lay at her splayed feet and a rain of mangled pages tumbled down around her, covered with the dark saliva from her open mouth. She chewed in a repetitive fashion, rotten and pointed teeth levering up and down like an industrial grinder. At first, my gaze was fixed on her maw and the way her throat distended horribly as she swallowed a mouthful of printed paper. Then I saw her eyes and the way they narrowed and flashed when they saw me—then brightened and bulged open when they locked on what I carried in my arms.

Without warning, she leaped up from her crouch, hurling herself across the aisle towards me. Her arms were extended out, locked in position, while her grasping hands flexed and clawed at the air between us. Bits of her paperback meal drifted around her like snow or dandruff, occasionally sticking to her coat and the sweatshirt underneath as her drool plastered them into place. She screamed a jagged, hoarse scream and I automatically retreated, jumping backwards until I ran into the bookcase behind me.

In a heartbeat she was upon me. With one foot behind her and one stomping down on my instep, she grasped at *The Cancer of Superstition*, seeking to pry it from my arms. Her fingers clutched at it, savage nails clawing it so hard that they dug divots into the hardcover boards.

"Mine!" she howled as she twisted the book in my hands, writhing like a snake seducing its prey.

The smell of her filled my nostrils, dry and musty like a shameful secret long forgotten. Her breath stank, and I could see bits of paper stuck between her teeth. As she snarled, she extended the tip of her pointed tongue; there was a larger piece stuck there with the words "fly blown" printed on it. The whole of her was an assault on my every sense, and the thought of her in this place, in this good and kind place, was an abomination to me. Her presence was like a dead rat on the altar of a church, like sin and obscenity pushed into accompaniment with the most sacred.

I twisted to my left, hard, managing to tear myself and *The Cancer of Superstition* out of her grasp. Stumbling, I lurched back the way I had come, heading for the front of the store and the safety of the outside past the door. The bookcases flashed by me as I went, almost blind with fear and horrified confusion, before I felt a terrible weight land on me. The woman had leaped at me again, closing the distance between us with unnatural agility, and latched upon my back. She screeched in my ear, deafening me, and began to claw at me, drawing blood with her thick, ragged nails wherever she could get through to my skin.

I wailed and hurled myself forward, her unaccustomed weight throwing me off balance. Instinctively, I turned and, just as she lowered her maw towards me to bite a chunk out of my ear, pushed my weight backwards so that I toppled into the front counter. There was an awful smashing sound as the glass gave way and the heaviness of our combined weights bent the metal frame supporting the wood surface.

A shard of debris cut into the side of my leg and I shouted, furiously pulling myself forward out of the woman's grasp. I staggered to my feet and, after turning around, saw that she had been badly injured by the fall. One arm hung down uselessly at her side, obviously dislocated. Black blood seeped through her clothes in several places, and I could see where she had been run through with shards of thick glass and bent pieces of metal. With her free hand, she rooted in the remains of the counter, now destroyed, and came up with a glittering glass triangle as an impromptu blade. Her eyes were as dark as a shark's eyes, rolling over to yellowish white as she stumbled towards me.

I retreated, my breath gone, putting what I thought might be a crucial few paces between us as I made my way to the front door.

Dizzy with adrenaline and pain, I miscalculated the route, and instead of backing into the door, I managed to bump into the opening to the right-hand window display. An autographed copy of Philip K. Dick's *The Divine Invasion* toppled off its stand, and I hoped that it would be all right.

The woman raised her makeshift knife up high and skittered across the floor to me. She was entirely silent, now, all of her rage and fury seemingly channelled into keeping her moving while her wounds tried to shut her body down. I hoped that she would die before she reached me and immediately cursed myself in horror for having such a thought.

Realizing my error, and knowing that I wouldn't be able to get to the door to make my escape before she could reach me, I curled inwards, covering *The Cancer of Superstition* with as much of my body as I could. I didn't know why I was doing it; maybe it was my last attempt to preserve some memory of when I had been happy in this place. The last surviving reminder of all that I had ever found in here, and in stores like it.

I looked around, knowing that there was no choice but to make her inhuman appearance the last thing I would ever see. She stumbled from one foot to the other, blood raining down on her wild fan of hair from her raised hand, palm sliced deep on the edge of her glass knife. Her eyes were roiling pools of black and white, and their depths were filled with an alien hatred, while her mouth was a distended hole stretched wide in the mute expression of a language I had never heard.

She closed the distance between us, now mere moments from slaking her thirst on me before satiating her hunger with *The Cancer of Superstition*. The strike was imminent and I tried to gird myself for it—when Will returned.

He simply opened the door and stepped inside, as though nothing could possibly be going wrong in this chamber of nightmare. By that point, the woman's trajectory could not be altered. With a shrill, breathy cry of triumph, she threw herself forward over the last of the distance and plunged her blade into Will's chest.

He didn't make a sound at first. Merely gaped at her, as though this impossibility could not be believed.

Then she pulled the blade back out, and the force of its rough removal pulled him towards her, making him stumble into her waiting embrace. Blood fountained from the deep wound in his torso, right over his heart, coating her in a blasphemous baptism. Will wailed in pure anguish: desperation, surprise, and overwhelming sadness poured out from him as fear made his mind give way to shock. Exalted, she threw her good arm around him and pulled him to her.

Then, without pause or hesitation, she leaned towards him and bit out the side of Will's throat. The two of them tumbled to the ground in a display of perverted coitus, coated in each other's blood.

Time froze for me. It was as though the tide of their blood had washed into me, and I shuddered as it mixed with my essential self. Gone were the happy memories I had once treasured. The box of comic books I had been delighted to find was now stained with the blood of my friend. Huxley's autograph was wiped away by the lashing spurts of Will's vital essence. Even Falling Leaves itself was now corrupted in my mind, turned from a haven into an over-ripe piece of fruit that had rotted from within. What had once been sweet was now struck through with decay. All was ruin, all was anguish, and still the tableau twitched and heaved on the floor in front of me.

Will died within moments, and the woman followed him shortly thereafter.

Sometime after that, I realized that I was screaming.

I scrambled out the door on hands and knees, like an animal, the shock of the blizzard numbing me and freezing the blood seeping into my jeans from the cut on my leg. I crawled through snowdrifts before I was able to stumble back onto my feet, and in a haze I ran as best I could down the street. There was no clear plan of action in my mind, nor any destination—I simply needed to get away from there. And stay away, no matter what.

Eventually I found myself a few blocks towards the business end of downtown. A banking high-rise there was attached to a twenty-four-hour burger joint and in the lobby was a bank of payphones. I used one to call the cops, stammering out the sketchiest of stories. That my friend was dead. That there had been an attack on Falling Leaves bookstore. That there was blood. And that my friend was dead, and dead, and dead again.

A squad car came around minutes later, siren blaring and snow tires rolling heavy through the blizzard's leavings. One police officer came into the lobby, sidearm drawn, while he signalled his partner to head down the street towards Falling Leaves.

I began to cry, hoping I could get the words out for him. It was then that I realized I was still clutching *The Cancer of Superstition* to my chest. I wrapped my arms around it and, tilting my head towards the ceiling, wailed my dismay out into the night's wild storm.

Eventually, the officer was able to get some semblance of a story from me. After he heard what I had to say, he called for backup, then an ambulance. His partner's voice came over the radio, thin and crackling, verifying in police code what I had already described. Not knowing what else to do, I sat down with my bloodied hands, now washed clean by the snow, and began to read.

The officer tried to take *The Cancer of Superstition* from me then, saying that it might be evidence.

I wouldn't let him.

I wanted to keep it pristine.

That was three years ago. I've read through *The Cancer of Superstition* multiple times. I haven't been able to find out anything about it, other than a brief conversation with one of the few friends who checked up on me after I let my phone bill lapse into disconnection. He said that it sounded like a book that wasn't supposed to exist. Possibly, I could have found out more, but I haven't looked.

The police investigation into Will's murder was short and pointless. They weren't able to identify the woman and said little about her beyond the fact that they thought she had died attempting to pull off an improvised robbery. Somehow, she believed that Will would still be in the store, they said, getting ready to deliver the day's take to the night deposit. When she realized that he was just returning from the bank, rather than about to head there, she had gone into a rage and murdered him for stymying her plans.

They said nothing about her deformities and less about her bizarre behavior with the books.

I was questioned in hospital during my brief recuperation, then released without charge. All they said was that I shouldn't attempt to leave town, which I found preposterous. There's no reason to go anywhere.

It took me a while to think about that night with any measure of dispassion. Over time, though, I've made sense of it all to the best of my ability. Much as I eventually made sense of *The Cancer of Superstition*. I reordered all the sections. I considered the different parts and the way that one script turned into another without warning. I thought carefully about the reasoning and the implications of that reasoning. And, most of all, I went over and over the editing. The lines that had been cut, ignored, or ended abruptly so that another could continue on.

Without even realizing it, I started taking a different route to my job at the factory. I started going to a different grocery store and stopped drinking at the bar around the corner from Falling Leaves. In fact, I gave the whole area a wide berth, never even going back to the second-run cinema that I had loved so much.

Indeed, I don't go anywhere at all any more, other than work and home. One building is the same as any other, so there's no point going any place other than where I have to go. I certainly don't go back to Falling Leaves. Or any other bookstore, for that matter. I haven't been to a single one since that night. What was known of old and long familiar, as Freud put it and the authors of *The Cancer of Superstition* repudiated, became just frames, and paint, and bricks, and mortar. Whatever that woman was, whatever else she wanted, if she wanted anything at all, she taught me one thing: no place is safe. No place is special. There is no bastion of peace and happiness in the world, no location where the horrors of the world are kept at bay by an inherent serenity. Nowhere is good. Nor bad. Or anything else.

It took me a while, but I'm finally able to look in the mirror again. My eyes are different. Large, black irises, running from edge to edge, where they meet the yellowish whites.

I'm not surprised, though. After all, the scales of false belief have dropped away from me.

So I don't go to bookstores anymore. Nor am I a collector anymore. As soon as I was well, I set about making the changes I thought were appropriate. I pulled down all my bookcases, scattering their contents throughout my apartment. I broke up the wood and threw it board by board into the fireplace in my tiny living room. Then, while the flames roared, I set about taking care of all of my books. I couldn't bear to look at them anymore, nor did I need to read them ever again, so I disposed of them.

I tore the pages from the spines and stripped the covers from all of the ones I could. At first, I thought it would be easier if I closed my eyes while doing it, but I discovered that it made no difference whatsoever. The white pages scattered all over the floorboards of my apartment reminded me of a winter landscape, until I realized that my rooms couldn't look like anything other than what they were: an apartment filled with loose paper.

It was harder to destroy my books than I would have thought. Scooping up their remains and shoving them into the fireplace was easy enough, but the crackling they made as the flames curled them up sounded too much like chewing. So I gathered them all up into cardboard boxes and put them, one by one, out on the curb behind my building. Occasionally I would pull back my bedroom curtain and look out at them, but I didn't feel anything at all. There lay my comic books, my novels, my rarities and special editions. There lay my past, and my memories, and all the joys I had been foolish enough to believe existed in the world.

Slowly, over time, the winter took them all. One by one they went away, and with them went my erroneous beliefs in the places I had purchased them. The wind and the snow disintegrated them all bit by bit, tearing pages from chapters and dust jackets from boards, until they had been entirely obliterated by the unremitting facts of material existence. Then they were gone, and I felt nothing.

I knew then and I know now that I won't need them anymore. I have divested myself of illusion. Or, rather, I've had my illusions torn from me by unmistakable savagery. Once my books had been symbols of something that I believed existed, but I have been proven a fool. There is no need for belief, since there is nothing to believe in. There is only the truth of our existence, as cold and impermanent as a hard-packed snowdrift. Truth cannot be avoided, and there is no place to hide. So I do not hide any longer. I avoid the places that remind me of my superstitious ways, though I know I will go back to them once I'm able to see them for the meaningless places that they are. There is no sanctuary, no home for the sacred, because the sacred does not exist.

To assist my awakening into the true home we all inhabit, I have divorced myself of the totems that I had once thought so holy.

I rid myself of every book I have ever owned.

All except for one.

MORTAL COILS

Eric Bradshaw

Today was a good one for business. The day was bright and I was able to walk to most of my appointments. Several of my clients had orders for me to fill, some of which I was able to send out this afternoon. Irving, a young doctor whose acquaintance I had made in our school days, had a rather large order that will take some days to fill. His practice is growing quite steadily thanks to his reputation for both skill and discretion. He is not only the personal physician for my sister as well as myself, but a good friend.

I paid a visit to my sister Joanna in the evening and was pleased to find both she and her newborn daughter in good health. She had convinced her husband, Zachary, to name the girl Mary after our late mother. Mary looked the very picture of a happy healthy baby and I felt confident that she would grow up to be every bit as beautiful as her grandmother before her. She had her father's brown eyes, but a twinkle in them revealed that she would have all of her mother's wit and good humour. I said as much to Joanna, who seemed quite pleased.

After a time, our conversation turned away from the child and Joanna revealed that she had a favour to ask. Her friend Beth had come by the day before to see her and the baby. Over the course of their conversation, however, Beth had confided that she was worried about her husband, Howard. Joanna intimated that Howard was behaving oddly and that Beth feared he had taken ill. She asked me to pay them a visit, hoping that through my work in the medical supply trade I might be able to recommend a suitable doctor if in fact Howard's health was in decline. I promised that I would call on them the very next day. Joanna was very grateful for this and, after chatting for a little while longer, I bade her goodnight and returned home for the evening.

Unfortunately, the good weather did not persist. The sky was overcast the next morning but stalwartly refused to release more than a few drops at a time. Remembering my promise to Joanna, I sent a note off to Beth telling her that I would pay both her and her husband a visit that afternoon, advising her to reach me at my office if that should prove inconvenient. The remainder of the morning passed uneventfully. I met with some distributors to place orders for Irving and was pleased to learn that, with a bit of luck, I should be able to meet his order sooner than anticipated.

After lunch, I decided to walk to Beth's. The general gloom of the day still persisted but the threat of rain had dissipated. As I had just conducted business on Irving's behalf, I pondered the ethics of drumming up more business for the both of us by recommending him to Beth for her husband. Though I did not yet know what ailed the man, I was sure Irving would be up to the challenge.

Although my hostess greeted me with all due propriety, I could not rid myself of the feeling that something very odd was occurring in the household, regardless of Howard's condition. I had gathered from Joanna that both Howard and his wife were near my own four-and-a-quarter decades. Yet to look at Beth, one would more likely have placed her at nearer my sister's age, and Joanna is younger than I by a full ten years and more. Stifling my surprise, I introduced myself and she kindly invited me into the sitting room. There, after exchanging a few pleasantries, I asked Beth to elaborate on the causes of her concern for her husband.

She confided in me that her husband had been behaving rather oddly for the past several months. He was an optician by trade and was always tinkering with new kinds of lenses. On one particular day this past February he had come home from his workshop wearing a set Beth had never seen before. The lenses themselves did not seem odd in any way, but Howard constantly rubbed at his arms as if there were some stain he was attempting to remove. When Beth had approached him to see if she might assist, he had leapt back and refused to allow her to touch him.

For the rest of that month and then all of March, Howard refused to allow anyone to touch him and had not once laid so much as a finger on his wife or children. Indeed, the mere presence of another individual provoked a nervous agitation in the man. All that time, the new lenses remained perched on his nose, always before his eyes. Beth had optimistically attributed this worrisome behaviour to some new stress at work. During these two months, however, she had also observed two more alarming new features of her husband.

Howard had begun to grow quite wan, which came as scant surprise, as he had taken to working long hours at his workshop and spending still more time locked away in his study. In itself, this caused Beth little worry. Howard loved experimenting with new methods and materials for making lenses and would often fall into bouts of frantic energy when a particularly novel approach sparked his interest. However, when Beth discovered the marks on Howard's arms, she began to wonder if he wasn't working on something altogether separate.

One evening in March, when Beth had brought dinner up to his study, she found him engrossed in his research, his sleeves rolled up to his elbows. It was then that she first beheld the numerous cuts and scratches that adorned his forearms. When questioned about the cuts, Howard gave a vague response that they had to do with his experiments and were nothing to worry about. However, the cuts persisted and soon multiplied. The sleeves of his shirts often bore traces of encrusted blood. While Beth wanted to believe what her husband told her, when she took this behaviour in concert with Howard's agitated demeanour she grew fearful that he might cause himself some harm.

But around the beginning of April, just when Beth was beginning to get anxious enough to consult a physician on her husband's behalf, all of these worrisome signs vanished. Howard ceased closeting himself away in his study and even reduced the amount of time he spent at his workshop. The blood no longer appeared on his sleeves and, as the weather warmed, Beth received ample proof that the injuries to his forearms had healed well. He had even overcome his aversion to physical contact and, most reassuringly, the new lenses were all but forgotten.

This return to normalcy was, however, short lived. While all had seemed to be well with Howard for some weeks, Beth had recently noticed in him a return to protracted hours of work. This time, Howard retired at a respectable hour but rose after only a few hours' rest. Beth would likely not have noticed this behaviour, generally being a very heavy sleeper, had Howard possessed any measure of stealth. In the mornings, he had always been wont to rise before her. Instead, he had roused her late in the night on several occasions over the past few weeks as he left their room. While this had seemed odd to Beth, she had not seen anything particularly alarming in it until the most recent episode only three days ago.

On that particular night, Beth's curiosity had eventually persuaded her to expose her husband's nocturnal activities. She had only just entered the hall when she saw Howard exiting the nursery. To her horror, the moonlight had caught the blade of a razor in his hand. Unable to fathom any respectable reason for Howard to be in the nursery in the small hours of the morning, with or without bared steel, her mind leapt at once to the worst possible scenario. She barely managed to stifle a scream as she fell back into the deeper shadows of the doorway. There she stood, trembling with fear and able only to listen to Howard's footsteps as he slowly made his way downstairs and into his study.

Only after the house had been silent for several long minutes was she able to force herself into action. Beth rushed into the nursery, dreading what she would find within. But instead of dismembered corpses, she found only her two children, sleeping peacefully, not a mark on them. The very next day she had rushed to my sister to seek advice, but in the end, she had been unable to bring herself to disclose the full, ghastly details. She admitted to me, somewhat sheepishly, that she felt rather foolish at having panicked with such little provocation, but for the life of her, she still could not fathom Howard's purpose that night.

Beth still harboured doubts about the safety of her family. While she was certain that Howard had no ill intentions toward the children, she feared that this new insomnia threatened a future return of his agitation. While I did not doubt the whole of her story, I did not fully share her concerns. To my ears, it sounded more like a bad dream brought about by the anxiety she had regarding Howard's behaviour. Nevertheless, it did appear that Howard was behaving oddly. His insomnia may indeed give way to frightful consequences if left untreated. Still, I was determined to meet with him in person before advising that a physician be consulted. I inquired when Howard was accustomed to return for the evening and promised to drop by to see her husband in person.

I spent the remainder of the day at my office, verifying accounts. The time was fruitful if not exhilarating. However, my afternoon was plagued by concern for Beth and her children. While I did not put much stock in the fantastic tale I had been told, I could not deny that the three of them were in very grave peril should it prove true. The sky grew steadily darker as the afternoon slowly wore on. Finally, as I supped, the storm broke. For a time, I simply stared out the window, watching the raindrops disturb the surface of a puddle as I wondered if the man I should be shortly meeting would prove to be a violent, razor-wielding maniac or simply an overworked optician.

Having finished my repast, I returned to Beth's house for my meeting with Howard. The storm had lessened slightly, but the rain was still falling persistently. Beth answered the door herself, looking rather relieved to see me. She hurriedly invited me in and scurried off to announce me to her husband, who was once more ensconced in his study. I followed her through and waited outside the door as she informed Howard of his visitor. It took but a moment for her to reappear and usher me into the room.

Howard's study was more of a workshop. The room was dominated by a large workbench littered with various tools and apparatuses. Lenses and wire frames lay scattered about the table in various stages of completion. A small mirror stood near one corner of the bench. There were some shelves of books against one of the walls but they seemed to be an afterthought to the room and there was no place for one to peruse them at leisure. Instead, several bookstands stood on the workbench.

Howard himself stood near at hand, clearly in the midst of some labour. As with his wife, I was astonished at his youthful visage, more akin to one half his age than one who has seen nearly half a century. Further, there was no evidence on his face of the long hours his wife alleged he was keeping. For the moment, no spectacles adorned his face. Instead, Howard wore an expression of equal parts bemusement and irritation.

"Ah, Mr. Comstock," said Howard, extending his hand in greeting. "My wife tells me that you and I have much to discuss," he continued as I clasped his offered hand, "though for the life of me, I cannot imagine what. You are a medical man, are you not?"

"Not precisely. I trade in medical supplies, and as a result know many physicians in the city," I replied.

"I see, well, please make yourself comfortable," he said, offering me his chair, which I accepted. "I fear our conversation may be quite short and unproductive, as I am quite sure that I have no need of medical attention. Still, can I offer you some refreshment? Tea perhaps?" He pulled his watch out of his waistcoat and consulted it for a moment before returning it. "Or some sherry?" As I now occupied the only chair in the room, Howard satisfied himself with a hastily cleared corner of the workbench.

Howard proved to be a most civil gentleman, though I must confess that from the first I had a sense of unease in his presence. I could not help but feel that Howard was torn between a desire to avert his gaze from my person and a reluctance to reveal this desire. I declined his offer of refreshment and explained that his wife was concerned that he was having trouble sleeping.

"Oh, that," he replied with a chuckle, eyes settled for the moment on a pair of pliers mid-way between us. "I assure you, I am sleeping quite well. I simply find that I do not require as much rest as I used to. In fact, I feel quite the picture of health."

And he truly looked it, even if he was sleeping scarcely half the night. Still, my unease persisted. There still remained the matter of Beth's fright of the night before last. I feigned satisfaction in my inquiries and engaged in light conversation with him, hoping that if some mania lurked within Howard it might make itself evident.

Instead, the more we talked, the more steady and rational, if terse, he proved.

As we conversed, I allowed my gaze to travel across Howard's workbench and noticed something that my earlier, cursory inspection had missed. I saw a completed pair of spectacles set apart from the general clutter of the bench.

"Are these the spectacles your wife said you had been labouring over for so long?" I asked as I plucked them from the bench for closer inspection. There seemed little about them to set them apart from the others littered about, save the fact that they were completed.

"Yes, I have been working very hard on them of late," replied Howard, a sudden tension springing into his voice as he rose from his perch on the workbench. For the first time that evening, I had attracted the full measure of his gaze. "Please be careful with them. In fact, it would be best if you set them down at once."

But it was too late; I had already settled them upon my own face and adjusted the small mirror to admire the effect. But what I perceived through the lenses caused me to snatch them off with a curse. In the mirror I could see my own face but not adorned solely with the spectacles. A great tentacle-like appendage seemed to have entwined itself around my head and neck as it dangled from some higher perch.

"What the devil was that?" I exclaimed as I searched my head with my hands and the ceiling with my eyes for some trace of that ghastly extremity. But neither sight nor touch availed me in my search.

Howard attempted a laugh that was thoroughly unconvincing. "Oh, it's just that old mirror. The dratted thing is full of microscopic fractures. Can't see the cracks themselves of course, but they do distort the reflection in a rather disturbing manner."

The lie was, of course, borne out immediately when I returned my gaze to my reflection with the spectacles still in my hand. The tendrils had also vanished from my visage. I spared Howard a scathing glance before turning back to my reflection, slowly raising the spectacles. This, however, was not enough to pin Howard in place, and this time he was able to seize my wrist before I could put on the spectacles. His grip was firm, and as I turned back to him, a curse on my lips, the earnestness of his gaze silenced me. "Please, Mr. Comstock, put them down."

For a moment, I felt persuaded to do as he asked. After all, he was a professional and likely I held in my hand the culmination of several months' work. But then his eyes darted to the wrist that he held and, for the briefest moment, a grimace or shudder passed over his face. Though the change of expression lasted but a moment, there was no denying the shift in his grasp. What had once been strong as a vice was now as light as possible, making just enough contact to hold me still.

I caught his eye and held it with my own and, making my voice as commanding as I could, said slowly, "Howard, what did I see with these spectacles?"

"Dashed if I know," replied Howard with a heavy sigh. He let my hand go and nearly fell back to his position on the edge of the desk.

"Nonsense. You've had these spectacles for months. Surely, you know something." I examined my reflection through the spectacles once more. The tendrils were there again, thick as a noose about my neck. A hand raised to my neck could find no tangible trace, but revealed a wrist likewise entwined with tendrils. Even with the spectacles on, the tendrils had a glassy transparency to them.

"I know no more than what you see. Well, except how to remove the damned things." My gaze now left the mirror and travelled along my body. I found great coils of the things at my shoulder, elbow, hip, knee, and ankle. The rest of my body was hardly free of tendrils though. Slender threads adorned nearly every inch of me. I turned again to Howard, barely able to look away from the tendrils for an instant. "I think you had best start from the beginning."

"I suppose you won't be satisfied with anything less now." And so he launched into a tale far more bizarre than the one told to me by his wife hours earlier.

Howard had become an optician because of a childhood fascination with the manipulation of light, how something as simple as a piece of glass could change one's perception of the world. In recent years, he had become increasingly interested in devising a method for expanding the visible spectrum. To that effect, he had been tinkering with the compound used for making the lenses. Finally, this past March, he had succeeded, only to make the same horrible discovery that I had: tendrils fastened all about his body. Further, he had found that everyone was likewise entwined.

Howard had been so revolted by this discovery that he was unable to suffer anyone to touch him. He had resolved to find some method of separating himself from these appendages. This had proved to be a monumental task, as they were not physically tangible. Any attempt to grasp them was utterly futile. Likewise, his attempts to cut through the appendages proved fruitless. Undeterred, he had begun trying every kind of blade imaginable and even ordered custom blades of new alloys. Finally, in April, an alloy of chromium and nickel had proved capable of severing the appendages.

"What? You mean to tell me that these tendrils can simply be sliced off?" I interjected at this point. "They seem to be completely intangible to me. Why should nickel and…What was it? Chrome?… be able to cut through them?"

"Nickel and chromium. I haven't the faintest idea why that alloy should prove effective. I can only assume that the two metals have some alchemical property when used together." Continuing his tale, Howard told that ever since that day he had been using a razor of the alloy to keep himself, his wife, and his children free of the hanging tentacles. The effect had proved most invigorating. Howard found that he had renewed vigour and a decreased need for sleep. He even attributed his youthful appearance to the absence of the tentacles.

During this curious tale, I at times looked at my reflection again through the spectacles, to remind myself that I could not simply dismiss such a mad concept. When he reached the part about finding the alloy, Howard offered a demonstration. With the two of us awkwardly sharing the spectacles, he carefully severed the large tentacle around my face and set about removing the remaining coils.

As Howard had indicated, the effects were most remarkable. I could see Howard removing the tendrils, though I did not feel as though anything were being removed. Still, I could not deny feeling invigorated. It was as though, after spending an afternoon in the torpor of a stuffy, overheated room, I had stepped out into the cool, crisp fresh air of an autumn evening. The severed pieces quickly vanished. My eye was first drawn to those that fell to the floor. They fell slowly, as though gravity had but a partial hold over them, and the floor failed to arrest their descent. These were the sections of tendril that had been entwined about my person that Howard had separated from whatever greater body of which they were a part. The other parts of the tendrils bucked about for a moment or two after they were severed before retreating upward, straight through the ceiling.

The removal of the tendrils being finally completed, I burst out, "But what the devil were they? To what do they connect?"

"I do not know the answer to either of those questions," replied Howard, slowly shaking his head. "I can only guess that they are some sort of parasite, feeding upon us all somehow."

"But did you not look?" I persisted. "From here my vision is blocked by the ceiling, but surely you would have followed the trail to the end."

"I did, much good it did me," he said gloomily. "I went outside and followed the tentacle upwards with my eyes, but never found an end. I can only thank God that it was overcast that day. That small grace permits me the belief that there is simply some manner of creature in the clouds sending down these creepers. But I cannot shake the suspicion that should I look heavenward through those lenses on a clear day, that the tendrils would extend forever."

"Good God," I whispered. "Into the heavens themselves."

"Or beyond," Howard went on. "I do not expect you to believe my story, not right away, but I realize now that I had to share this discovery with someone."

"You mean you've not told anyone else?"

"To what end? To be laughed at or committed?" Howard asked scornfully. "I am rather surprised that you have not sent for a straightjacket yourself."

"But not even your wife?"

"And tell her what?" he said vehemently. "That there are invisible tendrils attached to us all, likely sucking the very life out of us, but that my special razor is keeping us safe? She already believes me eccentric. Telling her more would surely convince her that I am mad as a hatter."

"Yes, I can see it might be best not to tell her just yet, but surely, if the rest of the world is entwined in these, you should show the people how to free themselves."

Howard shook his head remorsefully. "My family is free of them. For that I thank God. This small thing seems to have gone unnoticed. But if there would be a national or even worldwide shedding of these tendrils? Perhaps then you would see to what those tendrils lead. Take those spectacles with you. Now that you have had a glimpse, I cannot in good conscience endeavour to keep you blind. I shall have a new razor made and sent round to you at once. You must decide whether or not to make use of it. For now, I think it best that you rest yourself. You have had quite a shock this evening and there is much for you to ponder."

I agreed with him, but took a moment more to pull myself together. Whatever I decided to believe about those spectacles and what they revealed, Beth deserved her peace of mind. So I bade Howard farewell and left the study. It took only a little convincing to persuade Beth that Howard was perfectly fine and that she and her children were in no danger at all.

The rain had stopped and I decided to walk home. The spectacles tucked carefully in my pocket, I gazed at the stars as I made my way through the empty streets. In Howard's study, it had been very easy to be caught up in the images revealed by the spectacles. Out in the street, doubts and suspicions abounded. What had I truly experienced? A vision through suspect lenses that could not be verified by my other senses. But as I looked up at the stars, I could not help but wonder what might lie out there. As I sit here now, writing this account, I still have not decided what to believe. For myself, I think I could condemn Howard to lunacy.

But as I gaze at the spectacles as they lie on my desk I think of my newly born niece. For myself I dare not believe but, for her sake, can I willfully disbelieve? My sister and I have grown up completely unaware of these parasites and, even now that they are revealed, I know that they were always a part of our lives. But what sort of life could my niece have completely free of the parasite's influence? The spectacles have proven torment enough. I dread the arrival of the razor.

THE DARKNESS

Christina Koblun

WEDNESDAY

The darkness waited. I could feel it pressing its face against the glass as I finished up the last few keystrokes at my computer. I glanced at the bottom right corner of the screen. 4:56 pm. It was early today. A month ago, it hadn't joined me until I was halfway home, but now, early January, it escorted me to and from the office five days a week. It was getting hungrier.

A thumping noise started approaching my cubicle from down the hall. Pam was leaving, right on schedule. Everyone in the office technically worked until five o'clock, but Pam consistently started her guilty shuffle to the door at 4:58 every day. No one bothered her about it, even though she tended to arrive five minutes late more often than she arrived early in the mornings. She was at the mercy of the city's inconsistent bus schedule, and she had kids she had to pick up and drop off from daycare. As the thumping grew louder, a rustling joined it. Sorels and a puffy parka: trademark noises of a Winnipeg winter.

"Cold one out there tonight!"

It had occurred to me on multiple occasions that Pam could probably leave the office just after five and not have to cut out early if she didn't insist on stopping for small talk every day on her way out the door.

"Yeah. It's been a cold week."

If there was one thing I had learned about Winnipeggers in my six months here, it was that they loved to talk about the outdoor conditions. In summer, it was the heat and the mosquitoes. In winter, it was the wind chill and the anticipated snowfall.

"Supposed to go down to minus 40 tonight."

Pam was pulling on her toque and scarf. The next step would be her mittens, and then I would quickly be free of this asinine conversation. No one stayed indoors for long once they were dressed to go out. The layers that made the outdoors bearable quickly overheated a body indoors.

"Brutal."

"Yeah. Well, I don't want to miss my bus! Have a good night!"

"Stay warm."

The thumping and rustling began again, and, a moment later, the click of the front door told me she had gone. I glanced at the bottom right-hand corner of the screen again. 5:02 pm. The day was finally over.

I quickly packed my bags, shut down my station, and left the office before I could end up in any other conversations. I had no interest in visiting with coworkers at a job I hated. I blamed them all for having ended up here, stuck in this hellhole of a city in the winter that wouldn't end, with the darkness stalking me day in and day out.

It hadn't always been this way. People told me I was crazy to accept a transfer from bustling Vancouver to what Canada liked to call Winterpeg (as though I had a choice in this economy), but in my first few months in the city, I fell in love with its tree-lined streets.

Having purchased a condo in the city's southern suburbs but with a job downtown, I felt like I had the best of both worlds: the joy of the downtown in the day, with its plethora of food trucks and comforting bustle, and the safety of the suburbs in the evening, my condo building being bordered on one side by a neighbourhood park, on another side by a pleasant residential road, and on the other two sides by a vast, undeveloped field. At night, I would sit on my balcony in the cooling air and listen to the crickets in the field or take a stroll through the park as the sun set. In the beginning, I found my new position as a sales representative at a shipping company pleasantly challenging. I had the opportunity to speak to a variety of people every day and my coworkers were friendly and welcoming. In short, my job was satisfying, property costs were low, and the city was beautiful. I loved it here. But then the darkness came.

I suppose the geese came first. I woke up one September morning to a dozen of them in the field. It wasn't that alarming. I'd seen them in and around Vancouver. Even when hundreds started showing up, I merely marvelled and took pictures. And then they started leaving. I started having to start my car ahead of time in the mornings or scrape layers of dead frost from the windshield if I was running late. For the first time since I bought the car, I tried the heated seat setting. One Friday, as Pam came back into the office from her lunch break (three minutes late), she casually said, "That will probably be the last one of the year! It's cold enough that the vendors will probably pack it up this week until the spring." Sure enough, the next Monday, as I left the building to walk to the bank on my lunch hour, Broadway was deserted. Gone were the tables of jewellery and the long lines of people waiting to order poutine or Thai food. A lonely hot dog vendor was bundled up inside a bulky jacket, hopping from one foot to the other to stay warm. The wind whipped through the tunnel created by the buildings, gathering up scraps of paper and dust from the street, which turned into weapons in its grasp.

Even then, I didn't realize the danger. Sure, the cold was a little miserable, but there was daylight during my trips to and from the office, and I found a camaraderie in the anticipated cold, as though we were warriors preparing for battle. Coworkers would entertain me with horror stories of two-foot snowfalls and minus 45 nights, and I began to be excited by the prospect of testing my mettle against a true Canadian winter.

The first time I noticed the darkness, it still filled my room after my morning alarm went off. It took me by surprise. As my morning drive only took half an hour, and I didn't have to be at work until 9, I was used to the sun being up by the time my alarm went off at 7. But it was November. The clocks had rolled back, and the darkness was here.

It has been here ever since.

At first, it was just the ordinary loss of light that was expected with the beginning of winter. Sure, it felt a little different when mixed with Winnipeg's cold, which snapped at your cheeks and shook your body to its core, but I was used to shorter days in the winter, and I had purchased top-of-the line outerwear to help me get from my front door to my car every morning. But it quickly got worse. Soon, I was having trouble pulling myself out of bed in the morning. In the evenings, I would find myself motionless on the couch, ignoring the phone and crying at random. I'm not an idiot. I know the symptoms of depression, and I know you will tell me that's what it was, but you need to listen to me. It's something worse. Something about my role as an outsider to this city gives me the different perspective needed to see the danger in this seemingly eternal darkness.

I could feel the darkness as soon as I left the parking garage at the bottom of our building on Wednesday evening. It started as a tingling on the back of my neck, and then it moved itself down my back, until it sat like a heavy weight on the entire upper half of my body. Any happiness I had been feeling—any euphoric relief at the end of another workday—was quickly sucked into its impenetrable mass, leaving me a lifeless form. The grocery shopping I had optimistically planned was quickly cancelled, and it seemed to take all of my energy just to get home and heat up a microwaveable dinner.

This is how I knew it wasn't depression. This lifelessness that was forced upon my body on a daily basis was inextricably linked to the arrival of the evening's darkness. I knew there had to be something sinister at work here. Something that no one else could see. It was as though an enormous, shadowy being blanketed the city every evening and only released the icy streets from its grasp with the rising sun, but no one else found this abnormal.

THURSDAY

My alarm went off at 7:15 and I couldn't move. I focused on lifting my arm. My body felt as though it was being weighed down by some invisible attacker lying on top of me, arm to arm, leg to leg. I squinted through the shadows, trying to catch sight of the heavy form, but the darkness stretched into every corner of the room. I tried to turn my hand up and feel along my arm, but there didn't seem to be anything there. I considered screaming, but what was the point? Rationally, I knew there wasn't anyone in the room, but somehow I could still feel the weight of the intruder spread over my body, pressing me down against the mattress. Every attempt to move failed, and I spent the next hour staring up at the ceiling that I couldn't see and hoping the daylight would bring relief.

As the sun rose and daylight spilled in, I felt the form stand up and move away. There was enough light in the room that I should have seen something, but there was nothing. I didn't even catch an indentation of the bedcovers as it moved away. It was simply there one minute and moving away from me the next.

I sat up, drawing in several deep breaths and trying to reason through what had just happened. I had known the darkness was a threat, but it had never before taken a physical form. Could it be getting stronger? Or had it all been a dream? One of those half-awake, half-asleep experiences that always feels so real?

The clock read 8:05. Time had definitely passed since my alarm went off, but had I really been awake and unmoving for that full 50 minutes? It seemed impossible.

The only thing of which I was sure, was that I wouldn't be making it into work that day. There was no way I could get ready and get myself to the office on time, and after my troubling morning, I had no problem calling in sick.

The rest of the daylight passed in a pleasant haze of domesticity. I made an unconscious decision to treat the incident as if it were a dream and move on with my day. I turned on an audiobook I had been working my way through and managed to complete several loads of laundry, a scrubbing of the kitchen, and a pot of chili large enough to freeze several meals from the leftovers. Overall, it was a pretty good day off. I rarely got to appreciate the coziness of my condo. So many days involved a quick rush to the office in the morning and a rush to put dinner on the table once I got home before I crashed on the couch for the evening. I never had the time to appreciate the way the sunlight danced into the kitchen, seeming to warm it even in the middle of winter. The kitchen was why I had picked the condo. I remember thinking how much it felt like a charming country kitchen, with its blue countertops and pine detailing. It had been such a boon to get the corner unit, positioned to catch both the rising and the setting sun, bathing the condo in the maximum amount of daylight, and I was happy to have a day to appreciate it.

But the darkness was waiting. Around 4 pm, it started with a sensation as though I was being pulled down from the inside. It was like my chest was trying to fold in upon itself—not painful, but uncomfortable. Then my limbs became heavier and heavier, as though I were trying to move through water, until I couldn't pull myself off the couch to bring the folded laundry into the bedroom. It was then that I saw the creature for the first time. It was watching me from the corner of the living room closest to the window. I must have turned my head at just the right time, or maybe it had been getting stronger for months and was only now starting to take a visible form. Either way, we were separated by only one dying beam of the setting sun. Its features were difficult to discern as they blended into the surrounding darkness. The only way that I knew it was there was that it was somehow darker than dark. It seemed to be formed of an extra-dense darkness. It wasn't a static shape. Instead, the edges of its body flowed back and forth with the surrounding shadows. At one point, I was sure it opened its mouth, and in that moment, it seemed to start to fold in upon itself, its mouth drawing the rest of its body into a void, circling like a whirlpool. But then it seemed to close its mouth and the moment was over.

I know now that I should have jumped off the couch and turned on every available lamp, but I was frozen with fear and disbelief. Instead, I watched as the sunbeam slowly disappeared, allowing the form to drift closer and closer. It didn't move like any creature I had ever seen. Instead, it seemed to pour itself through the room, re-forming its shape with every movement forward, until it sank down beside me on the couch and wrapped itself around my body.

Its touch was like a cold fog, but it was heavy. It didn't seem to breathe. It was in constant motion, as though it wasn't confined to a specific physical form and instead its edges floated in and out of existence. It brought with it an overwhelming sadness. I sat on the couch, unable to move out if its grasp, and was forced to feel every grotesque emotion I possessed. When it held me, I knew I was ugly. I knew I was unloved. I knew I should do the world a favour and kill myself, if only I could get off the couch.

FRIDAY

I woke up drowning in black. Even the streetlights outside couldn't penetrate the gloom. I wasn't sure how I had made it to the bed. My last memory from the evening before was of the darkness closing around me as I sat on the couch. Just like the day before, I couldn't seem to move. However, unlike the day before, I could see what was wrong. The darkness lay on my chest, stretching out across my body and weighing it down with its inexplicable mass. Today it had eyes. I knew because I could feel it peering down at me. It was so close, I could smell it—a sulphuric stench. I could taste the smell in the back of my throat, causing me to gag with every breath. I wondered how long it had been here before I saw it. Had it been getting closer all these weeks, staying hidden until it was already too late? Like an optical illusion, now that I had seen it once, I would always be able to see it; I would never again be unaware of its presence.

Once again, I was forced to lie still and wait until it lifted itself off of my body as the rising sun's light penetrated the room. At that point, I was able to get myself out of bed and dressed for the day. I didn't even think to call in to work. I had more important things on my mind.

Unlike the day before, the darkness never left. Instead, it spent the day watching me from the corners. Even though sunlight splashed into every room, I couldn't push the shadows completely out. All day, I felt the creature's presence like tiny sparks on the back of my neck. I started to watch the clock in fear. There weren't many hours of daylight to work with. The darkness wasn't going to stay trapped along the edges forever.

I quickly realized the only way to combat it would be light. At 3:45, I walked around the house turning on every overhead light or table lamp I owned, while the darkness mocked me from its ever-widening patches. I spent the evening watching TV from beneath the shelter of a floor lamp, watching the creature prowl along the edges of the circular beam, occasionally pressing itself up against the edge, as though testing its power. Sometime around 2 am, I realized I would need to sleep to keep up my strength and I tucked myself into bed, but I left the overhead light on. The creature watched me from the shadows of the closet.

SATURDAY

I woke up at my habitual time of 7:10 to find darkness surrounding me. At some point during the night, the light bulb must have burnt out. I could feel the now-familiar heaviness in my limbs and knew there was nothing I could do except close my eyes and pray for sunlight.

The next time I woke up, it was just past eleven in the morning. The darkness seemed to have left, and I tried to get myself up and dressed but I stumbled with exhaustion. I decided to try and rest in the shelter of the daylight and slipped back beneath the comfort of the covers.

It was then that I realized my mistake. Somehow, the creature had hidden itself in the bed, sheltered from the light under the dense cover of the duvet. I didn't notice it until it was already wrapping itself around me, and by the time I realized what was happening, it had me trapped in its embrace.

It was then that I knew it was getting stronger. This time, it didn't stop at a physical hold over my body. Instead, I could feel the fog moving through my skin and into my head, slowing my thoughts to a crawl. I felt the effects of fear—the racing heart, the sweaty palms—but I couldn't organize my body into a response. And then I felt my eyes drifting closed and I knew I had no chance.

The next time I opened my eyes it was 8 pm and darkness covered everything. There was nothing I could do.

SUNDAY

I needed help. By 10 am, still in bed, I managed to formulate that thought. With every passing hour, the darkness was spreading further and further into my body and it would soon be too late—if it wasn't already. I willed myself to move, first one leg to the ground, then the other. I didn't fool myself into thinking I was stronger than the creature. I knew that for some reason it had let me go.

The fluorescent glow of the bathroom light seemed like heaven. I bent my head over the sink and quickly brushed away the chalky feeling that a full day in bed had deposited on my teeth. Then, out of habit, I moved on to brushing my hair.

The first difference I noticed was in my eyes. Their dark colour was a change from my usual blue. I leaned forward and opened them as wide as I could, but that didn't change what I was seeing. It was as though my pupils had expanded so that they completely eclipsed my irises and I was left with perfect black circles. I blinked but they didn't go away.

I opened my mouth to scream, but the noise died in a strangled gasp as I saw the edges of my mouth begin to fold in upon itself, as my body began to implode. As soon as I closed my mouth, the implosion ceased. I tried to say something—anything—but the same image was reflected back at me and no sound came out.

The creature hadn't truly let me go. It was inside me.

MONDAY

I waited all day and all night, sitting in the fluorescent haven of the kitchen, for the creature to leave my body but instead its strength has grown. The battle is lost.

It no longer needs the shadows to operate. It controls everything. Work calls but it doesn't answer my phone. I know what I have to do, what it wants me to do, but I am resisting as long as possible. A few minutes ago, it got the bottle of pills out of the bathroom cupboard, and I can feel it pushing me towards the liquor cabinet. The kitchen knives have begun to exude a magnetic pull. It will toy with me until the very end, but death is inevitable.

Please, let this serve as a warning. There is a danger lurking in this eternal darkness. I do not know if the creature will ever let anyone see this but I had to try. Please, look to the shadows. Look closely. The darkness is waiting.

FOXDREAM

Elin Thordarson

I.

Jimmy Boswell pulled through. He was comatose for weeks. The exact number of consecutive days had been tallied on the chalk-boards in the city's pubs and in the arithmetic lessons in the city's schoolhouses, and every day another number was pasted in the windows of the offices down Newspaper Row. Now the exact number is lost to civic memory, but Jimmy Boswell actually pulled through. Up in the rooms he kept above his bicycle and automobile shop at the corner of Hargrave Street and Ellice Avenue, the greatest athlete Winnipeg had ever known lifted open his still-swollen eyes more than a month after the automobile crash. He said he'd come to the end of the dream of the fox leading him up the escarpment just north of the city and seen the hieroglyphs there. He opened his waking eyes to the camera flashes. The competing city newspaper photographers' camera mounts had been fixed for days on Boswell's minutely flickering face. The smallest of muscles. Only the threads of musculature. The powers in him were returning, reawakening, preparing in the athlete a new health, a new strength, a new life. The magnesium blazed white, the filaments crackled. Each photographer vying for it. Each hoping they'd captured this long-anticipated moment.

"Well done! Another record set, Jimmy!" Breaking the weeks-long city silence was a young journalist chasing the wrong story again, pen to notepad already. He was promptly hushed by the medical staff on site, followed by the other journalists. This was Winnipeg, 1906.

II.

This was October. Well into the October of 1906.

Before there ever was a city here, there had been an ancient spiritual site right at the confluence of the two rivers. Right where two rolling bodies of water converge. Its name: Wi' Nipe' K, or Dark Waters, for the intense mystery of the rivers' mélange. The grass along the riverbanks grew ten feet tall then, and clicked away with cicadas. The ash-leaf maples and burr oaks clung tightly to the mudbank and pushed their way through like slow, twisting arms out of the clay. The deer and bison cut their curving trail along the plateaux. And the glinting, silver, muddy rivers attracted the flights of ravens that went on to establish some of the most powerful and expansive parliaments in the history of provincial ornithology.

By 1906, however, the bison had been pushed out to a place called Silver Heights. The ravens had been ousted from their court and replaced by the Winnipeg Brahmin, the city's first traditional upper class. The Alloways, the Ashdowns, the Bawlfs, the Bells, the Chowns, the Currys, the Galts, the Houghs, the Nantons at Kilmorie, the Strangs, the Strevels, and the Tuppers at Ravenscourt. Instead of trails and river bends, spirits now had hallways, parlours, and basements to haunt as up went scores of showpiece mansions inhabited by these men who filled a philosophical *tabula rasa* with plain and practical ideas. By 1906, Winnipeg had become the largest and most important hub in the exchange and distribution of world commodities. Like ancient Thebes, Winnipeg had become a seven-gated city of trade. Aboard chugging locomotives, hauled in by beasts wearing full corporate regalia, or spirited in under coats, in bootlegs or in plain disguise, it all had to come through the gates of Winnipeg City. As a result, socially, Winnipeg took the palm. But for every bit of lightness and every cotillion and quadrille that spun across the parquet floors, there were things done under the smashed-out lights behind the great warehouses and stockyards, gaping wounds that dragged themselves into back alleys behind the banks. But that's just the way people are.

In 1906, there was nothing official in place to stop the city news-papers from running front-page photographs of the strangulation victims on the all-too-regular basis they surfaced from the city's underbelly, found dumped outside the city gates. Unrecognizable as altogether human faces from the half-litre of blood that swam beneath them. They seemed more like frogman from Japanese folklore.

The swollen nostrils and the shattered hair spread across the white linens provided by the overloaded city morgue were each pho-tographed like a punch. In the rooms above the bicycle and auto shop, the Great Flying Boswell (a 1903 Canadian rowing 8s champion and national tandem bicycling champion, a record holder for caps in rug-by matches and a prolific hockey player, gliding between rover and goaltender positions and, let's not forget, one of the city's first auto-mobilists) lying there could have been likened to any of these all-too-regular photographs. The gash that split his forehead in two during the rollover caused a cumulus of swelling, a thunderhead that swal-lowed up the lengths of his eyebrows and billowed over both eyelids. The swelling descended the bridge of Boswell's nose, marring his "renaissance profile," as the newspaper sportswriters had often called it, and settled into his neck and then his chest. But this was after the race, in the city silence that followed for weeks.

III.

In 1906, Winnipeg may have been famous worldwide for the steady commercial activity checked at each of its seven gates, but there was another set of gates. An eighth. "The Gates within The Gates—The Dream within The Dream," another famous headline off Newspaper Row. Happyland (American Entertainment Corporation brings you… Happyland!!) was an amusement park—"The Tivoli of the Prairies!"—a pleasure garden that stretched along Portage Avenue between the streets Aubrey and Dominion and that extended all the way back to the Assiniboine River. Its six-hundred-foot-long gates were designed, as the Dorians had done before, with the divine proportion in mind. The golden mean, found in the mollusk shells that littered the silt of the riverbanks, in the florets of the hyssop, the ironweed, the wild strawberry, and in the very division of the human body: the lines of the massive gates were divided such that each division had a fixed relationship to every other division and to the whole itself. As one passed from the exterior to the interior, the scene was completely bewildering in its beauty and splendour. Architecture commingled with history along the great plaza. The eye met styles representing all periods in architectural development: Byzantine, French, Ionic, Arabic and Gothic.

The blend of exotic aromas of the various tobacconists' stalls as one paid one's penny admission called visitors to far-off places to which they'd never been or would never go, to the beedi merchants in the markets of Delhi, of Samarqand, and Samarra. Popcorn and peanut vendors strolled the grounds, with a warm savour wafting from their carts. Artisan balloon sellers trailed along as well. A miniature steam-powered locomotive, on a rail twelve inches wide, took visitors on a slow-moving tour of the park, making a stop at the lively dance palace and the Old Mill, a kind of "lover's delite" boat ride where couples drifted into dark places together, interrupted from time to time by lights snapping on above baskets of flowers. There was a fig-ure-eight roller coaster, the only one of its kind on the tall grass plains, and there were the tranquil Japanese tea gardens. Big Top acts like Barnum and Bailey Circus brought African elephants onto the prai-rie landscape and showcased for weekend Happylanders their famous diving ponies. The baseball diamond at Happyland was essentially the main draw. It held national tournaments and at night was illumi-nated by electric lights. In fact, the entire park boasted its electrical capabilities in the newspapers. And all the attractions at Happyland were accessible by a network of white-painted boardwalks driven into the ground. The effect was a sense of floating, three feet above the thick grasses imported from Kentucky. Each of the boardwalks were touched up with paint every night after close so as never to break the illusion of a floating dreamland with the regular wear of everyday use.

Happyland was true to its name. For the citizens and work-ers in the busiest economic centre in the western world, Winnipeg's Happyland was a joyful return to their nineteenth century Canadian childhoods, remembered as spiralling round robin after round robin of baseball tournaments in the mown tall grasses of summer.

The automobile race had started at Happyland.

IV.
Manitoba Free Press—Vol. 34. September 4, 1906.—No. 52.

"Jimmy" Boswell Seriously Hurt.

Sad Accident Attends Annual Automobile Road Race—Daring Chauffeur Sustains Injuries That May Result in Permanent Disablement—Anderson First, Bawlf Second, McCulloch Third.

"Jimmy" Boswell, one of the city's best-known amateur ath-letes, was seriously injured yesterday morning during the Labour Day automobile races. Near the town of Stonewall at the escarpment, his machine upset, throwing the occupant out. Boswell fell on his head and was rendered unconscious. Up to an early hour this morning, he was still unconscious, but every hope of his recovery is entertained. This unfortunate event marred what would otherwise have been a most successful race. The race was won by Herb Anderson, W. Bawlf was second and McCulloch third.

The racers started from Happyland at about 10.30 yesterday morning with intervals of two minutes between the machines. They took the western route to the escarpment past Stony Mountain and all went well 'til near the turnaround point. Boswell was driving well and had worked up from seventh position to fourth, when four miles out from the turn he encountered a bit of winding road through the bush. It was somewhat rough, but with careful handling was not considered dangerous. On one of the turns he came to grief.

Beyond Boswell, there was no person present at the time of the accident, so that it is difficult to tell exactly what happened. However, from a careful examination of the road at that point, it appears that Boswell was taking the crooked road at a good rate of speed. At the turn where the wreck happened, he cut the corner sharp, as usual, but when the rear wheels started to skid, he struck a rock, throwing him on the ground. When he alighted again, he struck another boulder and the car was thrown over. From the position in which it was lying, it must have almost upended.

About this time Jack McCulloch came along. He was leading in the race and, having made the turn at Stonewall, was on his way back. McCulloch pulled up as soon as he saw the wrecked car beside the road and was greatly amazed to find that the injured man was his chum. Throwing aside all thoughts of the race, he set to work to see what he could do. He appealed to a neighboring farmhouse for aid, and while they were fixing the injured man up, Anderson came along in his Columbia. As this was the only car in the race which carried a tonneau, Boswell was put in and with the two men supporting him, the race for Winnipeg and medical aid was begun.

Fast Run Home.

Anderson did not spare his car, and he drove with such good effect that he won the race. Two doctors were summoned, and Boswell was taken to his home. When an examination was made, it was found that he had been struck heavily on his forehead, which was frightfully gashed. There is danger of injury to the brain at this point.

The machine that he was driving looks a wreck. When it turned over, the seat was smashed to matchwood, as were all the other wooden parts. The steering wheel was bent forward over the bonnet. However, the machine was righted yesterday afternoon and though the gears were wrecked, the engine was still in working order. After the car had been started by hand, it came under its own power, making an average of twenty-five miles an hour the whole distance back to Happyland.

v.

September 1906 rolled into October 1906. It was the silence that defined that time. It was unseasonably warm for a Manitoba October. The sunshine throughout the afternoon exposed the particles normally unseen. The smallest of insects, the spider's thread, the dusts and ashes of the earth. The season had reached the point just past the zenith of its biology. The slowing point, heavy with age, right before the rapid and colourful descent into the beginning of winter. The farmers outside the city gates were burning the brush. Its aroma, the collective and longstanding local portent for autumn's arrival, commingled with the fragrance of sawdust and horse piss. This is true. Down in the streets, at Ellice and Hargrave, people who had watched Boswell win rowing championships, regattas, hockey trophies, cycling pennants, rugby cups, and those who had watched him cross the finish line at Happyland, limp, seemingly lifeless, grotesquely red, his skull showing through his hair like a dinosaur egg, threw down layer after layer after layer of sawdust in the streets below his window to create a muffler. This kind of silence was required for Boswell's hoped-for recovery. Winnipeggers' love for him was real. They truly worshipped him. He was a god to them. A Quetzalcoatl. Boswell, the feathered serpent. A trickster god. As all the greatest athletes are. Tricksters. They have to be mischievous enough to win. To deceive their opponents, to deke, to fake, to dodge. It was all sleight of hand. It was all shape shifting.

This bloody injustice (even if Boswell did miraculously cross the finish line in the winning automobile) spread sorrow in wide circles. The whole city grieved this bodily harm done to a man who'd been instrumental in some of the most triumphant moments in the collective memory. The citizens of Winnipeg in 1906 could all say with certainty where they had been when Boswell had scored what came to be known as the Boswell coat trick. Never replicated. Three natural hat tricks. By his ninth goal, in the end of the nail-biter of an ice hockey match in Winnipeg's arena on Osborne Place, no more hats remained on the heads of any of the supporters—so coats, like giant, silent ravens, began to float down onto the ice surface. Boswell brought the people of Winnipeg together in ways that the warehouse foremen, the bank managers, the politicians (all Brahmin) could never touch.

During the autumn of 1906, grown men tiptoed carefully past the building on their way to work, children were told by their mothers to "mind Jimmy now" and devised elaborate war games played entirely through hand signalling to each other over long distances. This system proved instrumental when many of them were sent over to Europe a number of years later. Automobile traffic, what little there was of it in 1906, was strictly prohibited at that intersection. Bicycles didn't ring their bells and washing was taken off the line promptly whenever the snap of those sails rose over the silence of the quarter. Not even the midnight sighings coming from the Masonic temple down the block could be heard during that time. The sounds of the massive drays and blood horses pissing in the streets as they brought the cartloads of sawdust through the city gates every day was completely muffled by the blankets. As a result, the entire street corner smelled of fresh-cut wood and horse piss, whose pungent odour became unforeseeably trapped in the sawdust, no matter how many layers were thrown on top.

VI.

"I dreamed the fox," Boswell replied before falling back asleep. It would be another week before the newspapers would get the full story. Published as a serial.

It was nighttime in the dream. A greenish hue, like a jewel tone. Like the backing on mirrors. The smell of stone after a good rainstorm. The gentle shivering of a Manitoba autumn twilight. The dream became civically famous for its opening instant. Boswell was following a fox through the ferns. This alliteration was used widely in the city's schoolhouses for decades, until the meaning of the subject-noun Boswell had become lost. Tramping up a slight incline through fronds of bracken. The detail of which was so vivid it's said that Boswell suffered from headaches for the rest of his life because of it. Headaches so bad that Boswell never competed in any sport ever again. He spent the rest of his days sharpening skates and fixing bicycles and chewing aspirin. "I saw every last stitch of every last frond," he'd told his doctors.

Sometimes all Boswell could see of the little fox was the white end of the foxtail flitting through the bracken. It was a signal to follow—Boswell knew that without having to be told. When Boswell fell behind, the little fox waited, nipping at the burrs that clung to its tail, until Boswell was just close enough to follow along.

Boswell had told the newspapers all about the episode of climbing the hill. But he never had the words to talk about the dream prior. Boswell remembered. Before he'd entered the dream following the fox, there was a long period of blackness, but before that he remembered the crash site. In his dream, he remembered dreaming.

"Do you appreciate art?" the fox asked, stopping and turning to Boswell. The fox nearly underfoot. Boswell stopped too. What could a fox mean by art?

"Art?" he replied.

"Yes, art. You know. That moment when the essential is unconcealed? Of course, for you, the lid is slammed shut. Like a too-heavy lid on a larder. Or when there's something preventing you from opening the door to the chicken coop to allow you in fully. To all its fleshy riches. Or the rabbit hutch." The fox's eyes gleamed with some long ago and humorous memory.

Jimmy thought. He knew he felt a sense of exiting his finite existence, of rising above his giant body while rowing on the rivers. The magnificent push and pull of the water's tension on his muscles, his sense of when to resist and when to yield, his body in perfect function. Closest to nature. And for him it was a preternatural capacity.

A kind of rhythm, a counting, lifted his mind out of his body above the water. There were times at the Winnipeg arena that in defending against an oncoming offensive attack, Boswell could wait and wait and strike the puck away at the exact right moment. He had simply stepped into his opponent's sense of time. And below them was another cavern of time and below that another. He felt cut loose from himself. Boswell could sense how masterfully and infinitely ordered all of reality was. Mathematically sound. Like the mollusk, the frond, and the gates of Happyland.

"I appreciate sculpture best," the little fox tossed over his shoulder as he made to keep going up the incline. "I have something I want to show you, finally." His light step relaxed into a happy little gambol up the hill. Boswell worked out the meanings of his thoughts the entire length of their trek. That his athleticism was a kind of speaking with mute Nature.

When they'd reached the crown of the escarpment, just below them Boswell could see the crash site and way south the lights of Happyland. The bracken exhaled its green fragrance and the sky fevered with lightning in the distance. The gentle Kee-way-din wind cooled the sweat on Boswell's arms.

"Nothing, I mean nothing, in Nature retrogresses," the little fox said. "Everything endeavors forward. There is only one genuine philosophy and it's inscribed in hieroglyphs here."

life is a power.

INTO THE MADHOUSE

Josh Gerard Moore

A carnival is an unsettling place after hours. Once the last patrons have shuffled out and the gates are locked, the only visitors left are the rats and other vermin. The lights go out and the cacophony of tilt-a-whirl theme music and shouting barkers fades to nothing. Silence claims the fairgrounds, broken only by the wind and the scurrying of the pests that emerge to feast on the scraps discarded by gluttonous thrill seekers.

Or that's how it should be, Cassie told herself. *What am I doing here?* she wondered for what seemed like the hundredth time.

The smell of corndogs and cotton candy that lingered in the air only punctuated the eeriness of the vacated fairgrounds. Instead of the riot of flashing lights and giddy laughter that were the mainstay of the carnival, Cassie was surrounded by shadows and the looming silhouettes of abandoned rides. In the darkness, she could imagine the towering metal structures were giant mechanical insects ready to rend her limb from limb with their jagged metal claws. The moonlight cast the usually bright backdrops in a sinister monochrome. Cavorting clowns became ghouls waiting to devour lost children.

Circus animals, once friendly and playful, were transformed into the grim inmates of a madman's demented menagerie. Cassie shook her head to clear her thoughts and dispel the demons she was beginning to see all around. With reality resituated, she promised herself that she would try to rein in her imagination.

She decided instead to focus on following Simon as he passed ride after ride looking for the target of his intended mischief. The duffle bag slung over Simon's shoulder was lumpy and misshapen. Its contents were a mystery to Cassie, but she doubted that whatever he had planned could be worth the risk involved. Part of her was a little exhilarated by the slight surge of adrenaline that trespassing had provided, but mostly she was just annoyed that she had allowed Simon to talk her into this. Even better would be to ask why she was *always* letting Simon talk her into shit like this. He'd flash that stupid crooked smile and it was almost like hypnosis. Suddenly she'd find herself agreeing to lower him into the cellar of an abandoned farmhouse without ever thinking about how he was going to get back up, or she'd be dragged through a forsaken graveyard at midnight in the middle of nowhere, or she'd end up helping him break into a carnival in the dead of night so he could pull off some stupid prank. Yeah, she really needed to learn to just close her eyes, take a deep breath and say no.

Rousing herself from contemplation of Simon's powers of beguilement, Cassie realized that she'd lost track of him in the darkness. As misguided as he could sometimes be, his presence had nevertheless been reassuring and without it Cassie once again found herself dwelling on the way the shadows turned the carnival into a panoply of twisted and vaguely threatening forms.

"Simon?" She whispered his name to avoid alerting any security guards that might be on patrol in her vicinity. "Simon, where are you?"

He did not respond.

She scanned the darkness, searching for any sign of her missing boyfriend. All she could see were empty food vendor stands and carnival game booths. To her left was an attraction where patrons could win prizes by throwing darts at balloons. Row upon row of stuffed animals lined the inside of the booth. The friendly, familiar characters were intended to excite little children into cajoling their parents to spend exorbitant amounts of money trying to win a doll that was likely worth a couple of dollars. But in the darkness, Cassie only saw thousands of glaring eyes hovering above malevolent, slathering grins.

Cassie was on the verge of bolting when Simon popped out of the shadows.

"What the hell are you doing?" he blurted.

"Jesus! You nearly scared the shit out of me! I was looking for *you*, asshole!"

"Seems to me you were staring at those stupid stuffed animals. Why? Do you want one? I could probably get this cage open..."

Simon started shaking the cage that was securing the booth but Cassie pulled him away.

"Don't be an idiot. That's nothing but cheap crap."

"Suit yourself." Simon let go of the cage. "Anyway, I found the Haunted Castle ride. It's just around the next corner."

"Good, let's get this over with so we can get the fuck out of here. This place is giving me the creeps."

"Really?" Simon laughed at her. "It's just an empty carnival. What, are you afraid of the dark all of a sudden?"

"Shut up!" Cassie punched Simon in the arm as hard as she could. "I didn't say I was scared. Just creeped out. This place is supposed to be lit up and full of families laughing and having fun. Empty and dark it's just...weird..."

"Haha, you're scared," Simon taunted in a singsong voice.

Cassie stuck out her tongue at him and pushed him in the direction of the Haunted Castle. "Stupid jerk."

As they turned the corner, Cassie could see that Simon was right. The Haunted Castle ride was at the end of a row of similar attractions. It was right next to the House of Mirrors. Cassie used to love those when she was younger. The sight of her image distorted into ludicrous shapes in the warped mirrors would send her into paroxysms of laughter. The thought of navigating the maze of mirrors in the dark, however, sent shivers down her spine. Cassie was careful to avert her eyes as they passed, lest Simon suggest they take a detour through the maze.

Once they had moved beyond the House of Mirrors, Cassie let out a relieved sigh and realized she'd been holding her breath. Somehow, the thought of vandalizing the funhouse ride was preferable to the prospect of navigating hallways lined with darkened mirrors.

The so-called Haunted Castle looked pretty pathetic, even from the outside. The façade of the ride was built of plywood painted grey with black mortar lines in a feeble attempt to make the walls look like the stone masonry of a very small fortress. A sign stretched across the top of the wall proclaimed that this ride was indeed "The Haunted Castle" in what Cassie assumed were meant to be spooky-looking letters. The right side of the marquee was dominated by a poor likeness of the Grim Reaper. Overall, the exterior of the ride looked cheap and tacky, which didn't bode well for what might be found inside.

Simon was already climbing over the railings that would funnel patrons as they lined up to enter the ride. In no hurry, Cassie casually walked through the winding path and pushed through the turnstile at the end rather than vaulting it as Simon had. By the time she reached the top of the metal steps leading to the ride's loading area,

Simon was already pulling his bolt cutters from his duffle bag. He'd used the same ones to cut a hole in the Carnival fence earlier that evening. With a great deal of effort, Simon was eventually able to cut through the padlock securing the entrance to the ride.

"Gimme a hand with this," Simon requested as he began to lift the overhead gate that blocked the way to the ride's interior. With Cassie's help, the gate moved slowly upward. As soon as the gate was high enough, they both ducked under and it slammed shut behind them. Out of curiosity, Cassie tried to lift the gate again but it wouldn't move.

"Shit! It's jammed."

Simon joined Cassie in her frantic effort to open the gate, but it still wouldn't budge.

"Oh well," he shrugged. "Guess we'll have to find another way out, but not until I've fixed this place. See, this is exactly what I'm talking about!" Simon gestured towards what appeared to be a mannequin under a white sheet. "It's fucking pathetic!"

After a few bewildered moments, Cassie's eyes adjusted to the dark enough for her to notice that two eyeholes had been cut in the sheet. This was supposed to be a ghost. What it really looked like was the laziest Scooby-Doo villain ever. Simon was right. It *was* pathetic. Maybe not pathetic enough to risk criminal charges for trespassing, breaking and entering, and vandalism, but Cassie didn't have the same artistic sensibilities as Simon. Cassie wasn't personally offended by the ineptitude of travelling carnival folk, but Simon sure was. So much so that here they were breaking into an amusement park ride in the middle of the night so that he could right this terrible, terrible wrong.

Simon was already pulling the sheet off the mannequin. The form underneath was an androgynous blank. Simon's grin was as wide as the Cheshire Cat's.

"This is perfect! I can totally make this work!" He fell to his knees and started digging in his duffle bag like a child rifling through the presents under a Christmas tree. But this would be a morbid Christmas indeed. He had five large jars full of fake blood. Never satisfied with the brands available through retail, this blood was his own concoction of corn syrup, food colouring and a few other ingredients that he kept to himself. He also pulled out several bundles of different coloured fabric and ragged old clothing, a pile of old wigs, various sets of fake teeth ranging from fangs to some that were merely crooked and discoloured, a roll of flesh-coloured latex, and finally a large sheet of foam rubber. Creature makeup was one of Simon's favorite hobbies and Cassie had to admit he was quite good at it. Once he had these items arranged as he wanted, he handed Cassie a flashlight.

"Here," he said. "Be careful where you shine this. I don't want beams of light shining out letting every security guard in the park know we're here, but I am going to need light to work, so try to keep it pointed at the mannequin but angled further into the ride." She held the light as he directed and Simon smiled. "Sweet! Now I'm gonna make me a kick-ass fuckin' zombie that's gonna scare the shit out of the next person to ride this thing."

Simon shoved his duffle bag aside and got to work modifying the mannequin. A metallic clanking noise came from the bag as it slid across the floor. Her curiosity piqued, Cassie snuck a look at the bag's remaining contents. Inside was a variety of rusty tools and knives as well as a hatchet. Cassie guessed that Simon intended to use these as props in his horrification project. On a whim, she picked up a butcher knife. She'd been on edge ever since they'd broken through the park fence, and even though she could never imagine using the knife, it still felt reassuring in her hand. With her mind now somewhat at ease, Cassie felt more comfortable taking in her surroundings.

She was near the mouth of a narrow corridor. There was a single rail running along the middle of the floor that would guide the passenger cars through the ride. The walls were a uniform black, and she could see spotlights hanging from the ceiling. These would undoubtedly light up as the cars approached: an attempt to startle the occupants with various "scary" vignettes set up along the track.

Simon had taken a ride through this Haunted Castle once himself and had been utterly disappointed. When he complained to the carny afterwards the man laughed and said, "I'd like to see you do better." Little did he know that Simon was exactly the sort of person to take him up on that challenge.

She shone the light down the corridor and she could see a few rubber bats hanging from the ceiling and a horrible fake-looking spider at the centre of some cheap cotton webbing. There was also a skeleton that stood only about three feet tall. Perhaps the skeleton of a child could be creepy if it wasn't so disproportioned and obviously made of plastic. It looked as though someone had merely bought a bunch of cheap Halloween decorations from the Dollar Store and haphazardly hung them up on the walls of the ride. The deserted carnival grounds had been scarier than this.

The corridor turned to the right about twenty feet from where Cassie stood. Propped in the corner was a cardboard coffin with a ghoulish hand reaching out from under the lid. The hand was clearly just a rubber glove from some crappy costume that had been attached to an empty shirtsleeve. They didn't even bother to fill the sleeve with anything that might give the impression that there was actually an arm inside. It just dangled limply from under the lid of the coffin. If Simon was gonna make this shit scary he had a lot of work ahead of him, which for Cassie meant a lot of time holding a flashlight.

"Hey, watch what you're doing!" Simon grumbled. "Shine the light over here. I can't do this shit in the dark."

Cassie pointed the flashlight back at the mannequin. Simon had barely even started working on it. A few smudges of fake blood and a half-completed latex gash in the mannequin's skull were the only changes she could see in the figure's appearance. At this rate, it would take Simon a week to finish redecorating the entire ride.

"Jesus, Simon, this is fucking boring! Why don't we just forget about it and go home?"

Simon wheeled around and slapped her hard across the face.

"Maybe if you'd help me I could get this done sooner! Now hold the fucking flashlight so I can see what I'm doing!"

Simon's violent outburst shocked Cassie. He'd never hit her before. She would never even have imagined him capable of such a thing. Rage swelled within and her vision turned red. She felt like kicking him in the balls then stomping on his head till his mashed up brains oozed from his cracked-open skull. Instead, she threw the flashlight, which struck him in the middle of the face with a sickening crunch.

"You broke my nose you fucking bitch! I'll fucking kill you!"

Cassie wasn't going to wait around for Simon to make good on his threat. While he was distracted assessing the damage to his face, Cassie ran off into the darkness. She turned the corner and sprinted blindly down the next section of the ride. She could see the light from Simon's flashlight bobbing behind her. Indistinct forms seemed to be reaching for her from either side, but all she could think about was getting as far away from Simon as possible.

Somewhere behind her, Simon cried out in pain and she heard a muffled thud. The light danced erratically then was still. He must have tripped. As she reached the next turn, she could just make out a doorway on the left side of the corridor. The words "Keep Out" were written across the door in letters meant to look like dripping blood. Assuming this was merely a disguised emergency exit, she pushed through and heard the door click shut behind her. Simon must not have seen her, because she heard his pounding footsteps as he ran past on the other side of the door. He was yelling frantically now. "Cassie! I don't know what happened, I just lost my head. Cassie, please come back!"

With her back pressed hard against the door, Cassie began to catch her breath. She waited in silence for some sound of Simon returning, but all was deathly quiet. Tentatively she tried to open the door. It was locked from the other side. She had escaped from Simon, but where was she now? All she was certain of was that she wasn't outside as she had hoped.

Wherever she was, it was pitch black. The first thing she was going to need was some light. She had a flashlight app on her phone, so she started fumbling through her pockets.

"Aw fuck," she cursed under her breath. She just remembered that her phone was sitting on her dresser at home. The battery had been almost drained, so she'd left it to charge.

Okay, no light, she told herself. *Well, this is going to be fun.*

She knew that sitting here feeling sorry for herself wasn't going to accomplish anything, so she picked herself up, checked the door one last time to be sure that it was truly locked, and started moving down the passageway, running her hand along one wall as a point of reference. Soon she started to realize that the passage was descending. The decline was gradual at first, but after a few minutes, she was half sliding down what seemed to be a steep slope.

This doesn't make any fucking sense. I must be almost thirty feet underground by now.

The fair was set up in a huge concrete parking lot. Cassie couldn't understand how this ride could have a section that went underground. Despite how crazy it seemed, she had no choice but to continue her descent. As she moved deeper, the air got warmer and more humid. The texture of the walls was changing as well. Where before the walls were entirely unremarkable, now they felt moist, bumpy, and a little bit sticky. The tunnel floor had become spongy and damp as well. She couldn't help feeling like she was walking down the throat of an enormous beast.

The walls were not all that was changing. Cassie became aware of a dim red light that slowly grew in intensity as she moved deeper down the tunnel. As the light became stronger, a rhythmic thumping noise arose which grew louder on pace. The rhythm was almost soothing at first, like the heartbeat you hear when you press your ear to a loved one's chest, but as she moved further along the tunnel it swelled until she could feel the beat pounding in her eardrums.

Without warning, the tunnel levelled out and almost immediately opened up into a large chamber, the sights inside almost enough to break Cassie's already tenuous grip on sanity. The walls of the chamber were made of the same spongy material as the tunnel. Spaced evenly along the walls were a series of sconces with oil lamps hanging from them. Whatever type of fuel fed these lamps made the flames burn red instead of orange. As she scanned the room, Cassie's eyes were drawn inexorably to the source of the pulsing rhythm. A dozen people were seated at a long wooden table. Each person held a knife in their left hand, and they were pounding them on the table in a steady beat. They were all dressed in identical black robes with raised hoods. Although their faces were shrouded in darkness, Cassie could still make out the mutilated features of a few of these strange people. From what she could see, their heads were completely hairless, lacking even the shadow of stubble promising new growth. Their eyes were sewn shut with thick black thread and it appeared that the surrounding flesh had long since healed around the sutures. Perhaps worst of all, their lips had been completely cut away, revealing teeth that were stained black and protruded from bleeding, diseased gums.

The skin that ringed their grotesque maws was jagged and torn in such a way that it looked as though their lips had been removed forcefully and with a dull blade.

Cassie found herself becoming entranced by the gruesome spectacle of their tortured faces coupled with the steady rhythm of their pounding fists, but movement to her left broke her from her torpor. Opposite the table of fiends stood the largest man Cassie had ever seen. He was at least seven feet tall and as wide as two men. The brute wore a robe similar to the others but the sleeves had been torn from his, revealing enormous arms that were wrapped in barbed wire. The barbs cut deeper into his flesh with every movement he made and the wounds dripped with black blood. He walked over to a row of low cages that ran along the left side of the chamber. There were thirteen cages and each one held a small, terrified child. As Cassie watched, the beast stopped in front of a cage containing a small boy. The man pulled the screaming child from the cage and, gripping the child's ankles in one giant fist, carried him across the room and slammed him unceremoniously onto the centre of the large table. The child's head hit the wood of the tabletop with a loud crack and he abruptly stopped screaming. Cassie would have assumed the child was dead if not for the steady rise and fall of his small chest. The blow to his head had knocked him out; Cassie would not have been surprised to find that his skull was fractured, but this was probably for the best. The child would not have wanted to be awake for what happened next.

As Cassie stood dumbstruck by horror, the unholy congregation rose from their seats and all at once they reached forward and slashed twelve deep gouges in the child's arms and legs with their knives. The child did not wake as his blood began to pour out onto the table. The blood flowed across the tabletop and was channelled through a series of shallow troughs carved into the wood to a drain hole at the end of the table. Cassie could see a pipe running from the drain into the floor but she did not want to know where the blood was going.

As the child bled, the ghoulish people began to chant in a language that Cassie did not recognize. The chanting was soft at first but steadily grew to a roar as the child's life pumped out onto the table.

Cassie could do nothing but watch in horrified fascination as a large hole began to open in the wall at the far end of the chamber. The hole appeared to be a giant sphincter that quickly gaped wider and wider until it was large enough for a person to walk through. The instant the orifice stopped expanding, something long and snake-like began slithering out into the chamber. The snake-thing was wide and flat. With a sickening realization, Cassie knew that she was watching the tongue of some unfathomable monstrosity questing out for its dinner.

Upon reaching the end of the table, the tip of the tongue rose off the floor and split into four obscene proboscises that latched onto the child's tender flesh. The tongue began pulsing with a nauseating suction. The child's skin turned grey. Cassie assumed the child's remaining blood was being syphoned away, but there was no desiccation. Instead, an inky blackness was radiating out from the points where the monstrous tongue touched the child's skin. The black substance was replacing the child's blood in some form of diabolical transfusion.

The entire process lasted only a few short minutes, but for Cassie it seemed to take an eternity. Its work done, the tongue detached itself and retreated into the depths from whence it had come. The sphincter closed behind it. On the table, the child's body had become a bloated mass of grey flesh, spider-webbed with sickly black veins. The body's appearance did not, however, deter the cloaked figures from ripping into it with their bare hands and shoving fistfuls of diseased flesh into their lipless mouths. Cassie vomited violently, but the demented dinner guests were too caught up in their feast to notice her retching.

"What's the matter Cassie? Not hungry?" Cassie whirled around. Simon was standing between her and the tunnel entrance. "This meal was prepared specially for you. Join us Cassie. Join us and be my queen. Feed and we can live together forever."

Cassie's head was spinning. She wanted to throw up again but her stomach was empty. All of it had been a trap. Simon made up all that bullshit about wanting to fix the Haunted Castle just so he could lure her down here to do what? Be his bride in this morbid freak show? Fuck that!

Like the flick of a light switch, rage replaced fear. Looking down, Cassie was surprised to realize she was still holding the knife she'd taken from Simon's duffle bag. She slashed at him, ripping open his throat. His neck became a fountain of crimson and he stumbled and fell to the floor.

Acting on instinct, Cassie grabbed the nearest lamp from the wall. Clutching it by the chain, she swung the lamp over her head a few times and hurled it at the freaks still huddled over the dead child. No sooner had the strange fuel spread out from the broken lamp than it burst into flame, engulfing the table and all of its feasting occupants. Screams erupted from the conflagration. These joined the desperate cries of the remaining caged children so that the cavern filled with an agonized chorus.

Cassie surveyed her work. The table was a chaos of red flames and flailing demons turned torches. Simon lay in a pool of his own blood. The children continued to shriek in terror. Cassie was just moving to free the children when the giant burst from the flames. He was burning just as surely as his compatriots, but the fire didn't seem to faze him. Cassie wanted to save the children, but her instinct for self-preservation was stronger. She took off running back up the tunnel. She ran faster than she thought she could. Her descent had taken a lifetime but she seemed to reach the door at the end of the tunnel in a heartbeat. The door was still locked tight. In amazement, she realized she had still not let go of the rusty knife. She held the knife out in front of her, hoping that she might be able to fend off the behemoth. The tunnel was pitch black. Not even a hint of the red light reached this far. She could hear something scrambling up the passageway. She began blindly stabbing, stabbing, stabbing at the darkness…

———•◦•———

"Hey, watch what you're doing!" Simon grumbled. "Shine the light over here. I can't do this shit in the dark."

The light swung back towards him. He'd barely gotten started and already Cassie was flaking on him. How hard was it to hold a damned flashlight steady?

"Jesus, Simon, this is fucking boring! Why don't we just forget about it and go home?"

Simon turned to respond, but he didn't know that she had crept up behind him and he accidentally struck her with the back of his outstretched hand.

"Oh shit, Cassie I'm so sorry. I didn't realize you were standing so close to me. Are you all right? ……Cassie?"

She was just standing there with a blank expression on her face. It looked as though something had broken behind her eyes. Without a word she kicked him in the groin. Pain radiated through his abdomen and he crumpled to the floor. Cassie had raised her hand. She was holding one of the knives from his duffle bag. The knife seemed to move in slow motion but it bit deep into his shoulder with the force of a freight train. The knife made a wet sucking sound as she pulled it out of his flesh. She raised it again. He tried to shield himself with his arms but it was no use. The next slash severed three of his fingers and opened a deep gash in his gut. He tried to scream but he had no breath. His blood looked black in the dim light. Her onslaught was relentless. She was laughing now. Laughing as she stabbed and stabbed and stabbed.

Blackness closed in on Simon from every side and she continued to laugh. She laughed as he gasped his last breath.

———•◦•———

Eugene's day was off to a bad start. He arrived at the fairgrounds early; he enjoyed walking through the carnival at the break of dawn when no one else was around. The early morning quiet provided an almost meditative counterpoint to the chaos that would soon surround him as patrons filled these avenues with laughter and screams and the cries of children whose desires were continually quashed by frugal parents.

This morning, however, Eugene's ruminations where cut short as he approached his final destination. Eugene operated the Haunted House ride, and before he even entered the turnstile, he knew that something was wrong. From the outside, everything appeared normal, but he could hear the faint sounds of the ride's soundtrack playing inside.

"Aw, fuck!" he fumed. "Those sonsabitches left the ride running all night!"

With growing irritation, Eugene rushed to the door and stopped. The padlock was cut. There was something more serious than lazy coworkers going on here. He had been operating this ride for more years than he cared to count. Eugene knew every note, every scream, every peal of frantic laughter that comprised the ride's soundtrack better than he knew the sound of his own voice. Something was out of place. The soundtrack ran through its usual cycle of "spooky" noises, but underlying the all-too-familiar cacophony, he could just make out a sound that didn't belong. He could hear a girl laughing.

Eugene's irritation slowly kindled to anger verging on rage. *If some fucking lowlife kids have been messing with my ride there's gonna be hell to pay!* Over the years, this ride had become the most important thing in his life. Eugene was a simple man who led a simple life. He wasn't particularly smart. He'd never shown any great aptitude for any profession or trade. When he'd first gotten the job working at the carnival, it had merely seemed better than some of his other alternatives. When the carnival owners eventually put the Haunted House into his care, it had given his life a purpose. It might seem meager to some, but it was a purpose nonetheless. This ride had become like a child to him, and he was damned well going to protect it!

As Eugene made his way through the ride, the source of the irregularity presented itself almost immediately. It was as obvious as a nail being driven into his eye. Framed within a red spotlight sat a young girl, and at the sight of her, Eugene could feel bile rising in his throat.

On closer inspection, he realized that the light wasn't red after all. The girl was covered in blood. Where her eyes should have been there were only two empty pits. Long deep scratches were gouged into the flesh below her empty sockets. She had clawed her own eyes out.

Piled around her was a grotesque assortment of body parts and blood-soaked clothing. Cradled in her arms was the head of a young man. It didn't seem possible, but somehow this tiny girl had ripped the boy to pieces. She was giggling and performing a demented puppet show with entrails.

The sight would haunt Eugene's dreams for years to come. The sound of her hollow, mirthless laughter would be with him for the rest of his life. But more than anything else, one thought kept running through Eugene's mind. *Not again.*

ALL ROADS

Zacharie Montreuil

According to Brother Riel, M. Bonheur washed ashore on the coast of
Normandy three days past, frantic and unwell. I know not how, but
the Cardinal somehow learned of his arrival and immediately sent for
him to be collected and put to question as to his journey and the where-
abouts of his ship, the Ponctuel. *The bishop here is unaware that I shall*
set his answers to paper as best as memory serves. Bonheur spent sever-
al days insensible, but to-day, his fourth day in our care, he has become
remarkably pliant and well-spoken. I shall record his tale and look to
it later.

Bonheur is singular, fascinating, well-bred and educated, born to a
wealthy family before it was despoiled of its fortune and he pressed into
the militia. And he is almost certainly mad. But looking back upon his
account I must wonder if his tale is the product of a fevered mind or the
living truth—how such fanciful blasphemy could effuse from a Christian
brain is curious indeed. I would much like to see this world he speaks of,
and perhaps put his account to proof, though the bishop has more than
once repulsed my requests to set foot there. Indeed, I have never seen our
master so affected as he is now; since attending Bonheur's tales, he has

roamed almost in a frenzy. Surely he does not believe the frightful blasphemies that inhabit this soldier's tale?

The Account of René Bonheur follows.

———•◦•———

Good Brother, you do not know me as the Lord knows me and my tale. I do not know how I came to be here in France again, but let me recount what I am bid to tell: I am with total conviction that not an untruth or uncertainty is contained herein. What I speak of I saw with my own eyes, a presence I felt upon my own flesh, my very soul. No intemperate drink was carried on this voyage and we took no sustenance from the poisonous land, which some say breeds waking nightmares. I have had schooling, but I am a simple man who does not tell lies or fancies. Mark me close.

I found work on the *Ponctuel* after the army disbanded my regiment, which I had joined after no small pecuniary misfortune attending my father's ill-brained death. My days of impress were fine days. I had a home amongst military, and good purpose, and we carried on with surety. And so good company came out of ill cause of war, but like all things, that war ended, and we found ourselves beggars. I rode amongst some gentle traders into Dieppe in the hopes of finding need for a privateer, supposing that shooting a man over water was rather similar to shooting one on land. I'd never been upon the water save for a short paddle across the Seine to reach Dijon, but I had hoped that a way around a gun carried as great a merit as a way around a mast on a fighting vessel. Surely this country had some place for a good God-fearing Catholic man who has shed and let some blood for it?

The *Ponctuel* was an audacious-looking little craft with an equally audacious-looking little crew. What I assumed was the captain (I to this day barely understand the complexities of the informal navy) lazily whittled himself a pipe as he sat Turk-like atop a sheet on the mud. I was glad that the smell of burnt powder still lingered in my nose, for he looked as though he would smell especially foul. I am certain that when he was a child he had been given to wolves, which had gnawed half of his face before deciding to upraise him. When I addressed him, he dropped his pipe and nearly stuck himself in the thumb with his knife and said an oath, to my dismay.

I enquired if there was any work for a gun hand on the vessel, to which this wolf-man replied that it was destined for the New World and did indeed have use for a soldier to subjugate the Naturals there when not selling them things. I told him I'd no knowledge of this foreign place he spoke of beyond marginal hearsay, and he replied pleasantly enough that that ignorance might profit me. The ship would leave in a fortnight and I would travel with them to the New World and keep duty as a soldier and perhaps a huckster for a year or two. I'd little love for the Old World, which had used me with so much liberty. Perhaps the New one could promise better fortune. A price was settled on, and I was to be fed each day of my service. I was welcomed aboard the vessel.

This *Ponctuel* wooden bowl was laden with all manner of pots and cutlery and guns, things that the savages were said to delight in and pay for handsomely. Transporting this hold of peasant finery were twenty-two souls, including myself. Most of these were indentured wretches bidden by their masters to go trade and wander in some hostile far-off place until their debts were paid.

And it was also laden with two brave warriors of Christ, men of the Society of Jesus, swathed in black. They lightened our journey much and gave me comfort when they offered me the Eucharist or said a gentle sermon below deck in the low light. The Jesuits on most days kept to their own quarters, but to see them roam across the decks or below was always a source of pious warmth to me.

These two men had been to the New World before and had returned to France in order to report their findings to their masters. One by the name of Jacob told me of a new Eden, God's own country untouched by rude instruments and teeming with life nourished by fair weather, with bountiful harvests seeded and tilled only by gentle wind and rain.

The other, the elder, Matthew, who was deformed with scars in the face, said that his fellow Brother had not been far inland. He intimated to me his life amongst the savages, whose souls he had slaved to harvest but had plucked not one. The people he had been with, he said, had skin of tree bark, spoke in soft music, gave away all of their possessions at a whim, and treated each man, woman and child of their village as a brother, sister, and daughter or son, and they killed for the slightest offence, ate raw flesh (sometimes of men) with their fingers, and clad themselves in scalps taken from the heads of their foes. Three of this brave Jesuit's brothers had been captured, tortured to a hair from death, and eaten while they still lived (Matthew spoke little of them, though Jacob had told me the awful story). I saw and heard much ill regard for the race of Men in Matthew.

Of the voyage's early portion there is little to say, as I was of little use to anyone with the scantest knowledge of sailing, and thus felt rather foreign about the little ship. I spent my days below deck, dicing under the noses of our Jesuit brothers with a mildly aggrieved conscience. Only in one instance did I find myself needed. We drew the attention of Spanish privateers and repelled them bravely. I shot one of them in the shoulder and sent him wailing home. I myself managed the assay unharmed, but two of our men died of wounds. Realizing that we could not find land ere they rot, they were put overboard. The Jesuits, to my surprise, gave consent.

A burial at sea is a very strange thing. When one is nestled in the earth, he has a place appointed to him, and it is sacrilegious to stir him. This is even true of the graves that I saw in the districts of Paris during my short stay, where a plague had briefly emerged. The dead were all rudely ejected into a common pit, but once they found their home, they were undisturbed in their rest, perhaps all the better for their close community.

But when a dead man is put into the sea, where does he remain, if ever? I was met in dreams with the horrible sight of corpses tumbling through the deep ocean, no place to rest their heads, forever rolling aimless under the waves. Perhaps it was the rocking of the ship itself that put me so ill at ease, for in the early days there was nothing I craved more than ground that did not wander and list. To be always adrift, that became the greatest discomfort, which led to further dicing to procure my attention.

It is difficult to explain to those who have never been to the ocean the disquiet that a landscape without hills or trees or mountains may bring to one who is accustomed to them. They are natural protectors, screens which may shield us from what evils may be present in a county or a nation over. But on the ocean, on a windless night under a bright-lit sky, one can see forever, and can be seen equally so. For such a vast place, the waters seem most permitting of chance encounters, as the few souls that wander its wide paths may collide without hindrance, like an ill planet meandering once in a lifetime over a sole, ill-fortuned birth.

I saw many strange things above deck in the night. Odd creatures drifting just under the surface, the endless black sea that greets the eyes and shows the sun his twin, and the moon a long and serpentine sister...all of these novel sights and personalities can weigh the mind unbeknownst and make it list. So perhaps my own perceptions were skewed by this strange angle of a mind so besieged with novelty when I espied a visitor in the water as I gazed along the sea one lonely night. I looked down into the depths and saw a pair of lights, unmistakably like gazing eyes. Perhaps this sight was of my own making. Though I doubt I could have imagined the image these objects made as they rose from the meagre waves, turning from a wavering aspect as they pressed up through the surface into two solid points of light, incredibly bright and yet never combining. It put me in mind of how an intense flame might become two distinct entities if the source were placed at a distance and seen from two holes. Though there was no warmth or glow to speak of.

These points of light were eyes indeed, if not in countenance then in the certain *feeling* that one feels when one is under the gaze of another. Not as the eyes of another man, but perhaps an animal, dumb and dull, although with a greater aspect of *knowing*…yes, bright and knowing eyes, inhuman but wholly understanding, not of me but of what they saw, my fleshly housing and the wooden thing that I stood upon. As they rose from the water, there came soundlessly with them a black form, visible only in the way in which it occluded all reflection from the water's surface, a shape perhaps like a man, but long and lithe and many times greater in length than any man but not in girth. Indeed, as I regarded this rising shape I came to realize that it did not rise at all so much as it *grew*, lengthened, until the head of the thing came parallel with my own, not two arms' length from me. I think there was no sound in the encounter, not even my own fearful breath, but for a distant and hollow ringing. I can recall nothing well but those transfixing points of light and the black body that possessed them.

I do not know what I felt then. Curiosity seemed a distant and meaningless thing…but no, I know it now. The sensation was so strong as to envelop me in a way that was too great to comprehend at first, as when one views a mountain so close one does not recognize its massive shape. It was the sense that one feels when one regards a pest, when surprise is turned to loathing, to disgust—but in reverse, I the pest, and it, the disdainful being. Those eyes, they spoke with no anatomy of a man's face, no hint of communing with me their own interior, but they seemed to look on something beneath contempt, looking on me, a thing so insignificant as to not warrant a passionate thought. How does the intruding rat feel, when he flees the cold into a house only to find the hateful eyes of man upon him? Had I met the denizen of this world's house, or a wanderer like me? Did we intrude, or had our once distant paths merely crossed by chance, or fate?

I told no one of the visitor, lest they think me mad and find reason not to pay me. I myself am confident of my own soundness. The mad do not recognize their own madness nor question their own soundness: in Pirrote's account does he not find that no madman would ever recognize his own distemper when questioned? I am set upon this fact. What I met was not so strange considering our later encounters. Many men were involved in them, and they would corroborate the facts I do lay out, were they present. Unless we shared in each other's madness, blind men leading the blind...

Strangely, it never once occurred to me that this thing that came to me was a design of Satan. I have the fear of God, and yet I do not see his agency in things beyond perhaps the celestial bodies when I am in a mundane mode of thought. Some see the world glazed with the Lord's influence each waking moment. This visitor was perhaps a product of miracle, and yet the thought never crossed me, and such an aggrieving presence seemed anything but an emissary of God...or perhaps it lay outside his influence entirely, if such a thing were possible, like a comet knocked from its place in the firmament.

I mused in this way for the days and sleepless nights before the morning which marked three weeks at sea. I climbed to the deck to find upon the ocean, directly before us, a great grey wall of mist. The crew above worked despondently, their eyes constantly drawn to this threshold, for it was indeed a threshold, a great seemingly flat canyon of fog that stretched farther than my sight could reach, both long and high. The *Ponctuel* was drifting on the windless ocean straight towards it. It occurred to me that this fog must have been wrought by the visitor. Perhaps it was turning us away. Or merely informing us of our encroachment. It is for this reason that I am certain the first encounter was not a mad fancy...surely the two, the being and the realm, were connected.

The wolf-eaten captain, whose name I had learned to be Hicks, stood on the fore not far from me, and I heard him murmur that we'd no choice but to move through—to delay would stretch our now-waning provisions thinner. Beside him stood Brothers Matthew and Jacob. I could see the white skin of their backs through the patches of robes that had been eaten away by rats. They, like the rest of the crew, gazed uncertain at the fog.

"What do you say that this calamity is?" the captain asked, turning to Jacob.

Jacob replied, after a moment's contemplation, "Perhaps merely a turn of strange weather. The New World is made of surprises."

The captain swore an oath in reply. "Ungodly thing. Unnatural." Brother Michael grimaced indignantly at the foulness of Hicks.

Before he could speak, Jacob uttered, "The Lord has brought us here and shall see us through it."

Much to my unease, I felt less inclined to the sentiment of Jacob than to that of Hicks, though perhaps my judgment had been skewed by the fear of the visitor that was beginning to rise in me, having been curiously absent upon the thing's arrival. I had never before seen fog upon the sea, but I suppose it cannot be so different from that which rolls over the field, an ethereal thing that twists and bends and shows light through itself in patches like a thinning quilt. This wall before us was a solid and unblinking flat grey sheet. My musings on it were interrupted as the bowsprit pierced the veil, and the devilish threshold began its slow conquest of the vessel.

It first swallowed Hicks and the Jesuits, and some of the men stepped back as it enveloped them. Finally, it was not an inch from me, and the vessel's motion pushed me through. Most curious was the thickness of the fog, for unless my senses deceived me (and I concede my trust in them was beginning then to wear thin), my passing through that incorporeal screen felt the same as pushing a finger through the film that sits atop old cream, a nearly insensible forcing. Once through, I could only barely see the two black figures of the Jesuits, and they stood not ten paces from me.

The thick grey air was windless, and I was called below to assist with the sweeps. Looking out from the little oar-holes, which were a man's height from the water, I found that my sight could not reach the sea, so thick was the fog. Men muttered that it would breed rapid pestilence, which only added to my ill ease. The lapping of the waves and the slice of the oars were oddly silent. Perhaps we had tipped off of the world in entering the threshold, and we merely rowed through the empty spaces of the firmament now. Perhaps I would never meet anyone again save for this doomed crew, not because my death would preclude the meeting, but we had simply left the realm of men and wandered into some place beyond all others' reach.

Why was I rowing? My trepidation constantly mounting, I felt no desire but to keep the *Ponctuel* from her appointed meeting place, wherever that could have been, and yet I rowed just the same.

When I had passed my oar to the nearest empty hand, I came up on deck and was met still with that consuming fog that made the world seem only to extend an arm's length in front of me. I leaned over the side of the ship and looked out to the soundless abyss and saw nothing but grey. But I felt sure that the visitor's sight pierced through water and mist alike, a thousand miles away perhaps, its

gaze intent on me, and yet all the same uncaring for the living ato-
mite it looked upon. I could not see it, but indeed felt its eyes. Deep
in the fog, it watched me. How pitiful it must have found me, if it
cared to feel pity or even could, a man trapped with so many other
souls yet utterly alone, adrift in this ethereal grey ocean that extended up and down to the ends of eternity.

I know not how long we travelled. But after what felt a lifetime
of rowing, of windless days and nights that melted into one another
with a sun that gave nearly no light, of dwindling food and minds
ravaged with ennui and anxiety, we made land. Or rather, we *hit* land,
for we had no way of discerning shore from sea, and the *Ponctuel* one
morning (I suppose it was morning, from the position of the ineffec-
tual sun) simply gored itself on a mass of stone. Our dismay at the
Ponctuel's pains was overcome with the joy of landfall, and we made
our exit from the wreck, though alas, the fog was close to the land as
surely as it was to the water. The *Ponctuel* had laid itself on some sort
of escarpment, and we crept off the deck of the boat onto the grassy
shore; so firmly mated with the land was the ship that it allowed us
an easy and level departure.

I stepped off the bridge and looked to the land that greeted
us, glad for my feet to meet it despite its same dreary condition.
Stretching before us, and to the sides as far as sight could tell, were
strange and dense trees. And not a sound, not the wind or the curiously still ocean, not even the creaking of our wounded vessel. Jacob
called out, "I have seen these trees and this lay of the earth before.
We have indeed found the New World. It's a miracle." And just so,
we had stumbled onto our place of meeting.

———————

Our first order was to retrieve the cargo and bring it ashore, lest the
ship slide off its berth and sink, as it threatened to, with all of our

goods. We got our treasure piled in a heap, and only then did we begin to survey the land we had made. We possessed a map of the New World's coast, but with all landmarks or significant features covered in this vexing fog , we would have to decide whether to set up camp and gather what food we could (which seemed improbable, as Matthew had told me that only the savages seemed to have any knowledge of how to harvest from the accursed place), or continue inland and hope that we happened upon a settlement. Our party was overwhelmingly in favour of the latter action. So we bid the *Ponctuel* farewell and took up our march. I carried my gun and kept it loaded. Hicks tasked himself with marking our path with red flags, tying them to these alien trees, should we have to return.

The New World was not so foreign, I think, as I initially fancied it would be. As I stumbled a ways off through the fog, I came upon a thicket of shrubs and trees not so unlike the ones we know, though the terrain was strange and craggy, so much so that I was surprised that anything could grow out of the rock in such a way. But much unlike our native land, there was no life in the place, not even an insect. I knew not what sort of animal to expect, though I had been told by Matthew that many resembled those native to our lands. And still the fog did not stir, thick as prison bars. This strange world greeted me ten paces from myself at a time, and I doubted that, even with Hicks' ribbons, we would ever be able to find our way back to the *Ponctuel*. All around me were trees larger than I had ever seen, emerging in cadres out from the mist. It all seemed oddly silent still, no birds or beasts or wind. Even my footfalls were muffled, it seemed, by the fog, excepting a sort of thrum that followed me, like the sound of a bell that hums long after it is rung, only noticeable if I turned my attention to my ears.

We wandered through the fog as a group, backs soon aching from our charges, and my finger never straying from the trigger of the gun. Though we seemed utterly alone, I was deeply ill at ease. What if the visitor was glancing through these strange trees at me? I worked to banish such thoughts, focusing on the procession of my feet after tripping on a protruding root and my ankle smarting for the rest of the journey. We walked, and sat and rested, and walked, and sat and rested, not a word exchanged through the seemingly empty grey air between any of the men, who were only occupied in looking in all directions, the Jesuits carrying their burdens bravely, their cloaks tearing threadbare in the thickets. I bent to drink from a stream, so thirsted as to be near collapse, and was surprised at the lovely taste of the water.

It was a hike of about half a day, I suppose, before the captain called us to halt, our numbers so tightly grouped and burdened that some men knocked each other over with a start. Slowly, we all moved to his side and found, to our great relief, a great wooden cross, standing perhaps two heights of myself amongst the trees on a gentle incline of grass. In the tenebrous fog it almost shone, the late sun nestled behind its intersect. That solemn, majestic cross. I felt my breath leave me for joy.

Many of us, myself included, knelt before the icon, relieved to tears. We did not know how long the cross had stood there, but we were uncaring then. There was God in this place. And where God goes, civility follows. The two Brothers moved to the fore and knelt, and said a prayer in the Latinate, voices shaking. Matthew walked to the cross and bent low and kissed it. But he then cried out with a wail of surprise and dismay. He urged us to come closer and see, and we gathered and craned for a view.

Then did I realize that some portions of the cross had been scraped away. I looked closer, and then found what had troubled the Jesuit so. Inlaid at some places in the wood of the cross were what I first discerned to be broken fingernails—three or four, even some whole ones, dug into the wood as an animal will with a claw. And then even closer I espied several embedded teeth, one of them whole, as though ripped straight from the mouth. I am no physician, but I felt they were most certainly the teeth of men. The face of the cross, peppered with the teeth and nails of a man, or men. The staining of the exposed wood I feared to be very old blood.

"The savages!" cried Matthew, startling us. "The savages have no love for Christ or the cross. They did this defilement."

"At great risk to their own bodies?" questioned Jacob. "Only a madman would do this." Most curiously, they not only stuck in at the base of the cross but higher up, higher than a man could reach. Did someone prop up his fellow to work this deformity?

"The savages," Matthew replied, "are prone to madness. Women eat up their children when their husbands are off to hunt. They did this to me," he said, pointing to the many scars that crossed his face, and indeed the hand with which he pointed lacked, to my first noticing, its own thumb. "They hate Christ more than they hate us. Mark me, they did this in a fit of rage."

I supposed that Matthew's own unfortunate encounters with the savages had given him more reason than any for ill will towards them, but I was nonetheless disinclined to agree with him. Something felt terribly odd about all of this, besides the obvious distemper that this ill sight bred. I know not how long a nail or a tooth may lie in a piece of wood before it may rot, but I felt that this strange artifact preceded any of the excursions of Europe into the New World. I felt an odd desire to touch the thing, reaching out my fingers to brush them against a sharp tooth half-stuck in the cross, before Matthew took my arm and urged me to follow the group, his face still brooding over the wicked sight. The thing, and my inexplicable caprice in touching it, set me uneasy. The perpetual gloam of the fog weighed the spirits enough, but this defiled cross, looming behind us, no longer seemed a welcome sight, but rather a sinister portent.

"All this talk of savages, but we haven't seen a one," piped a small sailor, whose name I did not know, as we scaled to the crest of the hill. "Or anything else alive in this goddamned place."

"God's not damned this place," called out one ahead of him. "He's forgotten it, and forgotten us. God is not here."

As our troop continued on, Matthew, who had moved to the fore, swiftly turned and took the second speaker by the back of his tunic before striking him on the side of his head so that he fell on one knee, yelping.

"God delivered me from this place," the brother said calmly, taking the sailor's bloodied ear in his fist, the rest of us turning to watch this spectacle. "Satan has tried to turn us back." In the fog, his face possessed a ghostly aspect, an enraged father. "This black air and the lifeless land are tricks of his employ, to turn the weak, like you, to his fold." He let go of the sailor's ear, though the man's face seethed with anger, only softening when Matthew took him by the arm and helped him to his feet. "Have faith. Soon we will be with kindred civilization, and they shall keep you safe. Have faith. The house of God is near." How formidable and fearless this young Christian Brother! We sailors and soldiers were worn to the bone by this terrible fog and wretched terrain but he continued, unwavering. It was most terrible when he disappeared.

Matthew had become the beacon in the dark, the captain and us all yoking our resolve to him as we staggered up the hill, half-starved now. Hopefully, whatever settlement lay in wait could provide for us wretches.

We reached the crest and expected (foolishly) to see a settlement before us, but the fog obscured anything beyond the near decline. So we again slowly trod down the hill; it was not long before one of us walked into a low wall at his knees and tripped over it. We quickly gathered to look.

"This is not how our settlements are walled," Jacob said, crestfallen.

Indeed, the wall was not built of wood, as I am told our places typically are, but of old and crumbling stone, a little higher than my waist at its highest points. It was jagged and weathered, and this sight made most of the men grow uneasy. I felt strangely indifferent. Perhaps I had no doubts now that we would simply starve to death out here. Or if we were found, it would not be a benevolent presence that greeted us.

We moved over the wall and soon found square buildings emerging through the fog, none taller than a single floor (though they may have been, once), the grey stone of their making barely distinct from the air, standing as ghostly ruins. The earth was strewn with their remains, each of them surrounded by a ring of toppled masonry. The sailors were all silent. It felt as though we were treading on hallowed ground, these structures more akin to gravestones than homes. We did not call out for any resident; it seemed obvious enough that this place had been emptied long ago. And there was nothing to signal any past inhabitance. It was as though someone had come here, built a series of toppled ruins, and departed.

Soon we discovered amidst the buildings the stout, familiar church in what we assumed was the centre of the town. Matthew remarked, "This place seems pagan to me, the pagans the elders write about, but whoever lived here were people of God."

We stood and looked about, uncertain of our path, until one of the men cried out that he could discern the sound of a river, scarce able to be heard even in the otherwise total silence. Most of the men determined to set out for water, but I, out of curiosity, elected to follow Matthew and Jacob into the church. The men set down their heavy baggage, promising us water if we remained to watch their belongings (from what, I still do not know). The captain was exhausted of the red ribbons he used to keep the way, but the earth was soft and muddy enough to keep footprints. We bid them fortune and farewell before entering the silent church.

The floor of the building, also stone, had collapsed in places into the soft earth, and the grey benches jutted wildly. But the simple pulpit stood defiant, atop it a stone cross, and behind it on the wall, a crude and worn likeness of the Passion, but strangely inverted, the head of Jesus at the floor, his feet up to heaven.

"This is very strange," Matthew said quietly, examining the cross. He beckoned me to look. Despite the obvious age of the effigy, the features of the face were worn away more than the rest of the body, leaving it relatively smooth. His thorny crown had been ripped from his head, and the eyes...hollowed out and curiously well-kept candles placed therein as though to make them glow, the face without feature, terribly familiar...

We said nothing, I myself stirred by this unwanted visitation, and we sat on one of the benches more or less level, and prayed a while for God to take us out of this place. Then we rose, and searched some more.

"It is curious," Matthew called out as he looked over a surprisingly preserved, massive old Bible sitting on the pulpit, open. "They took nothing with them, and no sign of battle. No escape or attack. Perhaps a plague?"

"No bones, no bodies," remarked Jacob slowly from the other end, sitting on the bench still, resting his head curiously, passively, on it. Matthew seemed to ignore his despondence, until the other Jesuit made a shriek. I turned from the faceless effigy affrighted to see Jacob holding before him a curved iron knife.

"What is this doing in here?" he said, his shock leaving him. I saw Matthew look down to the Bible on the pulpit, turn to me with a knowing gaze, and then stride away.

"Perhaps we should leave," the elder, scarred Jesuit remarked, going to Jacob and taking him by the hand, helping him to his feet before taking the knife and placing it on the far end of the bench. As I went to follow him, I looked to the sacred text and saw through both sides of its cover a cruel wound through the centre. Flipping through the pages, I found most of the images of the people, of Jesus and the disciples, of Adam and Eve, cut out, and then placed back in, upside down, like had been done with the effigy of Christ on the stone cross. Why such alterations? A whole world of people inverted? I did not like to look at them, and I quickly followed the brothers out of the church, though to be back in the open air in that awful sepulchre of a dead village gave me no comfort. I felt the hollowed eyes of the effigy follow me out the door.

"I think I shall stay," Jacob said, sitting down on a stone that had fallen from the church. In the fog his hair looked white, his face shallow from hunger, and I knew then, somehow, that he would die here.

"Please let me rest, Brother."

I wish I had not seen the contempt in Matthew's eyes that I saw. He turned and walked away. After a moment's hesitation, I followed to see that he was trailing the footprints of the others.

"Why did you leave him?" I asked the Brother.

He chose not to answer me, but spoke instead as he walked: "It is now clear to me where we have strayed. Who inhabited this place is uncertain, but God has set His face against them and the land for their apostasy. All the while he has warned us to turn away, lest we fall to their indolence as Jacob has."

I wished to say that the fog and the misdirection that it sowed brought us here, that it seemed not a guide but a waylayer. But then, was this the visitor's design? Had it lain down the fog after it had spotted me to lead us to this cursed place for reasons I could not discern? All of this turned in my mind until Matthew spoke again.

"Among the men there must be a carpenter or two. We shall return to the coast and fashion ourselves a vessel if this cursed place gives its trees to the task. Then we shall follow the land from the sea until we break the bonds of this pestilent fog and find New France. Then, we shall return here and redeem our faith in God's eyes. We shall wipe this black mark from the map, for France, and above all, for God. You shall help me, Bonheur."

I wished for nothing more than escape. I did not tell him that if he ever intended to return to this land, he could face it with his Brothers alone. I cursed myself for picturing it, for it was not a fate I'd wish on the worst criminal. I spoke up to ask what he would do should the captain refuse him. But he replied that he could not hear me for a ringing in his ears that had likely been bred by the fog's distemper. I was reminded of my own, the bell that had been silenced but still hummed.

He could not hear the river either, for he nearly trod into it all of a sudden, falling onto his back and soiling his robes in the mud. He stood to the side of the tracks of the men, and I as well, and we were astonished by our finding. The footsteps in the mud simply stopped by the edge of the river, as though the men had waded in and not returned.

"What is this?" I asked as I stood closer to him, so he could hear me amidst the strange ringing din. "What could have happened? Did they choose to abandon us?"

Matthew spoke not, simply looked down at the terminating tracks in the mud, then knelt to peer into the river's swift current.

"Is it possible they did not see the river until it was too late, owing to the fog?" I asked.

"All of them? I think not."

"Then what?"

Matthew did not reply. Instead he turned. "We must leave now. Perhaps there is a lifeboat aboard the *Ponctuel*. If need be, we can fashion a raft from the ship; there must be an axe that someone has taken along or left on board."

"And what of Jacob?"

"We'll find him."

But on return to that dead parish, we found no one. We called Jacob, scoured the ruins, but there was no sign of him. We chose to leave without him, we two the only crew remaining, taking with us what food we could carry from the collection that had been left by the others. We searched the outside of the wall for a moment before finding one of the red flags that Hicks had left, and then began to mount the hill, on the other side of which stood the cross.

We sighted it in the fog, which was miraculously beginning to clear, and we were relieved to have found our way. The hum of the bell was growing louder in my ears as we approached the cross. My body grew cold, and somehow then, I knew what awaited me. There, behind the cross, the eyes of the visitor, gazing at us.

Cold terror seized me. But brave Matthew stood at my side, and I grew emboldened. I stepped out so that the cross no longer remained between us. The eyes lay fixated on me, bright and cold. In the grey, its body like that of a misshapen man stood as a dark silhouette, like a shadow on water.

"What is it, Bonheur?" Matthew called out, sounding terribly far away in the bell's din as I raised my gun to point at the eyes. They did not move at my threat, only stared. Frightened as I was, I could not look away from them.

"Do you see it, Matthew?" I called out, happy that I had kept the gun loaded. He said nothing as those bright eyes dared me to shoot. I faltered, but did not look back.

"Matthew?" I called again, feeling for the trigger that I had sense-lessly let go. But the only reply was a shriek that echoed out in the sudden silence, and I started, dropping my weapon. I turned to see what had befallen the Jesuit.

He was gone. No man, only an empty expanse beyond the crest of the hill.

I turned back, suddenly frightened at the silence. The visitor was also gone, or appeared to be. Only the solitary cross.

I searched and found that Matthew's steps had ended in the soft earth not three paces behind me. It was as though he had turned to vapour and dispelled into the fog.

And then I came to realize that I was alone. None in this place but me and the visitor, watching.

The horror of those days and nights, trapped in the fog, befell me all at once when it had seemed so distant before. What could I have done? I could return to the village and try to keep myself fed, and perhaps the fog would relent. Perhaps the visitor would spare me, or I could hide from it in the ruins. Perhaps someone would find me. But I never wanted to return to that long-dead tomb of the abandoned village. I began to weep. I was alone, an ocean apart from anyone I had ever known.

As I have said before, I am not a man of God, but I put my faith in Him, and I went to the cross that the visitor had waited behind, that a savage or, to my horror, likely one of the villagers, had defiled with teeth and nails, and prayed. I put my arms round the cross, and wept to God for salvation. Eventually, my sobbing ceased, and I tempered my resolve and dried my eyes. If the visitor was watch-ing, then so was God. I looked at the cross, my reminder of Him. Remembering its defilement, I could not help but examine what had been done to it. My curiosity overtook me, and I used my own nail to scrape at the blood that had dried around the strange remnants to expose the scarred wood and noticed, oddly, that the marks of the nails and teeth only seemed present *below* what had made them. And the nails. They all protruded wrongly somehow.

And then I saw. Given the shape of the wounds in the wood, and the way that they terminated with the inlaid teeth and nails not at the bottom of each scrape, but the top...they could not have been made as one would when standing upright, scratching downwards, but only when *upside down*, as though one were clinging to it, and pulled upwards. My eyes moved up the cross, following a little path of those remains, leading up and up, and then the top of the cross, and above it, only the grey, endless sky.

My thoughts turned to the people in the book, feet in the air and hands holding to the ground, as though it were not the earth that held them down, but the sky grasping them up. Holding to their anchors with tooth and nail.

I fell away from the cross and ran.

My mind was without thought, beyond animal terror, but I now think to thank Hicks for those markers that he placed upon the trees, wherever he is now. I followed them without clear purpose, accompanied only by the silence of that damned wood, my own breath and footfalls loud as cannon fire. In a moment of weakness, just as I reached the valley's edge, I turned to look to the cross again, and even as it sat tiny in the distance, I saw the eyes of that fiend, standing alongside it, gazing upon me. I did not look back again, but I am certain that its stare followed me all the way to the coast.

Did it feel pleasure? Did it mock me when I found that all trace of the *Ponctuel* vanished, leaving only the black ocean and the fog? Did it laugh to itself as it obscured God's path from me and gave me instead its own, its path to ceaseless fear, fear and hatred of the empty sky, fear of slumber, of the dreams of endless falling upwards? Fear of waking to find myself, as I found myself after days of sleepless wandering, in the land I once knew and cherished but which had somehow turned as strange and dreadful to me as those occluded shores: the endless silent trees, the cross, riddled with teeth, dwellings given way to the emptiness of the encroaching sky...has it followed my steps back from this chance encounter, back here to dwell? To watch, and to be unseen, as though it wishes us to know our own insignificance?

———•—————

Bonheur spoke with no more coherence following this last remark. Coming to try him today, we found him gone, and alas, the Bishop gone too, without any message to suggest his reasons or whereabouts. Thinking further on this matter, I have determined to go to the Cardinal at once and present Bonheur's case to him, though I am increasingly fearful that whatever haunts, or haunted, Bonheur is beyond our own knowledge or means of defence. I pray the lights outside my window are the horseman's lanterns.

THE WEIGHT OF THOUGHT

Jeremy R. Strong

Years ago, I made a shocking discovery while on a canoe trip with four friends. We were taking an afternoon break on the bank of the river and the coffee I had been gulping down all morning had irritated my bowels (that is not the shocking discovery). I hiked a full five minutes into the bush, not wanting Paige, the girl with whom I was hoping to leave the trip on more familiar terms, to catch me in the act. What could be a worse segue into my planned seduction?

I had just crouched down when I saw an incredible thick gold chain that was looped around a brass ring that seemed attached to the forest floor. I brushed away dirt, pulled out roots and a few handfuls of grass, and eventually, revealed part of a door.

I was excited. I marked the site with my windbreaker and made tracks back to the river, stopping every few feet to break a tree branch to mark my progress. I remember feeling like Hansel from the fairy tale. If only I had known then how accurate that analogy would become.

"You won't believe what I've found," I told the group, and led them back excitedly through the woods to the door. Their faces first revealed a mixture of curiosity and bemusement, then later—at the door—wonder. Now, as I replay the scene in my mind once again, I can't decide whether I feel like predator or prey.

As we cleaned away years' worth of growth and packed dirt, the others picked up my excitement. Paige, a PhD student in archaeology, seemed particularly excited, something I could understand. At that time, all of us were somehow connected to the same university; I was an associate professor. My field of specialty was languages. I was the youngest and most qualified in this part of the country, and, at that time at least, filled with self-importance and a naïve desire for the meager power afforded to teachers.

After almost half an hour of excavating, we uncovered the door. We excitedly began prying at the edges of the wood, but it simply crumbled away under our fingers.

"There's stone beneath," Paige exclaimed, breathless. She shot me a bright smile. I grinned back. I had always been shy and introverted but found myself feeling bolder. The brass ring pulled away the largest section of the wood, and beneath that was a smooth surface of polished stone.

"There are six hand grips carved into the stone," said Neil, a friend of mine from our student days. He and his wife, Jane, had been the instigators of this canoe excursion. Paige and Jane were both graduate students and had been friends for years. Also along for the trip was Michael, another friend of Neil's.

Michael stepped forward, flexing his considerable muscle, and slid his hands into the grips closest to him. He pulled hard. The stone didn't move. I had known Michael a few years at that time and had never been all that fond of him but had put up with him for Neil's sake. The thing I hated most about Michael, I think, is that girls like Paige used to pay attention to him and not to me. But once that door was revealed, Paige had looked to nobody but me.

"Martin, how old do you think this is? Older than the European settlement of North America?" She was excited and came close, placing her hand on my arm. "If it is, we could be making the biggest archeological discovery since Olduvai Gorge."

"Let's not get ahead of ourselves. We need to see inside." I motioned for everyone to use one of the six polished handgrips.

"You'll never budge it, man," Michael said. "I gave 'er my all."

"There are six hand grips for a reason. It's designed to be lifted by six people," I said, bending my knees and preparing for the weight of the stone.

Michael stood puzzled for a moment. "But there's only five of us," he said. My natural instinct was to ridicule his idiocy, but I realized we needed his strength.

"Well, though I'm not surprised you couldn't lift it alone Michael, I was hoping you could do the work of two people on this one." It was the right thing to say. He swelled with pride and flexed again, grinning at Jane and Paige.

We lifted on three. After a few seconds and some grunting, it came out of the ground.

"Okay, set it down here." I was certain the slab would fall and break someone's legs, but we managed to walk ourselves over to the side and lower it carefully. We took time to catch our breath, except for Paige, who was already perched at the side of the dark hole, mumbling in awe.

I joined her. She looked at me, her face radiating excitement.

"Martin, it's a passage." And indeed, the stone border gave way to a staircase.

"This is limestone. Look at how precisely it's been cut." I showed Paige the angles and the places where the blocks fit together. The placement was so tight I wasn't able to slide the end of my matchbook into the gap.

"Like the pyramids," she mumbled. The hole was dark, made worse by the lack of sunlight this deep in the woods. We couldn't make out the bottom of the staircase. I was filled with an unstoppable curiosity and a sudden lust for Paige, the combination frightening in its intensity.

"I need to get inside," I said. I began going through my bag. I had a steel flashlight, as well as matches and lighters. There was also a headlamp, what Neil teasingly called my miner's helmet; mostly I used that at night when I went camping, for reading in my tent. It had three spare batteries. What more could we have needed to explore the passage?

"Martin, Paige. I think you two should slow down for a second." Jane came to the side of the tunnel. Paige was already donning the headlight, checking to see that it worked. I was filling my pockets with other provisions.

"Why? I've never been so curious or excited in my life." And that was true, though there was something else I couldn't understand at the time, pulling me towards the secrets of the passage. I think it was strong enough to pull Paige along with me as well.

"Well, for one, if this is as big an archaeological discovery as you two brains think, then you might want to be a bit more careful about disturbing it. Also, there's a safety issue."

"Safety issue?" Paige said, eyebrows up.

"Yes. It could cave in. There could be holes you could fall into."

"There could be traps, doctah Jones!" Neil laughed.

"I think you've seen too many movies," I said. Paige giggled. The sound of her laughter made my blood pump harder.

"Martin and I will go down for a look. When we come back up, we can take turns going down and you can all get a chance to check it out." Neil and Jane seemed to find this acceptable. Only Michael looked agitated.

"I want to check it out too," he said, getting up and grabbing his own backpack.

"Of course," I said. "But if there are any safety risks, it's better to only have two of us trapped, and not all. Then we can help each other. And if there is a cave in, we'll need someone strong on this side." I hoped playing to his vanity would keep him out for now. I wanted to go down there alone with Paige.

To my amazement, my argument worked, and the three of them sat down on the stone door to watch us descend.

———•·•———

The staircase went deeper than either Paige or I expected. I ran my hands along the smooth walls as we descended. There was almost no moisture and the walls were coated with a light dust. The stairs were in perfect shape: smooth and hard. No breaks and no crumbles. This told me that water had never seeped inside. That was a good thing in terms of preservation, but how it had been accomplished, on a floodplain no less, was a puzzle to us both.

"Amazing how far down this leads," Paige mumbled, three steps ahead of me with the miner's lamp. I hadn't yet turned on my own light, wanting to preserve it in case we needed to explore deeper.

"Slow down, Paige." I reached forward and put my hand on her shoulder.

Finally, we reached the bottom. The passage stretched out further than the beam could reach. I snapped on my own light, which had a more powerful beam, and still the passage was smooth walls, floor and ceiling, away into the dark.

"We've really found something here, Martin," Paige breathed and turned around to face me.

"I counted over seventy steps," I said absently, feeling a magnetic pull come over me. Suddenly images flashed into my mind. Paige naked on an antique four-post bed, masturbating. Paige under me. Paige on top of me. The images were so powerful that they knocked me back against the wall.

"What's wrong?" she said, and came closer. I saw a change come over her. It was her eyes. They seemed to darken.

"Nothing," I said, though I felt strange and disoriented and a strong desire to go further into the tunnel. I could tell that Paige felt it too. We started walking.

After some time, we came upon a dead end. Our initial disappointment gave way to curiosity. The wall seemed made of one solid block of stone, about the same dimensions as the stone door that it had taken six of us to lift, only wider. The difference, however, was that the wall had a circular opening, precisely in the centre. Next to the round opening was a lever.

"What do you suppose this does?" Paige asked, reaching for the handle.

"Don't touch it. I think we should go back and get the others first."

"So soon?" she pouted theatrically, rubbing my stomach with her hands. So we didn't go back right away.

———•·•———

Back in the light of day, we told the others what we'd found. Neil and Jane had gone back to the river to secure the canoes and bring all of our supplies into the clearing where Michael was making a fire. We were going to stay here for the night.

"I want to see it," Neil insisted. Jane and Michael agreed. I told them I thought the tunnel was very secure.

"There isn't even a crack in the stonework. There's no danger of collapse." Of course, now that I was out, all I could think about was going back in.

"So you don't think we need to go two by two anymore?" Michael said, snidely. I wondered if he had heard us down there.

"No." My face had flushed. They were all looking at me. "In fact, before it starts to get dark, I think we should all go and look. Paige and I found something interesting. We could use your opinions on it."

After setting up the tents, the five of us headed down into the tunnel. Paige led the others, and I brought up the rear, studying the walls in more detail. They certainly were smooth. The only thing I noticed that I hadn't seen before was that where the ceiling met the walls, the grooves were deeper. They were uniform, but the gaps were wide enough to slide a pencil inside. I let the others get further ahead of me while I inspected this. I wasn't certain how the walls could hold up the ceiling when it appeared that they didn't even touch the massive ceiling stones. I shone my powerful flashlight inside. The gap extended for at least six inches and then all I could see was stone.

We trekked on, the others waiting for me to catch up.

"What are you doing back there, Martin?" Neil asked, falling into step beside me. The tunnel was easily wide enough for three to walk side by side.

"Something is bothering me about the way this tunnel is designed." I showed Neil the gaps I had found. He frowned.

"Air vents," he said simply.

"But what about moisture?"

"The top stone will have been carved to curve over secondary side stones that we can't see. There is likely a gap between those stones and these wall stones, kind of like weeping tile. Clever, really." He ran his hand along the smooth, dry walls. "That way, any moisture that develops seeps in between the two walls and back into the ground."

"Neil, you should have been an architect." I was fascinated at his explanation.

We walked on and I knew we were nearing the strange wall. I could hear Michael talking quietly to Paige up ahead. It was just then that Neil stopped in front of me to tie his shoe. I happened to look up and shine my light at the same time.

"Stop!" I yelled, my voice echoing and bouncing all around us. Up ahead, they quit talking, but I could see Paige's headlamp reflecting off the wall with the hole in it.

"What is it?" Jane called, nervously. I studied the script on the ceiling again. The message was written in at least three languages. Two of them were completely alien to me. But I could easily make out the third and final script.

"There's something written here. It's a warning." In Latin, of all languages, and in which I was, of course, proficient, was inscribed:

Only six of true courage should pass this mark.

The others came back, grudgingly, to where Neil and I stood examining the text. Jane drew the characters out on a piece of paper. It was much easier than standing, necks craned.

I told them what the Latin translated into.

"There were six hand grips in the stone door," Jane said.

"I was spending most of my time studying the walls. I may have missed more text," I said, starting back.

"Whoa, hold on. We just want to see this weird thingy you were talking about at the end. Then we'll head back," Michael said. He was starting to annoy me.

"Fine. But I think we should agree that nothing should be touched," I said. I could see Michael roll his eyes in the dim, but the others seemed agreeable. Neil in particular seemed worried, his eyes darting around.

We closed the final distance to the strange wall. I saw them all gathered around it, talking excitedly, discussing what the lever did and what the purpose of the hole could possibly be. I was standing back, thinking.

"It's a door," Michael said. "The lever just opens it."

"I don't think it's that simple," Paige said. "This hole is bothering me." She shone the headlamp inside. All that could be seen was more stone. Then, incredibly, she grabbed the wall and stuck her head inside.

Terror overpowered my curiosity. "Paige, no!" I screamed, rushing forward to pull her out.

Two things happened then. The first is that Paige pulled her head out of the hole, talking excitedly. The second is that I stepped onto the final stone floor block. The four of them were gathered so close to the wall, they were already all standing on it. The moment I stepped on that enormous stone block, all of us felt it. There was a rumble and the stone beneath our feet dropped a full six inches. Jane screamed and Neil began to hyperventilate, already on the verge of panic. There was the unmistakable sound of steel on stone, like flint being drawn for fire. Michael and Paige yelled and jumped back as, inside the hole in the stone, a blade drew quickly down and up. Bright orange sparks danced from the hole.

"What the hell just happened?" Neil screamed.

"Whatever trap this is, we sprung it," I replied. I walked to the wall. "This blade that came down was part of the triggering mechanism, but it was also meant to kill at least one person."

Paige looked as pale as the stone dust on the floor in the light of her headlamp.

"Let's get out of here," Jane said. Of course, we all agreed. But by then, I think I knew that there was no leaving.

We ran as fast as we could, single file, back towards the entrance. All the while, the loud rumbling that had begun with my stepping on the final floor stone continued.

I heard Jane and Michael swearing up ahead.

"Martin! There's a wall here," Paige yelled, still shaky from having had her head in some kind of ancient guillotine mere minutes before. I caught up to them. Just before where the stairwell should have been, there was now a smooth stone wall, blocking the exit.

"It's moving," I said simply, hating to be the first to say it. "Slowly—but toward us."

"Oh my god," Jane cried. Neil was another story altogether. His breathing had become erratic; his pupils were dilated.

"He's having a panic attack," Paige said, pulling him away from the wall and sitting him down. She pulled out her own asthma inhaler and tried to get him to take a pull. Michael started forcing his weight against the wall.

"Don't bother, Michael. That won't work."

"We have to try. This thing will push us all the way to that other wall and crush us." At least he understood that much.

"Look here." I pointed to the ceiling. There was more Latin carved there. "We need to find and write down all of the Latin on the ceiling before the wall moves to cover it." I had already read the words there. Jane began copying it down.

"Good. You copy, I'll move ahead. Michael, help me." He gave me a sour look. I grabbed the headlamp from Paige and tossed it to him. "You want to live, then run ahead and find the next engraving in the ceiling." He did, but only after a lingering, hateful look.

Altogether, there were four pieces of writing, not including the final warning I had stumbled on before. In order, they said:

The weight of six
The weight of thought
The weight of heart
Shall release the weight of soul

The five of us were grouped near the last inscription, the one that had warned that only six true of heart should pass. I was sitting on the smooth stone, trying to think of a way that we could survive this, while the rest of them argued in panic.

"Shut up everyone." I stood up. The rumble of the stone was closer now, perhaps almost to the halfway point. There was no way to know when it would emerge from the yawning darkness. They looked at me, hollow-eyed and terrified.

"We have to go to the end wall again. The only answer is there. The longer we wait here, the less time we have to figure out what it is." I led the way. They followed.

"Come on. The first line says the weight of six. We know what that means: the weight of six people standing here triggers the trap."

"But there's only five of us," Jane said.

"I weigh quite a bit," Michael piped up.

"Michael's right. Plus, if this place is as old as I think it is, people were smaller back then. Thinner too. The five of us likely weigh the same as six would have, thousands of years ago."

"Thousands?"

"Definitely. Before Christ."

"How do you know that?"

"The Latin. It uses primitive characters, before the language was fully developed."

The rumble of the wall was closer. Paige came to stand with me and look at the Latin. I had written the English translation underneath.

"What do you think it means?" she said.

"I have an idea," I said quietly.

"Well, share with the rest of us, please," Jane said, tears in her eyes. "I don't want to die in this hole."

I stepped forward, ignoring her for now, leaving the paper with Paige. I felt the edge of the hole in the stone.

"This is like a guillotine," I said, mostly to myself. The others didn't say anything. It wasn't sinking in for them yet. "And this," I said, gripping the lever, "controls it."

They yelled at me not to pull it. I did. The steel flashed again as it dragged down against the stone. There were more sparks.

"See?" When I released the lever, the blade rose with it.

"Okay. So if that doesn't make the trap worse, and it doesn't open a door somewhere, then what good is it to us?" Jane said.

"The fact that it doesn't open the door is bad news," I said. The rumble was getting closer.

Michael and Neil came closer. We were all gathered around Paige, who was frowning over the paper.

"Okay, genius. So if that thing is a door, then how do we get through it?" Michael said.

Paige looked at me. I shrugged. "What do *you* think?"

"One of us has to put our head in there." She pointed. "And somebody has to pull the lever."

For a minute that felt like an hour, there was silence, interrupted only by the rumbling drag of the wall.

"Oh no. No, no, no. We are *not* doing that," Jane said. Michael and Neil were silent but both pale. Neil was shaking.

"There was something written in Latin down inside the wall," Paige said quietly. We all looked at her. "But I can't read Latin," she added.

I was suspicious, but I didn't think they would pull the lever. I was counting on their hope of discovering a method of escape that would leave us all alive. I wore the headlamp and put my head inside the hole.

There was smooth stone on all sides except the bottom. I felt right away a sense of suffocation and fear. But when I looked down, I saw that Paige was right. There was Latin carved at the bottom, about two feet down. The stone was angled so that a severed head would roll down and to the right, into a dark recess in the wall. I wondered at where that head would then go. I breathed a sigh of relief as I pulled my head from that dark hole.

"It says 'Fear not the Face of God' at the bottom." The thing I didn't understand was how someone would be able to read what was written there, especially without a flashlight. I said as much.

"Maybe they never intended it to be read," Neil said, still breathing heavy. Behind us, the moving wall was now in sight, coming towards us in the glow of the large flashlight.

"We don't have much time," I said.

"So, how do we know that this is a door and that by one of us sticking our head in there, it will open?" Michael said.

"We don't," I said. "But we do know what will happen when the wall gets here."

Jane started to sob.

"How do we decide who dies?" Neil said through interruptions in his ragged breathing.

"It won't be me," Michael said. "I ain't losing my head. I say we all try pushing this wall. Maybe we can break the track it's on or something. Buy some time."

We tried that. All of us pushing and sweating. It didn't even interrupt the motion of the thing. Then Jane suggested we throw something into the head hole, see if that would work.

"That's a good idea," I said. We settled on one of Michael's shoes.

"It's probably a button or something at the end. The head hits the button and opens the door," he insisted. At the time, I thought it was worth trying. I was about to throw it in the hole.

"Stop!" Paige said. "Don't do it." The wall was so close now. The rumble was loud.

"Why?"

"Because, if it doesn't work, then you might jam whatever kind of mechanism it is. Then we all die." She drew something on a piece of paper, and then passed it to us.

"You think it's a track?"

"Yes. Heads roll, right? They're round. The trap is obviously designed for a head."

"So the head rolls to the end of the track, presses a button and what?"

"The door opens," Paige said, sounding unsure.

"Okay. So if I throw the shoe in?"

"It doesn't roll. Just gets stuck halfway on the track. Then when we put a head down, it gets stuck against the shoe. We all die." I could see her point.

"So, you volunteering?" Michael said, his voice shaky. The wall was closing fast.

"No," she said. The five of us looked at each other wildly, like we were all trying to decide who to grab.

"We draw straws," Neil said finally.

In the end, we all agreed. There wasn't enough time for a better solution. Michael tore one of the sheets of paper from Paige's notebook into five long strips. He showed them to us, and then ripped one in half. Then he turned around and hid them behind his hand. When he turned back, the four of us stood in front of him. The moving wall was mere feet away from Michael's back. Paige drew first: a long piece. I didn't have time to start a debate about who should be holding the straws. The one holding the straws had the best odds. I reached out after Paige and plucked a long one. Neil and Jane hesitated. Then Jane reached out.

"Wait," Neil said. Jane stopped.

"If you draw short…I'll be the one," he said, his voice shaking. Jane started crying.

"No," she said weakly. But she drew. Long. Her sigh of relief was a truly horrible sound. Neil paused for a long moment. Michael had started to sweat. He was shaking too. You could see the paper strands vibrating slightly in his big hands. Neil took a deep breath and drew quickly. He held the final long strip.

After a moment of stunned silence, Michael fought like hell. All four of us rushed him. I took a punch to the jaw and heard Jane cry out in pain. In the end, we managed to grab a limb each. Neil hit Michael hard in the back of the head until he lost consciousness. Jane was sobbing wildly but helped every step of the way.

We got his head in the hole, and Neil and I held him there while Paige moved to the lever. The wall was so close now that in a few more seconds it would hit Neil's ankles.

"Do it, Paige!"

She pulled hard on the lever and the blade came down with that same scraping flint sound. Even over the rumble of the wall, we could hear the wet plopping sound of Michael's head hitting the stone inside. Then rolling. Then nothing.

The rumble got louder and the wall was so close we were crowded side by side, all pressing together.

"We're going to die," Paige said, grabbing my hand. I reached out my other hand and could feel the moving wall: we had maybe twenty seconds left before we would be mashed together like grapes in a press. That's when I felt empty space behind me. The wall had begun to pull quietly sideways. It was opening.

"Here! It worked. Here!" I cried, pulling them back with me through the opening passage. We all cried out in relief. The wall slid away and I had only a moment to try to study the mechanism before the approaching wall got too close.

The tunnel continued, straight and true. I knew this meant the wall would keep coming. We looked for more inscriptions on the ceilings, then the walls. There was nothing. It wasn't nearly as long before we came to another wall, identical to the first.

"No," Jane sobbed, sitting down in front of the wall. "Not again." We sat down to think. I estimated we had less than fifteen minutes.

"There must be another way," Neil said. "We can't draw straws every time." I tried to think of a way to save us all. I read and re-read the Latin translations. Back in the dark of the tunnel, I knew that the trap was dragging Michael's body.

"I'm stumped," I said quietly. I didn't know what to make of the inscriptions. I passed them around.

"Any ideas?"

They all took their turn with the paper. While they did that, I ran back and tried wedging things in the crack under the moving wall. A pen snapped like a toothpick. A steel compass just dragged along noisily, sparking. My Swiss army knife cracked and broke into pieces, creating more sparks and noise. Then, in desperation and hoping the others wouldn't see me, I tried wedging Michael into the moving groove. His fingers. His arms. It didn't work. The blood made everything slip out. I returned to the group.

"I can't stop the wall." They were solemn.

"We decided. I'll be the one," Neil said, looking defeated.

"You're the only one who can read the Latin," Paige said simply. "You are our only chance at figuring this out."

We argued for a while. I went into the head hole again, this time more paranoid that they were tricking me. But nobody ran over and pulled the lever. My friends didn't double cross me. The Latin said:

Only one will gain ultimate knowledge.

I told them.

"I guess that means that you're the only one not losing your head," Jane said sourly, looking at me.

"Now hold on. I never agreed to be immune from this. We should draw straws again." But they refused. Neil insisted on being the one to die.

"Also, I hate to point this out," I said, "but there needed to be six, remember? Six of true courage, it said. So if one is left standing…"

"Then five have to die," Paige finished. "But we won't know for sure until we get there. So it still makes more sense for us to go one at a time, rather than all get crushed."

Nobody disagreed. The wall came closer. Neil and Jane started saying goodbye.

My friend Neil was brave right to the end. He didn't fight us. Didn't argue. He kissed Jane one more time, told her he loved her. Told me to try to get them out alive, if I could. I swallowed the lump in my throat and promised him I would. He put his head inside. Paige pulled the lever right away. Jane screamed.

The way opened. The next wall was the same. Jane sobbed uncontrollably the entire time. Paige gave me a look that said *Jane goes next*. We thought about trying to throw something in again, even about carving off part of Michael's body. But my knife was broken and smashed now under the moving wall.

Unexpectedly, Paige made a grab at me again, while we were further away from Jane. "It has to be her, Martin," she whispered, her eyes feverish. "She's already useless. You can read the Latin. Together we can figure out how to beat it. We can both gain the ultimate knowledge." Her hand tightened even more on my arm. I nodded. She was right. Jane was making things harder. She certainly wasn't helping us figure out how to get out of this. Still, I felt shame growing. I had promised my friend.

Jane was slumped in defeat against the guillotine wall, eyes red. I estimated ten minutes until the wall crushed us. After only three, the two headless corpses came into view, seeming to slowly crawl towards us out of the darkness.

"Jane, we were talking," Paige started. I felt my pulse quicken. Were we really going to do this? Drag her screaming to the hole in the wall and sever her head?

"I know," she sniffed. "I know you think it should be me. You're right. I'm nothing without Neil. Just promise me you'll wait a bit longer. I'm so afraid." She burst into tears. She wasn't going to try to fight us off.

"Jane," I said. She simply stood, waiting. "Just check if there's writing in this one." She hesitated but still did it, placing her head into the hole. I felt my legs start to tremble, but the wall was getting too close. I had to stick with my decision.

Paige pulled the lever. Jane's body twitched slightly then fell with a thud to the dusty ground. I heard the now-familiar sound of the head rolling into the hidden wall cavity. Blood spurted out against the wall.

I grabbed Paige's arm and we kept moving. I glanced down, reading the Latin message revealed by the receding wall and scrawling it on the paper, just in case. But I wouldn't forget.

Only one will gain ultimate power.

The rumble of the wall behind us continued. Of course, we came to another wall. Like the previous walls, this one had exactly the same guillotine hole.

"If there is another wall after this one, then we're both going to die anyway," Paige said.

"It sure looks that way," I said.

"Why don't you read the inscription?" she suggested. I started forward, and then stopped. She was right next to the lever.

"I think not," I said.

"Oh, come on, Martin, I wouldn't do that to you!" She looked genuinely hurt. I shrugged.

"You don't seriously think that one of us is going to gain ultimate enlightenment down here, do you?" she asked.

The rumble continued behind us. The wall was coming.

"No. I think we are both going to die down here," I said.

"The choice now is death by beheading or crushing," I said. "So let's think, at least make sure we haven't overlooked anything." I pulled the paper out of my pocket and we studied all the earlier clues again.

"The weight of six referred to the six people being present to start the trap," Paige said.

"Wait a second," I said, then read the words on the page aloud.

"So? I don't get it," Paige said, looking back. We could make out a small hand, rolling towards us out of the darkness. The headless corpses of our three friends were coming, on their slow but sure course, to meet us. The headlamp was getting dim. I didn't like the thought of one of those lifeless hands finding my leg in the darkness. I changed the battery while I spoke.

"The weight of thought," I said. "If the first line refers to the weight of six people, and it was some kind of massive scale we were standing on, then—"

"The weight of thought means the weight of a head," Paige said excitedly. "A human head weighs eight pounds."

Bingo, I thought. She must know that because of her background in archaeology. But why didn't she mention it before?

We scrambled to figure out a way to reproduce the size, shape and weight of a human head. We didn't have much to work with.

Paige went to the bodies. She returned with Jane's canoeing jacket.

"This is waterproof. We can fill it with liquid, equivalent to eight pounds. Tie it up as round as we can. We have resources," she said, gesturing toward the fully clothed bodies inching into the light.

We used Michael's full one-litre water bottle. I used a scrap of paper to figure out the conversion. There are 2.2 pounds in a Kilogram. 3.63 litres is precisely 3.63 kilograms, which is just a little over eight pounds. So we needed exactly 3.6 litres.

I won't regale you with the gruesome details of how we achieved our weight target. But, with great difficulty—and nausea—we got what we needed from the available sources.

When we were done, the bundle was as round as we could get it. I held it upright, to reduce the chance of liquid leaking out. We both took a breath. I reached my arm in and rolled the makeshift head down the tunnel. As soon as my arm was out, Paige pulled the lever.

The seconds passed. We crouched in a terrified mess, screaming as we joined the bodies of our friends in one gruesome mash. I closed my eyes.

Then suddenly we were tumbling through. It had worked! I shone the light on the floor.

To enter you must make the ultimate sacrifice.

This time we ran. I didn't bother writing down the words. Paige asked me about the inscription, her breath coming in ragged gasps.

"Just more religious nonsense," I said. "The ultimate sacrifice."

We came to the final wall. There were two guillotine holes—and two levers.

"I don't understand. It wants two heads now?" Paige cried.

When the bodies appeared at the edge of the light again, I knew we wouldn't be able to replicate another head. Without my knife to use to actually chop up bodies, we couldn't produce anything heavy enough, no matter how desperate we were.

The ultimate sacrifice. One must pull one's own lever to pass the final challenge. But how could one know if the levers would always do the same thing? A really brilliant designer would find a way to randomize the risk of death. What sort of trick was it? I desperately began consulting classical literature in my mind. Lost in my most intense thought, I heard the grind of the approaching wall as if its reality were merely a distant storm.

Then I felt something else. Paige had stabbed me, and before I could even react, she had done it twice more. I guess she had kept a knife on her this entire time, without telling anyone. I could see the logic here: it's easier to behead a corpse than a living person. I was slightly hurt, but it was ultimately a prisoner's dilemma scenario and time was short. Although I might have volunteered to die by beheading rather than crushing, I was not ready to give up. So I overpowered my last rival and placed her in the position she had intended to place me in: a dead or mostly-dead stooge for an ancient madman's trap.

After a few moments, the mechanism sprung and the door began to roll. Paige's body tumbled forward, her blood spraying the moving wall. I slipped through the crack, hardening my heart. I remember telling myself then that I had no choice. I had just been doing what was necessary to survive. There was another inscription.

The weight of heart.

This was a repeat from one of the earlier lines on the ceiling, before the heads of my four friends had been removed and neatly drawn away into the recesses of the mysterious stone tunnel.

This time, the passage began to descend. The wall behind me had ceased moving at exactly the point where the final wall had opened. My fear of being crushed dissipated. But a new fear took hold: fear of the unknown. My legs were heavy, like metal blocks. My heart thumped like a drum. I walked downwards. Onwards.

After some time of winding passages, I came to a vast chamber. The room was filled with a strange blue light. I couldn't make out the source; somehow, it seemed to come from everywhere deep in this dark ancient temple. Obelisks and statues populated the room. In the incandescent glow, I was sure that they were creeping and dancing behind me when I couldn't see them. An ornate walkway led to the far end, where a final gigantic statue stood. As I approached this place, toward which all the other ornate architecture pointed, my feet stained the dusty grey stone with the mingled blood of my friends.

This statue was at least ten feet tall. It was in the shape of a man, but with the face of a horrible beast. I shivered just looking at it. There is no animal that would make an apt comparison. On the ground in front of the statue, these words were carved:

The heart must be given to free the soul.

I contemplated this. There was a cavity in the chest area of the statue. One of the carved arms held a long, sharp, golden knife. Was I supposed to cut out my own heart and place it inside? Was it another scale? After sitting forever in that unspeakable place, among the whispers of some forgotten age and held in the deafening silence of the statue, I figured it out. I thought of going back and cutting out Michael's heart. He was the one I least respected.

I stood and placed the heart neatly inside the empty cavity. If I had to, I could get others. I was a survivor, and there had to be a point to surviving. But as I listened to the first true silence in that bluish gloom, I wept. For the first time I considered my dead friends the lucky ones.

Then, there was a click from inside the statue.

The rest is foggy for the human part of me, so mingled are those final memories with the sensations of Our Awakening. But I do remember the room filled with blue light. I felt every inch of this body as though it were on fire. There was a deep laughter that rippled me with fear, though I was conscious of the fact that it was also my own laughter. I floated up into the air, and down into my new body at the same time. I felt my human soul torn apart and then remade. Moments before, I hadn't believed in the soul. Now in one searing but endless instant of terror, it was destroyed and sewn back together. Different. My flesh seemed to boil, my lungs to explode. My skin burned. But there was also the most supreme ecstasy, a quivering of every fiber that made a lifetime of orgasms seem only faded memories of vaguely pleasant sensations. A soul had been freed...but it was not Martin's. Even now, as I record this narrative, the memory of it is stirring the demon. I fear I won't be able to write much longer as Martin. Soon, it will wake. I must hurry to finish this. I feel it quaking in the dark space between the body and the beyond, held there beneath skin, bone, and soul, waiting to travel forward to feed.

I woke up on the forest floor. Changed. Possessed. I could feel the demon inside me, its essence melded to mine, endlessly hungry for endless sacrifices.

Long ago, I travelled back from those woods and I brought it with me. We indulged in horrendous crimes. It was easy: no one cared as we moved, wraithlike, through the dark underbelly of Winnipeg. I can only hope to write honestly now because, after all the blood and horror, the demon has grown quiet. Many of my victims still decompose in shallow graves along murky shores. I—We— have also shared certain important knowledge. Evil contaminates.

I have wormed my way back into society. I, or we, still kill often. Blood is necessary. But it has become sensible to disguise the connection between our crimes and this fleshly vessel. Perhaps you have read of some of our exploits. Perhaps we still stalk the streets of the place you call home. Perhaps we occasionally visit your part of the world, to taste of its delights. Perhaps one day we shall meet. But I no longer look like the Martin that went missing years ago. *What are we doing, Martin?*

After my possession, we were flooded with knowledge. Knowledge so deep and great, that some nights it made Martin cry with awe. Knowledge and power beyond Martin's imagination. We could read minds. We could see into the future in the curve of a glass or the corner of a cracked mirror. Our body would regenerate when injured. This is why Martin didn't bleed out in the first place. *But I wish I had.*

Over time, the horrors of sharing the same body and the same soul with a demon have proven trying. I am tired of watching people die, crushed in our grip. I—Martin—grew weary of feeling the blood course out over my teeth and down our throat, even while I drank it as if it were fine wine. I know that this body as host will someday be exchanged. It will corrupt, use and betray me, as it has done so many others. I've tried many times to end our life. It's not possible. But the demon loves pain and gets stronger every time I try. When the demon rests, I find myself often thinking about the final inscription:

The heart must be given to free the soul.

If only I had the courage then, to take that blade and cut out my own heart. Then, Martin would have died along with Michael, Neil, Paige and Jane, and my soul would be free. But now I am a prisoner of this demon.

Another confession, Martin? We take a special pleasure in making Martin remember his friends and how they died.

PAST THE GATES

Dustin Geeraert

> Much strangeness is in flight, and mighty fetches have
> come hither to us.
> I heard them whisper in the dark, I hear them still
> in the gray.
> —*Hrolf Kraki's Saga*

I

Conrad floated up through the ceiling, through the next apartment, and out into the freezing air above the building. Darkness
had descended for the season and the snowbanks towered well past
a person's height. No cars moved; it was very late. High above the
city streets, he drifted toward the deserted downtown. Skyscrapers
of stacked cubicles gazed down on the century-old churches that
huddled together against the cold. *It's amazing how real this all seems.
The buildings seem geometrically consistent. Maybe if I hadn't wasted so
much time studying architecture, I'd find the inevitable inconsistencies.*

He could feel the winter air, but the pain was abstract, irrelevant.
Maybe I can find the bus Aaron is on. He floated to the edge of the city;

it looked like a huge circuit board. Over the outskirts and toward the frozen fields he flew. The dark plain extended in all directions; speckled with blue and beige prairie lights, it looked like a flat photograph of space. He saw tiny headlights moving on the highway far below. *Maybe that's his bus.* Then something changed. *Hello,* a voice said in his mind. *I am the earth. I am the sky.* Suddenly, he was torn down from the sky with sickening speed. Crows cackled as he spiraled out of control and everything turned red.

———•◦•———

Conrad awoke with a jolt. Sirens screamed outside. It was still dark, but pulsating red light flooded into his apartment from the courtyard outside. He squinted through the blinds. *The street blocked off, an ambulance, and cops all over the place.* He sighed. *This city.* As if to add to this unwelcome commotion, the heater started rattling away. *Damn old buildings.*

Conrad walked over to the window on the other side of his apartment, away from the lights. He picked up a filthy old bong from the floor and set it on the desk, put a few pinches in the bowl, lit and inhaled. In the window, he saw his gaunt face lit by the pale firelight that snaked through the smoke and glass. *I need to shave.*

He exhaled a large cloud, which ghosted its way up the windowpane and dissipated in the darkness above. *At least the ceiling is high.* Low ceilings made him claustrophobic, and in a city where the craggy snowbanks loomed like miniature mountains and the darkness pressed down like a huge weight from above, any relief from claustrophobia was welcome.

A few more hoots and he set the bong back down. *I wonder where Aaron is right now.* Conrad pulled up Google Maps, looked at the city from above, and tried to zoom out to look at the highway system outside of the city. As he zoomed out the city got smaller, but nothing else appeared, everywhere else was a mere blank grid. *Lost in infinity.* The city could seem huge or tiny, but apparently there was no world outside of it—no countries or continents.

My internet seems to be working about as well as my heater. Fuck it. Conrad shut his computer. Now that his reflection no longer appeared in the window, he saw only flat blackness. *Maybe this city has finally gone back to whatever abyss it came from.* As his eyes adjusted, the snowy maze of walls and windows outside reappeared. He got up and walked over to his bed. As always, changing positions was a good sobriety test; he felt relaxed and even amused. *Whatever. Perhaps now I'll be able to sleep and fly around in my stoned dreams a bit more.*

———•••———

It was still grey outside when a loud static sound startled Conrad awake and a man's voice came through. "—that's just highway robbery, plain and simple," the man was saying. *Sure it is.* Conrad leaped up, switched his radio alarm off and walked to the window. He could see pigeons fighting over garbage while a squirrel watched from a nearby tree.

He put coffee on and showered quickly. He poured a cup full, dropped whiskey into it, and dressed. He slurped at it while checking his email. There was one new message. The subject line read, s.o.r.e.p. *New Fee Assessment.* "Greetings Comrades," he muttered, "chocolate rations have been increased." But the email said nothing so direct; instead, it read:

> As you know, the Strategic Optimization and Resource Enhancement Plan has been enacted with the intention of improving our institution in every way. For the sake of optimum efficiency, our Plan Optimization Committee has recommended numerous funding reallocations regarding areas

of redundancy. Some of our much-appreciated employees may experience workload reductions, while others may find themselves open to exciting new employment opportunities in Marketing, Finance, and Administration. In the coming weeks, our dedicated staff will explain the fuller details of primary aspects of our Strategic Plan to your Departments. For now, please see the links below.

The links led to websites full of smiling, professional-looking people. *Translation: no work next year. Yet somehow, Administration has the money for those projects they're building out in the corporate park, and the kind of security they have out there can't be cheap.*

He had recently received another email from University Admin looking for volunteers to be "Test Subjects" for a program he had never heard of before. Supposedly, it was psychological research on lucid dreams, so he would probably make a great "Subject," but even poverty couldn't compel him to volunteer for that. *That's got to be a military contract or something. Look at what happened with the Unabomber and MK-Ultra.* Conrad finished his coffee, threw on a bulky winter coat, and stumbled down the creaking wooden stairs. In the alley behind the building, a man was grabbing bottles out of the bins and putting them in a shopping cart, which could hardly be steered through the ice. *At least it's Friday. I am so going to bed after work.*

After work he slept for an hour. After cleaning up, he microwaved some leftover Chinese food, drank a beer, and cleared a path through the laundry and empties. He looked outside; there were still police officers milling around the building. *I hope they're not around when Aaron gets here.* Conrad snuck away and took a circuitous route to the bus stop to avoid being seen. *At least every hallway in this building smells like a different kind of weed, so they can't target me specifically. So what if my lifestyle is a train wreck, I'm not hurting anyone.*

Fog had settled on the city so that the tops of buildings could not be seen save for the lit windows. This gave the curious impression of windows into another world, suspended high in the void. The bus was late, as it always was during blizzards. Snow swirled around the streetlamps, flowing down from the darkness above into the weak mauve light below. Finally, after his mind had falsely interpreted many distant lights as buses, the real thing appeared out of the gloom. He stepped in and saw a young man energetically airdrumming. *What the fuck.* In the middle of the bus, an old man was wearing a gas mask. *He must know something I don't.* Conrad sat in the back of the bus, with his toque down and his coat collar up. Although it was early in the evening, a guy sitting at the back of the bus offered him a swig of vodka. He happily obliged.

By the time he got to the Greyhound depot to pick up Aaron, the snow crews had started to work. The depot was filthy and dimly lit, full of sad-looking old people and sketchy-looking young ones. An old lady asked for help using a vending machine. Conrad helped. He had time, since the Greyhound was late—no surprise there. He made polite answers until she mentioned Jesus. Then he excused himself, went to the window and stared at the empty lanes.

Finally, the Greyhound pulled up, exhaling exhaust into the winter night as Conrad waited. His head hurt as he watched a parade of persons emerge from the vehicle, none of them his friend. Finally, off stepped the man he had been waiting for. Aaron Lyall was of medium height and muscular build, with the shadow of a beard, blue eyes, and close-cropped hair.

"Did you get any sleep?" asked Conrad.

"Crying kids, laughing teenagers, some idiot on a cellphone, another idiot muttering to himself, so not really" replied Aaron. "Let's get out of here."

"I brought bus fare for both of us," said Conrad. It shouldn't be more than a twenty-minute wait, so we'll be back within an hour. Plenty of time for pre-drinking."

"Fuck that," said Aaron, gesturing toward a line of cabs out front and pulling a stack of bills out of his coat. "I got this."

"If you've got money like that, why not just fly?"

"Not allowed on any planes, remember?"

The cab driver wore a turban and a full beard, and was smiling benevolently as they approached the cab. Conrad gave the driver the address but Aaron rode shotgun. *I hope Aaron doesn't make any unwelcome comments; he's not exactly known for his cultural sensitivity.*

But Aaron and the driver seemed to be getting along well, breaking into mutual laughter several times. Conrad was still tired enough to start nodding off even though the cab was periodically flung up and down by the city's many potholes. Suddenly the car slid to a halt on the icy road. "This right?" asked the driver.

Conrad looked around. "Yeah." He pulled himself together, got out, and walked around the cab to the sidewalk. His breath floated upwards, dissipating into the void.

Aaron had gotten out of the car and still had his head inside the passenger's side window. "Fuck the war in Afghanistan, y'know" said Aaron. "Leave people alone, how hard is that?" He shook the driver's hand and dispensed a hundred dollar bill as he did so.

"Hail, friend!" said the cab driver enthusiastically, and drove off.

"So how you been?" he asked Aaron.

"Same as ever," Aaron shrugged. "Fucked up, having fun. I was thinking about it and I maybe even made six figures last year, but I still always have nothing."

"Did I ever get into the wrong profession," said Conrad.

"Where's your building?" asked Aaron, looking around at all the huge, run-down old houses, brick walls, fire escapes and oddly-shaped little parks with overflowing garbage bins and used furniture sitting around. There weren't a lot of lights on.

"It's close," said Conrad. "We can walk from here." He led the way over to a little park. They sat on the jungle gym smoking a joint and drinking from a flask, as if they were teenagers again. On the picnic table there was a tin can for butts; it was chained to the table. Squirrels scuttled up and down the trees, chattering and insulting one another. A crow atop a street lamp squawked loudly enough to echo across the street, declaring itself King of this polluted tundra.

A huge and misshapen building loomed in front of them. It was built of red brick with many old world village – style extensions added on and wooden stairways clinging to the sides, leading to various levels. The steep metal roofing was turquoise, and at one end of the building there was a round tower, like a castle. On one of the alley-facing walls, all the windows had been bricked in and the entire wall had been painted this same shade of dirty turquoise, a colour so ugly it must have been mixed maliciously or satirically. There was a doorway two floors up that had not been bricked in—the metal door, painted dark red, was still there. There was graffiti on it: an asymmetrically curving nine-pointed star with eyes in the centre. *A talented artist*, thought Conrad. *I couldn't produce that and once upon a time, I was pretty good.* Out front, the patios and Victorian porches were full of snowbanks and smokers. A neon green sign hung above the main entrance: *The Poisoned Chalice.*

"What's this place?" asked Aaron. "Looks like they had no plan, just kept building shit on whenever they felt like it."

"It started as some robber baron's mansion, then was converted into rental lodgings," said Conrad. "I think eventually the party just never stopped, and now it's a pub. Kind of dingy but lots of fun."

They walked into the front hall. It was dark and stairways led up and down in every direction. "Looks like a maze," said Aaron, squinting into the gloom.

"Follow me," said Conrad. He knew the place well, but he also had an intuitive understanding of the layout of buildings. This was helpful in a city made of tunnels and skywalks, where many old buildings with unorthodox layouts had been converted for new use. As a failed architect, Conrad had a rare ability to rearrange three-dimensional objects in his mind and still excelled at the geometric components of IQ tests. Eventually they reached a room that looked out on a deck and the alleyway beyond. Aaron had little sense of direction and lost his bearings in the building, which seemed even bigger from inside than from outside.

It was dim and dingy, and everything looked worn out. The floor was dirty and perhaps had looked good in the 1970s. The old wooden chairs were missing support bars, and the tacky green tables had holes torn in their coverings. It looked like someone had raided a cheap antique store or an auction that was held when an old hoarder died. There were awful paintings on the wall and under some of them people had scrawled captions in black marker. One showed a ship frozen in ice at night and underneath it said *Witness, you ever-burning lights above, You elements that clip us round about.* Another was a Mona Lisa that had been vandalized in many ways, including a Hitler moustache. Beneath that, someone had written *Oh What A Piece Of Work Is Man.*

By mutual instinct, they chose the dimmest corner in the room, near a ratty old pool table and shielded from view of the doors by a divider. "So," said Aaron as they sat down, "this is where you hang out. Real classy." *He can't really judge,* thought Conrad. *Sure, he's burned through money in upscale restaurants and exclusive clubs, but he's also scraped together money to get shitfaced at the kind of places where the beer is cheap, the floors are sticky, and someone gets stabbed every other week.*

It was still early, so a waitress was there before they knew it; a young woman with a nose ring and a lot of tattoos: bats and snakes, it looked like, in purple, black, and a dark green that matched her eyes. Her blonde hair was so chaotic and complicated that it reminded Conrad of the illustrations of looping roads and bridges in Dr. Seuss books. "How's it going, guys?" she asked.

"Interesting place," said Aaron, his arms on the table, tattoos of the words LIFE and DEATH visible. "Dark and scuzzy."

"Well, it might not be classy," she smiled, "but we like it. What can I get you?"

"How's the special?" asked Aaron.

"No one's complained yet," she replied.

"Okay, I'll get that."

"Me too," added Conrad. Outside, red emergency lights flashed.

The waitress arrived soon with their food: two mushroom burgers with chili. They ordered one last pitcher and the bill. Conrad ate while Aaron went to the bathroom. He came back more energetic and talkative. "I noticed that the pisser is a giant trough, classy for sure." Aaron devoured his food in a manner that would be physically impossible for most people. Now the table held only empty glasses, crumpled napkins, and flecks of gravy. "Nice graffiti in there, too. *It's All Lies!*"

Conrad laughed. "Some of the patrons in this fine establishment are a little crazy. Not me of course, although it is *mostly* lies. Sorry for being kind of out of it. I'm just tired."

"There's solutions for that," said Aaron, mischievously.

"I don't need to deal with shit any more, I don't want to be up for days, have problems with cops, or hang out with dealers."

"Well you already lost there," said Aaron, chuckling as he took a bag out of his coat.

"What the hell," said Conrad. "You took that on the bus?"

"Nope, got it from the cab guy."

"So you were in town for less than half an hour when you got coke."

"Friday night, why not?"

"God damn it, if I'm going to poison myself I need to do it quietly and privately! People might not care what you do, but I have to seem respectable."

"Sure, sure," smirked Aaron.

"I'm not sketchy," said Conrad defensively. "I work for the university. Never robbed anyone for drugs."

"It's early, this room is empty. They won't care, I mean look at this place. I'll bet you've smoked weed on that deck right outside there!"

"Okay, but that's different," Conrad sighed. "Besides, this table's gross."

"Well, that's why I've got my trusty reading with me," said Aaron. He placed a thin book on the table; the cover said *Jim Morrison— American Night*.

He began dropping powder onto the book and dividing it into two lines. "Happy Valentine's day," said Aaron, snorting a line through a rolled-up bill.

"Ah, well," muttered Conrad, "what is this quintessence of dust, anyway?"

Just as Conrad was halfway through the line, the waitress returned to the room. Conrad put his head back up and put the bill in his jacket as quickly as he could.

"Sorry," said Aaron.

"Sorry for what?" the waitress asked, setting the pitcher on the table.

"Just... sorry."

"Oh, I don't care if you do coke at the tables," she said. "Yeah," she added sarcastically, "never seen *that* before."

"Want any?" Aaron inquired, handing her more than enough money to cover their tab.

"Maybe next time," she said.

"There might not be a next time," said Aaron. "Never know. Could be the apocalypse."

"If it is, I'm sure it will start here. It's the last place people would ever expect," she replied with a knowing gleam in her eyes. "See you around."

Outside, sirens howled, a dissonant symphony of dysfunction.

II

They walked away from the downtown and through a winding avenue of old riverfront houses, many of which could only be seen in silhouette behind their imposing walls. The fog was thick; the globe-style street lamps and Victorian iron fencing gave their route an archaic, eerie atmosphere.

When they reached the river, they ducked under a bridge, then climbed up its cement base and stood in the sheltered space halfway from the ground to the lanes. The cement they were standing on was covered in cigarette butts, pigeon shit, broken beer bottles, and used condoms. They could hear pigeons cooing. "Jesus," said Aaron. "Imagine the people who fuck up here."

"I'd rather not," replied Conrad. Another joint followed and they emptied the flask. "Come on, we're close to my place."

"Just a second," said Aaron, taking a last pull and passing the roach to Conrad. Aaron stood quietly, with an odd, dejected posture that was unusual for him. Traffic passed above their heads. Looking up between the two separate lanes of the bridge, they could see the huge cross atop the nearby hospital. It was lit up the colour of blood and jutted above the city lights, suspended in sheer darkness. Finally, he said, "I have to ask you a favour."

"Name it," replied Conrad.

"I'm not going back; this isn't just a vacation. I need to stay with you for a while until I get my own place."

"What happened?" said Conrad.

"I'm not even sure," Aaron replied. "A week ago I had a really bad blackout. I woke up with a lot of blood on me."

Conrad laughed. "Not the first time."

But Aaron didn't laugh. "I think I really fucked up this time. People have been following me. Sometimes I'm not even sure…"

"Of what?"

"Take the cab driver I bought from earlier. We were joking around, but I could swear he knew me or had seen me before. Maybe someone gave him my description."

Conrad sighed. "Honestly, I don't know what to say. You just got here. You're worried about the first person you meet in this city being connected to… enemies, of yours?"

"You never know. Even some of the people in that bar we were just at were looking at me when they thought I wasn't watching."

"Do *you* ever know if you're justifiably paranoid or just on a bad trip?"

Aaron paused. "Not really. You ever feel like this isn't actually real? Like we're just in like… a fishbowl, or one of those little Christmas globes full of fake snow?"

"How could you tell?" asked Conrad. He tried not to snicker at how conventional it was for this subject to be discussed by the heavily stoned.

"I don't know. But sometimes it just seems like *this* can't be real."

"I don't accept *this*. But I don't know how we could discover anything else."

"I always thought certain people came from somewhere else. Especially you."

"Shit," Conrad said. "I'm just another lost soul."

"I think I'm losing it, man," Aaron said, shaking his head. "If you only knew the half of it..."

"You can tell me tonight, but let's get out of this evil weather," said Conrad. They leapt down onto the snow and climbed the stairs up to the bridge.

When they arrived at Conrad's street, it had been unblocked and cleared. A shopping cart was jammed into the street side of the bank, wheels up.

When they reached Conrad's building, they saw that a woman was standing outside smoking. She was about their age, perhaps a little older. She had dark hair, hazel eyes, and was wearing a long grey coat and black boots. "Conrad?" she asked.

"Yeah," Conrad said. A crow's call echoed through the courtyard.

"We met out here last time there was a fire alarm."

"Right, you're... Sylvie?"

She laughed. "Good guess. Sophie. What are you boys up to tonight?"

"Drinking is the plan. Probably going to go out pretty soon, but we were going to go up for a drink first just now. Want to join us?"

"Sure," she said.

"This is Aaron," Conrad said. Aaron nodded. The three of them climbed the broken outdoor stairs carefully. Inside, Conrad said "Sorry, it's still a mess." Down the hallway they went; he put on the light in the main room. An old couch and some ratty chairs were still covered in laundry and there were empties everywhere. He looked back to see if either guest was horrified. Sophie looked nonchalant and Aaron was smirking.

"Well," he said, clearing off the table except for his bong and weed, "welcome to the sty. Come on in, get high."

"I can't smoke that," said Sophie. "I don't care if you do, but it makes me paranoid."

"Fair enough," said Conrad. "I'll grab some whiskey; hopefully I can find clean glasses."

He returned and poured three stiff drinks. Aaron had already filled up the bong and lit it, gesturing in Conrad's direction before he'd even set down the bottle. As Conrad exhaled a nebula-like cloud that lingered beneath the broken fan, he saw that Aaron had tilted back his entire drink. Aaron gave his trademark smirk but put on a serious face to say, "Make sure to smoke weed when you drink whiskey, otherwise you'll be a violent drunk." He laughed, a lucid yet maniacal look in his eyes.

Luckily, Sophie didn't seem intimidated. She wasn't even backing away from the weed cloud, and had made reasonable progress on what Conrad had intended to be a significant drink. *No point offering a drink and then pouring a shitty little one.*

Sitting down, Conrad asked Sophie, "So, what do you do?"

"I'm a shaman," she said.

It might have been the weed, but Conrad laughed. "Sorry, are you messing with me?"

"Oh no," she replied, leaning forward. "I'm for real. I'm going to a conference of shamans in the city here next month. Biggest one on the continent." A bunch of pigeons swooped near the window, making a noise that startled the two stoners, but Sophie didn't jump.

Those filthy flying rats are like my pets. Well, them and the real rats. And the silverfish. Sometimes I talk to them, but they never talk back. Speaking of shamans, why is it even possible to get rich telling people their dead pets want to talk to them? At least Aaron can justify the money he makes dealing by the risks he has to take. But I guess we're all fellow travellers, rats, silverfish and pigeons alike. Breaking the spell of these reveries, Conrad asked Sophie, "So do you shamans just compare out of body experiences, then, or what?"

"You don't believe?"

"Believe in what?" replied Conrad, answering a question with a question—a tactic he favoured when stoned and trying to annoy people. Aaron finished the bowl in one giant hoot.

"Everything," she said. "Those we can communicate with, our past, our future."

"I don't know what to believe," Conrad said, finishing his drink. "Usually when I hear spooky voices in my head it's because I'm stoned or dreaming or both." *But instead of milking it, I just ignore auditory hallucinations, as any sane person would.*

Apparently, she wasn't easily threatened by skepticism. "You seem educated," she said. "But you don't know much about the most important things at all. You are... misinformed."

"*I* am misinformed!" He stopped himself before launching into a rant. Aaron was always telling him that it was a good thing to have other people come into his apartment. *Or you just shun the world and stew in your juices.* "Come on," he said, having reconsidered his approach. "I've had lucid dreams, even some that seemed like out of body experiences. What people who believe in spirit powers often don't know is how powerful the brain is. For example, right now there is a blind spot in the centre of your vision that you do not notice because your brain predicts what should be in that spot so instantly and convincingly that you can't tell where the edges are or even that there are any edges. I've had visions, talked to some 'spirits' of people who are gone, even heard other voices—but they are all generated by my mind and memories. I'm definitely not ignorant."

Sophie was silent for a moment, but Aaron was used to hearing this.

"Where did the voice come from?" she inquired.

"From above, from below. Everywhere at once," Conrad said. "It defies acoustics because it was a dream. It shows that the source of the voice was in myself."

Aaron had begun refilling the bowl. "Pass me that," Sophie said. Aaron was visibly happy to oblige, and once she sparked the bowl she inhaled more than either of her conversation partners. "The spirit gets weak over time, just like the body," she said. "That's why I'm worried. It won't be easy for me but I think it means something. People like you think you know everything, but I can *show* you that you're wrong."

Conrad laughed, but tried to make it sound good-natured rather than disdainful. "I know that I know very little. Significantly less than everything."

The blinds were open and the light was on. Suddenly, the darkness outside seemed especially intense. Conrad asked, "Do you think I should close the blinds or turn off the lights? We seem too visible."

Sophie said, "If the sense of protection helps you. But that's purely on your end. You're becoming frightened, both of you, because outside spirits are being attracted here."

Aaron was quiet.

"If you say so," said Conrad.

"I'm ready to do a demonstration."

"Of shamanism?" he asked.

"Of the powers that we have and the powers that surround us," she replied.

"If you can demonstrate *that*, why don't you go on TV and make millions?"

She paused. "That would attract unwelcome attention. Those people have all made deals and few of them are as protected as they think. Some of them are hardly human anymore."

Great, Conrad thought. *Conspiracy theories on top of supernatural nonsense. The two go together, I guess; at least she's creative.* "I couldn't agree more," he quipped. He closed the blinds, poured himself another drink. "So what are you going to do, spoon-bending? How about I go in the other room and write down a number, and if you tell me the number I'll give you $100, or rather Aaron will since he's not broke."

"I'll do better," she smiled. "Go outside and walk to somewhere nearby, but out of sight. Stand in front of an address for five minutes. When you come back I'll tell you the address."

Conrad laughed. He looked at Aaron. "Don't drink all the whiskey while I'm gone."

He got down the stairs and jogged for ten minutes, then cut across the street and went two blocks. The huge Victorian houses loomed around him, lights mostly off, a few windows leaking out a blue glow. He stopped in front of one that seemed especially dilapidated—its porch covered by a tarp on two sides, the windows boarded up, a yard full of broken garden gnomes, dead flowers and damaged flower pots with frozen dirt spilling out. He could just make out the number on the front of the house: 1042. The fence was broken and an old trailer sat out back. *Deliverance, prairie style.* No lights were on.

Conrad decided to mess with Sophie's plan. He walked back up the block and into the back alley, behind the trailer. He jumped the fence and started wandering around the back yard. He saw a woodpile, workbench, and some old tires stacked against a wall. All of this was beneath a balcony, also with tarps and sheets hanging, softly swinging in the winter wind. Hammers, saws and other tools hung on the wall. *Lots of work to fix up this piece of shit.* Then he noticed an old-style angled cellar door and felt an odd curiosity. *Have I been here before?*

The old wooden doors creaked and groaned. *How gothic.* He descended the steps. There was no light except the cold haze of the streetlamps floating down through the snow. He stepped forward; the whole basement floor was frozen with inches of ice, like some demented underground skating rink. *That'll be hell to clean up in spring.* Old furniture was stacked all around, tilted or fallen, and children's toys were frozen into the ice. Toy ponies and fairytale books ripped and tattered. He smiled to see a book he knew: *One Fish, Two Fish, Red Fish, Blue Fish* by Dr. Seuss. But the dolls were eerie. Dolls everywhere, all with the same unblinking blue eyes and vacant smiles. Many of them had the clothes torn off, some had limbs torn off and others had moustaches or genitals drawn onto them. *Puberty at the point of a black marker.*

At the end of the room, an empty doorframe beckoned. It was almost totally dark, but a little yellow light leaked through. He nearly slipped on the uneven ice but grabbed an overhead pipe. A dark space opened up ahead, and he saw that he was in a huge room with wooden pillars and bare walls. Debris was everywhere: toys, chairs, an old bicycle, bottles, tools, crates, wood. The light was coming from an old furnace stove at the end of the room. A couch and coffee table had been set up in front of it, as if in parody of a cozy living room. There was a sleeping bag on the couch. On the table were a half-empty bottle of whiskey, a huge machete, and an old book with yellowed pages. *What kind of crazy fucker lives here? Who sits on this filthy couch drinking whiskey and reading this shit?*

Conrad sat down and picked up the book. No title was printed on the binding so he looked inside. *The Ways of the Hidden Ones.* *Guardian Press*, 1919. It was signed: *Keep the world safe for democracy* (*or just safe*)—H. H. The table of contents said *Prehistory, History, The Present Situation,* and *Known Methods.* He turned to a random page:

> The Old Ones were, the Old Ones are, and the Old Ones shall be. Not in the spaces we know but *between* them, They walk serene and primal, and unseen to all but the Wise. The Wise know where They tread upon earth's fields, and why no one can behold Them as They tread. They walk unseen and foul in lonely places where the Words have been spoken and the Rites howled through at their Seasons. The wind gibbers with Their voices, and the earth mutters with Their consciousness. Their hand is at your throats, yet ye see Them not. Behold, Their habitation is even one with your guarded threshold, for many are the gates. Ever shall the Wise hear Them speak in dreams, for They choose of each generation the Prophets who shall prepare the glorious day of Their revelation.

Conrad knew religion when he saw it. *Invisible spirits, ghosts, gods that people need to worry about and pay an organization to deal with on their behalf: a tax on credulity.* Something about this passage, though, struck him as different. *This sounds more occult. Then again, it's not like mainstream religions make sense or aren't creepy.*

Conrad took his roach out and lit it. He burned his fingers a bit trying to get one good puff, but after that everything seemed less worrisome. He put his feet on the table. He browsed the book, impersonating a respectable gentleman of 1919 with his mannerisms, imagining himself in a suit, smoking a pipe, and reading the Bible by the fire. *Oh yes, precisely my good man, Civilization, most certainly! Shall we have a whiskey, sir? Indubitably!*

He nodded at the room and drained the bottle of someone else's liquor. Then he realized his hypocrisy: *Who sits on this filthy couch drinking whiskey and reading this shit? Me!* Conrad laughed and laughed. The scary schizophrenic wasn't some fifty-year-old Unabomber-type—it was him! *Quite certainly, sir!* The whiskey had warmed him, and having seen Aaron, the only person he truly trusted, had warmed his mood. His laughter echoed back from the darkness.

Then he heard a different noise, a sort of scraping. He froze. He could hear his own breath, see it puff and dissolve in front of the fire. Somewhere in the darkness, it was getting louder. Conrad actually grabbed the machete and crouched behind the couch, weapon in hand.

A glint of something pale appeared in the shadows. A naked little doll was walking toward the fire, its cheeks rosy, its permanent smile perky, its eyes an intense hazel colour. Its jerky motions reminded Conrad of a mechanical mockery of the military goosestep. Each time one arm and one leg rose and fell, he heard the strange scraping noise.

"Fuck you!" he shouted, leaping over the couch. He used the machete more like a bat than a knife; in a single hit the doll's head was separated from its body, which fell on the ground and continued jerkily moving, its arms and legs moving as if it wanted to go somewhere. Conrad hacked the still-moving limbs until the doll's body was a collection of broken fibers and flimsy plastic. Then he picked up the pieces and walked back around the couch.

"Into the furnace you go," he said with a crazed smile as he fed the doll to the flames. *Damn, I'm drunker than I thought.*

"You tried to trick me," a woman's voice said from the darkness. For a moment he was unable to process what he was hearing. "You tried to betray me." He recognized the voice. *How the hell could Sophie get here so fast?* Her voice seemed to be coming from everywhere at once, from the darkness all around him.

He crept across the ice, weapon in hand, listening intently. He only had to get through the next room and outside again. He entered the main basement and sighed with relief: the entrance was still open, and soft mauve light could be seen upon the stairs.

He sprinted for the stairs, leapt the fence, and ran for blocks. When he stopped at an intersection to get his bearings, an old man asked him, "Spare any change?"

Without thinking, Conrad brandished the machete. "Fuck you man, I've got problems!" he shouted, running away like one of the city's many paranoid squirrels.

Crows followed his hasty retreat, squawking and mocking.

III

Conrad burst into his living room. He was still holding the machete and set it down on the table. Aaron was sitting at the table drinking and nodded when he saw the weapon. Sophie was sitting back silently, her eyes closed. She appeared to have passed out. *Hopefully she just wakes up. Why did I agree to this?* He loaded up the bong and was about to light up when her condition changed.

At first, she just murmured in her sleep. *Think logically, not emotionally. Sure, she's kind of cute, but she's also crazy and a problem. Distance yourself.* He took a large drink from the bottle. Then Sophie started to twitch. At first, the tremors were small, but soon her whole body was thrashing from side to side, her head flung back, incoherent noises flowing from her mouth like a river of nonsense. *Damn it, speaking in tongues is the worst! Is this what I need to deal with?* Then he stopped himself. *Don't be hateful. She needs help, this looks like a seizure!*

With these better thoughts, he approached her and said loudly and clearly, "Sophie, can you hear me? It's time to wake up." He tapped on her shoulder; still she displayed no sign of comprehension.

Who knows what kind of liabilities there might be if she suffers a medical emergency in my apartment. He hated himself for even thinking that, but one financial disaster would crush him. *Asking her to demonstrate her altered-state mental powers sure was a great idea!*

He didn't know what to do. He put his arms under hers and lifted her up, saying helplessly "Come on Sophie, wake up." Her eyes remained closed and she showed no reaction. "Fine, you fucked with my head real good," he said. He held her up for a moment and then let her go. She slumped back into the chair; now she seemed to be having some kind of attack and was even spitting or foaming at the mouth. He put a pen in her mouth to stop her from biting her tongue. "God damn it," he said. "I'm about to call 911."

Suddenly her hazel eyes opened. Her expression was lucid. She calmly drew a tissue from her purse and wiped the spittle off her face. "Sorry," she smiled cutely. "Didn't mean to fuck with your head *too* much. You think us shamans are all just epileptics, right?" He was still standing. "It's not my fault if it doesn't take much to mess with you," she said. "Your class of personality is usually a bluff, so it's hard to tell where to stop."

Conrad was surprised to find that he had tears in his eyes. "You are one weird woman," he managed.

"Ah, you're a pushover," she said, giving him a tissue from her purse. "Here. The eyes are the windows to the soul, you know. Anyway, the address was 1042. You picked a creepy place for sure."

"That doesn't... prove anything," Conrad tried to assert.

"Don't bother," she replied. "No one can hide from us." She turned to Aaron, who had been drunkenly relaxing in the corner. "Not even you, Mr. Lyall."

Aaron's demeanor changed instantly. He grabbed Conrad and dragged him down the hall, to the other end of the apartment. "What the hell's the problem?" Conrad asked.

"I never told her my name," Aaron said. He looked into Conrad's face.

"You're getting paranoid again," said Conrad. "Calm down a bit."

But Aaron's expression only intensified. "People know I'm here," he said.

"No one knows you're here except me and Sophie," replied Conrad. "She doesn't know you. She's a nice person. A bit deluded, maybe, but she means well."

Now Aaron turned his whole body and grabbed Conrad's shoulders. "Then how did she know my name?" he hissed. "I thought you would be the last person to get tricked. Jesus."

"What the fuck?" asked Conrad.

"I'm probably fucked, there's probably nothing I can do," said Aaron. "I never wanted this. She's part of it. You have to kick her out. She can't be here while I'm talking about this. Or I could just leave. I don't want to put you in danger so if you want I will leave right now. I was never here." He started pacing back and forth. "Fuck," he muttered to himself.

"Look," said Conrad, grabbing Aaron's shoulders. "We go to the gates of hell together. I'll help you bury bodies. We are brothers in arms no matter what."

"Not the gates," said Aaron. "Past the gates. You should let me go, or you'll regret it."

"Past the gates," replied Conrad, "In that case, I happen to have some Kentucky Moonshine." He withdrew a large jar from the freezer, took out glasses, and poured. The smell was immediately apparent. They drank.

I don't know if I can calm him down. Haven't seen him like this in a long time. He decided the first thing to do was get Sophie out of the apartment, for her own safety. "Come on Sophie, I want to talk to you," he called down the hallway.

There was no answer. They went back down the hall. "What in hell," said Conrad. "This apartment's not exactly huge. I could hear my last roommate brushing his goddamned teeth. If she was here, we would know. How did she leave without us noticing?"

Aaron had an expression of utter paranoia. "Maybe you weren't paying attention."

"Are you saying," inquired Conrad, "that she opened that door and stepped out, right past us, and somehow we never noticed?"

"All I'm saying is I'm not surprised. You think someone like her can be easily trapped?"

"God damn," said Conrad. "Am I the only sane one here?"

"No," replied Aaron, and they both laughed. Then they drank more moonshine and scowled in disgust.

"Out with it!" Conrad said. "Explain our damnation!"

"Isn't that your job?" said Aaron.

That instant there was a pounding from the apartment door down the hall. Conrad whispered, "Oh *shit*." *Maybe a noise complaint or even the cops after this morning.* "I'll take care of this," he told Aaron. "If I have to leave I'll call as soon as I can." He turned off the lights, leaving only the entrance light on and the living room light—where the bottle was, even where the bong was. *They will assume this is what I want to hide, and that I was too stupid to hide it. They will look in that direction, not toward the kitchen.*

Conrad took a deep breath, smoothed his shirt, wiped his face, and opened the door. "Yes, is there a problem or can I help you?"

A tall man made even taller by his huge military-style boots stood in front of him. He had a goatee and grey eyes. His dark attire made him instantly recognizable as a policeman. *Well this is unfortunate.* He peered down at Conrad from just below the doorframe, silently.

"Was my music too loud?" asked Conrad. "I'll turn it down."

The large armed man was smiling as he said, "Oh no, it's not about that. No problems tonight. Just wanted to talk to you—you're Conrad Torben, right?"

Conrad's heart sank. *God damn.* "Yes, yes," he said. "About what?"

"There was a murder here the other night. We have been interviewing everyone in the building, and you're one of the last. This won't take long." Conrad stepped forward and was about to close the door behind him. "No," said the officer. "I need to come in. No one can overhear us."

"You mean, you suspect someone in the building?" said Conrad. "Jesus."

"I mean we can do this here," said the officer calmly, "or downtown, as they say."

"On a Friday night, seriously?" blurted Conrad. *Play naïve, that's what you are.*

"Not exactly one for civic responsibility, are you?"

"I'll answer whatever you want," said Conrad. "I know you guys have a difficult job. But like… don't judge my Friday night, y'know?"

He turned and stepped backward. "Sorry this place is such a shithole," he said, gesturing toward the living room. "I clean up on Sundays."

The officer walked toward the light. He ducked under the old-style hallway door and saw scattered chairs, a shelf full of random keepsakes and empty bottles. There was laundry on the floor and an open 40 sitting on a table next to a dirty bong.

"No judgment here," said the officer. "Nothing unusual for this building."

Was that sarcasm? Conrad was almost offended. He sat down, and the officer sat down across from him and took out a notepad and pen.

"Were you in your apartment on Thursday?" he asked. "In fact, if you could just tell me about your last 48 hours, we could get this over with quickly."

"Well, Thursday I was at work all day, and after that I went to a bar. I got home before midnight and went to bed, but I couldn't sleep. Then the sirens woke me up. Today I was at work all day too, got back around six and had a nap," he explained. "Woke up a couple hours ago, figured, hey, it's Friday night so I might as well have a drink."

The cop glanced around at all the empties, but let that one pass without comment.

"You couldn't sleep last night," said the cop. "Is that because you—"

He stopped speaking instantly. Aaron was behind him and had the machete at his throat.

"*Jesus* man!" hissed Conrad. "You're fucking us both over, don't you see that? Why not just let him go, *we didn't even fucking do anything*! He said something happened Thursday night *you weren't even in the city*! Why can't you ever calm down!"

"I *am* calm," said Aaron, with an insane look in his eyes. "He's here because of me, nothing even happened here Thursday, but I need to send *them* a message."

The officer was trying to appeal to Conrad with his eyes. Despite the logical side of his mind, he found the power reversal satisfying. "*Them?*" Conrad asked. "Who, the CIA? None of us is that important, no one wants to hunt you down, there's no cosmic war or grand conspiracy." He found the weed bag on the floor and loaded up the bong again, right in front of the cop. *Probably the only chance I'll ever get to do something like this.*

Aaron had the cop's weapon arm clamped quite effectively. Smiling serenely, he started applying the tiniest amount of pressure to the man's throat using the machete.

"Admit it," he said.

The cop's eyes moved up, as if he could see backwards, as if it would help if he could. He was out of moves. "What do you want me to admit to?" he choked out, trying to move his head back away from the blade but only hitting Aaron's chest.

"Just admit it."

"I can't admit what I don't know!" the officer tried to shout, as loudly as his neck's limited expandability and mobility would allow. "I just came here for an interview! I have a family! I'll let you go if you let me go, I don't even know who you are!"

Aaron's expression did not change as he remarked, "None of that is true. You did not come here for an interview. You do not have a family. You will not let me go. You *do* know who I am. In fact," he smiled crazily, "you came here because of me. *Now admit it.*"

"I can't even *see* you," said the cop. "All I was told was that there was probably a murderer in the building, that's all anyone was told, the evidence showed that."

"The Evidence," said Aaron, "indicates to me, that you came here alone, not in a police car, that you have never worked for a police department, and that until I make an example I will *never* get rid of pieces of shit like you." He trembled with rage and the machete trembled too.

I won't be able to play innocent witness, Conrad thought. Nevertheless, he smoked a bowl and blew it in the cop and in Aaron's faces. *Maybe they'll both chill out a bit. That demon weed might save a pig's life. But I need to do something.* "Okay," Conrad said, careful not to name his friend. "Relax the blade. At least don't kill him without even meaning to. I *do* trust you, but why don't you let *me* conduct an interview, you need someone more objective to figure out how we can fix this situation."

Conrad stood up and grabbed the 40. "Shot?" He drank. "Nod carefully if you're interested. I know I'd be, in your position. But hell, I'm interested anyway." Nevertheless, the officer was able to make enough of an affirmative motion that Conrad poured a significant whiskey down his throat as his Adam's apple gently rode the blade.

"Now," said Conrad, moving his chair close to the large, armed man who was now helpless. "He and I are both going to jail if we kill you."

"I am not going back to jail," interrupted Aaron. "Ever."

That was a dumb thing to say. Conrad continued, "But you are going to die first if you lie to me. Answer each question quietly and truthfully. Then you will give my friend a head start, and after enough time that I think he is safe, you can take me in, but I won't name him."

"Why would you still assume he's a cop?" asked Aaron.

"Well, he's wearing a uniform," replied Conrad.

"That's, what would you call it, *superficial*."

"Okay," said Conrad. "Did you come here to track down a man from another city?"

"No," sputtered the man. He was trying to control himself, but he was trembling. *God it feels good to be on the other side of the power dynamic, although to say that this will cost us is like saying that World War II was a polite disagreement.*

"Are you actually a city police officer?" asked Conrad. Aaron's eyes gleamed with righteous joy. He obviously thought that the moment of truth had arrived, after all his paranoia.

"No," the man said.

Holy shit, thought Conrad. "Then why do you want to know about the murder here? There was a murder, right?"

"There was a murder, but it wasn't random. It was targeted, or that's what the cops thought. That's why they called us."

"They called one guy, in a shitty fake police uniform, who showed up alone and let himself be taken at knifepoint?"

Even though the machete was as close to his throat at it had ever been, the man now squirmed indignantly and raised his voice. "What kind of budget do you think we have? Enemies of our world live among us even here, yet you sneer at those who guard you while you sleep."

"So even the vanguard of saving the world is subject to budget cuts," laughed Conrad. "But what do you mean? Guard us from what?"

"None of us knows, exactly," said the man. "The knowledge is too dangerous to understand. It has to do with dream states, separating spirits and bodies. There have been experiments. A few people have tried, with the best of intentions, but the test subjects never… come back the same."

Conrad laughed. "You might be part of a secret organization that protects us from invisible threats. Or maybe you're just delusional! Sign any million-year contracts lately?"

"We aren't going to *ourselves* possess the dangerous knowledge that we are dedicated to eradicating," said the man, sitting up in his chair and flexing his arms in an expression of anger, despite his better judgment. "What do you think we are, hypocrites?"

"Okay, well let's get to the point here. You aren't a police officer, and this doesn't have to be a police matter. I don't know anything— although I'll admit, I'm curious. My friend here doesn't know anything either, even if he thinks he does. He's just paranoid. He's had problems with police before and it's been a long day. You didn't come here for him. He doesn't know you and you don't know him, so we will just walk you to the door and pretend this never happened."

The man looked relieved. But before he could answer, a different voice interrupted. It seemed as if time had frozen. Out of the darkness, a woman's voice said "He"—Aaron started moving the blade— "came here"—blood spurted out of the man's throat as his body fell forward—"for *me*." Then time returned to normal and the man in the uniform had slumped forward, twitching as blood lurched in swift streams from his neck.

Standing behind him in shock, Aaron's arms were covered in blood. *This must be another nightmare, how can this be real?* Conrad was looking at Aaron's horrified face when suddenly his vision went black. He felt warmth pressing up against him and he realized that his eyes were covered from behind. "Guess who!" Sophie said.

"Sophie," he choked. She removed her hands. "Where were you?" he said.

"Hiding in the closet. Hiding under the bed," she smirked mischievously. "I can easily pass unseen."

She is insane, Aaron is insane, I am insane, and this is not happening. "It's my apartment, so both of you have the best chance of getting away with this, as long as we get rid of the body quickly and the one who is left stonewalls the fuck out of them. We don't need to sacrifice all our lives. But we have *no* time."

"How noble," said Sophie, sliding past him into the light. "It's fine," she said to Aaron, who was so frozen with fear that he hadn't even moved. Blood was running down his forearms and dripping off his fingers. He seemed entranced, outside of his own power. "I am not your enemy," she said. "I can protect you both. Make this go away."

Aaron was no stranger to the sight of blood, but this was different. His movements were jerky, as if he were a marionette. He looked at his arms confusedly and moved them as if in a sort of test. He dropped the bloody machete on the floor near the bleeding body. He still seemed unable to understand what had happened. Nothing enraged him more than the idea that he had been tricked or used; it took his mind a moment to shift gears, and he shouted, "You made me to do this! You tricked me! It's you who's after me, not him! He was innocent!"

"You did the right thing," said Sophie.

"This fucks me. This wasn't right."

"Well, if you're feeling upset, you can always go back to heroin," said Sophie.

"What do you know about that?" he said, still in shock.

"Not as much as you," she said, hazel eyes sparkling. "This isn't the first body you've abused, and it won't be the last." Then she straightened. "Look, let's stop fucking around. You only have one way out of this and that's through me. Otherwise you're done. But if you give me a chance, I can fix all of this. I have powerful friends."

Aaron had numbly walked to the bathroom; Conrad could hear the water as he washed the blood off himself. Sophie took off her shirt, picked up the machete, and casually started sawing the head off the corpse. Conrad noticed a tattoo on her shoulder that looked familiar; it resembled the nine-pointed star he had seen at the Chalice.

Blood was getting all over her arms, but she managed to keep her bra clean. Conrad was so shocked that he could hardly move. Finally he croaked, "What are you, an expert at disposing of bodies? You a fucking serial killer?"

"I'm a shaman," she said. "I'm a spirit warrior. And this head is worth something." Her work had unleashed a tide of blood all over the chair in which the man had been sitting and the laundry around that area; it had splashed on the furniture and the wall, and was pooling on the carpet. *Jesus, it's going to be like a damned wading pool.*

Still in her bra, Sophie walked to the bathroom. Aaron had just finished washing himself off and was standing there shirtless, staring at nothing. He had several tattoos, which Sophie stopped to admire as she walked by. Aaron saw the tattoo on her shoulder and asked her, "What's that?"

"The Sign of the Hidden Ones," she said.

Aaron returned to the living room, clean of blood. "Can I borrow a shirt?" he asked, carefully stepping around the headless corpse. "Actually give me two." Conrad complied, but Aaron used the second shirt to pick up and wipe off the machete, hooking it through his belt.

"Great idea, carrying around a murder weapon," protested Conrad.

Aaron pointed out, "We at least need to get rid of it." But then with a knowing look, he said, "She said something about 'the Hidden Ones.' Those are *demons*, I've read about them online. I'm not walking around unarmed tonight." Conrad realized all of this was somehow connected to the book he had seen earlier. *Better not mention it; it will just make Aaron even more paranoid.*

Sophie returned and put her clean shirt back on; she looked just the same as before. Now she placed the man's head in her purse; it fit snugly and her purse did not leak. *She seems like she knows what she's doing.* Sophie grabbed a large blanket from Conrad's bed and used it to wrap up the corpse. "This is purely for your end of things," she said. "If things go well, you won't need to worry about anything. We're just going to turn the lights off and walk out."

"So you're not going to help us clean up or dispose of the body," said Conrad. "Why the hell should we come with you?"

"I'm the only one who can help you," she smiled. "I'm going to introduce you to someone who can make your problems go away. Abban. He's kind of the king around here."

"Some foreign fucker is king here?" asked Aaron.

"That was a metaphor," Sophie explained, as if she were responding to a question about the official political status of monarchy in the New World. "We're not limited to anywhere in particular; spirituality transcends all cultures."

Aaron grabbed Conrad and said in a low hiss, "We can't go with her. She's got powers."

"No one has powers!" Conrad protested. "Only tricks, even if we don't understand those tricks. Either we trust her this once, or it's probably jail for life. Shouldn't we at least try?"

"I don't trust her, or anyone associated with her," Aaron said. But he stepped back.

"Where are we going?" asked Conrad.

"Your favourite place," she responded. "But look guys, you can't fuck around there."

"Never do," said Aaron sarcastically, raising the bottle and taking a huge drink. Conrad finished it, then they smoked a bowl and did a line. Aaron was so wasted it looked like his face was falling off, and he had a crazed look in his eyes.

Sophie walked to the hallway and put on her shoes and jacket. The two men put on their shoes and their jackets. She moved toward the door. They followed listlessly, mechanically. She started down the stairs. Conrad waited for Aaron to leave the apartment so he could lock the door. As Aaron walked past, Conrad could see that he had the machete in his coat. It was freezing on the stairwell and they could see the full moon blazing red in the blue midnight sky.

"Fuck the hidden ones and the king of shamans too," whispered Aaron, his bloodshot eyes looking like they were straining to escape from his head and bits of cocaine visible under his nose. "I'm not going down without a fight."

Conrad followed silently.

IV

They had entered the Chalice through a side or back way; it was hard to tell, given the odd contours of the building and the fog. In any case, it was an entrance that Conrad had never seen before. He recognized some general features of the place inside, but felt totally baffled by others. He tried to deduce where the rooms and hallways he was currently occupying could be, given what he knew about the building's floors which he often visited. But no matter how he rearranged the pieces of the puzzle in his head, he could not make the layout of the Chalice fit. It was as if he had entered an entirely different building that simultaneously occupied much of the same space as the Chalice he was used to. *There has to be an explanation for this.*

As they followed Sophie through these dark and twisting corridors, they were themselves followed by men who had obviously been hired for their size. They went up some tightly winding stairs and emerged into a large hallway with several different exits. On the left was a raucous bar scene, full of shrieking and shouting. On the right was a dark red door with a nine-pointed star full of eyes painted onto it. The guards here were even more imposing.

Their waitress from earlier walked through the hallway carrying a stack of empty glasses and just about dropped them when she saw Conrad and Aaron with Sophie. She looked worried. "Hi guys," she managed. "Didn't know you knew the boss."

Sophie opened the red metal door with the painted sign. Neither guard moved a muscle. She stepped into the darkness. Aaron stepped forward confidently. The guards did nothing. He had angled his jacket well and kept his posture natural. *Either these guys suck at their jobs or he's a genius.* Conrad brought up the rear. They walked through a strangely tilted dark hallway, like a madly extended entranceway to a plane. *Perhaps we're just too wasted to walk.* Suddenly they brushed through doors and lights confused their vision.

Straight ahead, there was a stage. On the stage, a twenty-something woman had the mic, with a few young men behind her playing ambient jazz, all of them wearing pretentious hats. She was reading "an autobiographical poem," which was apparently about plastic bags, dating, and phones. *Modernism never dies.*

They had a panoramic view. The place was packed with people dancing, talking, standing in circles. Every table was full. They all pretended not to notice the newcomers and Conrad pretended back, but a few people nodded to Sophie, and Aaron flashed threatening looks at each person who met his eyes. There were decks, there were galleries, the place was a massive arena of intoxication on three floors. *How is this layout possible?* Conrad wondered numbly.

Totally clashing with the modern décor and entertainment, many huge tapestries hung on the walls, shimmering in the electric light and moving ever so slightly. Aaron stopped for a moment as Sophie made her way through the crowds ahead. As Conrad caught up, he said quietly, "There's guards everywhere. Don't look, but behind each of the wall hangings there's a space big enough for a man. They're all pitch black but I'll bet there's guys with guns in there. I just need one chance, so when I make my move either back me up or get out quick."

Conrad nodded and saw what Aaron meant: behind one of the tapestries, depicting a glittering purple dragon, he thought he saw a shadow move. *This is sketchy as hell.* Huge weapons hung on the walls—axes, swords, halberds, the blades glinted in the sparkling light of a giant disco ball. Down more stairs they finally reached the stage in the main area.

Sophie was now a ways ahead of them, approaching a table full of people. There were people from all walks of life. One middle-aged man was dressed like a respectable farmer, complete with a cowboy hat. A tall black man in a suit looked like a businessman; another man was in full traditional Hindu garb with a full beard. *Is that the cab driver from before?* One young woman was dressed in punk style. There was a pint at every place and there were two open spaces beside Sophie; she looked up at Aaron and Conrad.

With nothing else to do, and obviously surrounded by security, the two of them walked to the table and sat down at the two empty seats. Aaron moved quickly and switched his pint with his neighbour's pint. Thinking again, he then reached over the table and switched this new pint once again. The other people at the table didn't react; Conrad switched his pint too.

Sophie lifted her pint and said, "Skål." The twelve people at the table clinked glasses; Aaron and Conrad finished their drinks. Immediately the ladies and gentlemen there began clapping them on the backs, offering shots, handing over chicken wings. *Why are these people so friendly?* Conrad kept up a good appearance, but Aaron's mistrust was clear.

They looked over toward the stage and saw a man sitting alone at a table. His pale eyes were fixated upon them. He was a huge man whose fat had outgrown his frame. His black leather jacket made him seem even bigger than he was. A crow was perched on one of his shoulders, a pigeon on the other. His skin was puffy and there were dark circles under his eyes, which were so pale as to be almost colourless. Rusty red curls spilled from his head, and his huge shoulders puffed out as he raised a glass toward the newcomers and his birds fluttered up into the rafters.

"Don't betray me," Sophie said. Then she walked down into the pit and over to the red-haired man. She bent over to his ear and said something, motioning toward Aaron and Conrad. She waved them over. Aaron slowed for a second to let Conrad pass ahead of him, saying quietly "I *am* going to kill him. Run if you can, I'm fucked for sure. Just wanna send a message."

With every step they took toward the man, the lights flickered. It got dimmer, so dim they could barely see his face. As they approached the stage some people were still dancing; the woman was singing and the drummer was playing, even though most of the instruments weren't working properly and the best the rest of the band could produce was distortion.

Walking down the stairs, Aaron stumbled and tripped; only someone as agile as him could have landed with a machete in his coat and neither impaled himself nor even revealed that he was armed. Conrad tripped over him. The lights flashed on while they were still on the floor; there was a needle on the ground mere inches from Aaron's face.

Aaron leapt up. Conrad wasn't so much helped up as launched into the air by a huge man with a beard and long hair. *Jesus, this guy's got arms like tree trunks; he looks half a giant.* Silently the thug motioned toward the table near the stage, where the red-haired man waited with a strange smile. The lights were mostly out, but staff were lighting candles on the tables and torches that hung on the walls. Aaron and Conrad made their way through the pit to the table by the stage, where Sophie waited with their mysterious host, now looking all the more sinister in the glare of a guttering candle.

Sophie gestured for them to sit down. "Gentlemen," she said. "This is Abbadi Abban."

The man smiled at them even as they saw that one of his eyes was lazy. "I've heard good things, gentlemen. I've heard you have a gift for me and there may be something I can do for you in return." His voice had an odd, musical quality to it.

"One thing is for sure," Conrad said. "We've got a problem. Sophie said you could help us."

"So long as you're serious," said Abban.

"We don't have much choice, do we?" said Conrad, while Aaron glowered.

"I suppose not," said Abban. "Unless you would prefer to deal with the formal authorities. But it's best for us not to talk in front of all these people. Follow me."

He rose and walked around the side of the stage. Sophie followed him. "Come on man," said Conrad. "Let's get this over with. If he can't help us we should start dealing with shit on our own as soon as possible."

Abban opened a small door, behind which a stairway yawned. It was dark but some slight firelight wafted up from around the corner of the base of the stairs.

The basement was huge. There was a fire blazing in a furnace in front of a couch, with a few chairs scattered around a coffee table. The floor was covered in ice and strands of mist were swirling around. Abban sat down on the couch and put his feet up on the table; Sophie put her purse on the table and sat beside him. Conrad walked over to a chair and sat down, in shock. "I've... been here before," he whispered. "But... I came in a different way."

"Yes you did," said Abban. "Sophie used the demonstration to lure you here; you found this place because we wanted you to."

She shrugged and smiled. "Sorry about the doll, that's just a little trick we do. I can teach you how to do it; you've got good natural projection abilities. You're already half a shaman."

"Each time you came here," continued Abban, "you entered through a different way. This place is one of several that intersects with your city at whatever point we wish it to."

"Bullshit," said Conrad. "That's impossible."

"Your understanding of metaphysics is like your understanding of architecture and geometry: a useful model, perhaps, but with little relation to higher realities. I've been to Their world, though not in this body of course. Their servants stand to benefit greatly upon Their glorious return. For those who reject Them, however, They have... different ideas."

Conrad shook his head slowly, his eyes burning with stress. "And people call *us* insane."

Aaron was still standing at the base of the stairs silently.

"Don't be shy, Mr. Lyall, come over here," said Abban. "I believe you have something of mine."

Aaron snapped into action; he tore the machete out of his coat and brandished it at Abban, who didn't seem worried. "Let's reason together," he said calmly. "You think I am one of 'Them,' the mysterious people responsible for your troubles. Yet where have your beliefs gotten you—here, in such desperate straits as this, in fact. And now you have murdered a police officer. The next time you are arrested will quite clearly be the last."

"*You're* the one who's set people to chase me all these years," shouted Aaron. "It was you all along! *I said no before*, I don't want any of this!"

"Perhaps we've been watching you," said Abban. "But no one is chasing you, Mr. Lyall. Even the police aren't chasing you, for the moment."

"I didn't mean to kill him!" shouted Aaron, with the agitation of a maniac who could endure no further provocation. "He wasn't even a cop, and I wasn't even in control! You made me, or *she* did!" he gestured with the machete at Sophie, who smiled calmly and gently kicked over her purse so that the man's head rolled out and fell onto the ice with a dull thump.

"Indeed he was not a police officer," smiled Abban. "That is worse for you, however, rather than better. His colleagues are not the sort to put their enemies on trial, and they will assume you are working with us. It is well worth joining our side; in the long run we shall surely triumph. You can't use police methods, or even espionage methods, to fight the nature of reality. They only resist us because they don't understand the situation—by their own design, of course. Their errand is futile. But in the short term, they are dangerous. They will find you eventually; they have shamans as well. Some of them are very likely here tonight. Only I can protect you.

"You're right about one thing after all, Mr. Lyall," he said. "This world—this city, in particular—*is* much like a goldfish bowl. The rest of your beliefs, however, are malformed delusions born of drug-fueled paranoia. No wonder you accept whatever this pretentious cynic," and here he gestured at Conrad, "tells you. You haven't the faintest clue—no more than your father before you." *He'd better shut up*, thought Conrad, *this is one of Aaron's sore spots*. But Abban only continued in his smug way. "We watched him too, but he made too many mistakes for our liking. After all the people that came after him, for a man with his experience to get rolled in South America— it's pathetic. Still, it was merciful. A mine collapse would have trapped him the next month anyway, and he would have been much slower in dying then."

In an instant, Aaron had darted over to Abban and slipped the blade sideways between his ribs, up to the hilt. He had struck with such speed that no one could stop him. Sophie leapt back and Abban sputtered blood from his mouth. "Fuck you!" screamed Aaron.

Abban's head was lolling back and forth and he seemed like he was trying to speak, but only a horrible gargling noise came out. Suddenly they realized that he was laughing.

His movements were jerky and oddly mechanical as he lifted his arm, reached for the handle of the machete, and slowly withdrew it from his torso. He laughed louder as blood leaked from his chest and his mouth.

"Excellent work, Mr. Lyall," he sputtered, still laughing as he set the weapon down on the floor. "It can be hard to stay on top of your game when you're high all the time."

Aaron was in shock. "Jesus, this guy's fucked up," he said.

"This flesh is but a vessel," Abban smiled. "Even if you were to destroy it, *I* would not be harmed. You are brave and will do excellent work for me. And you," he turned to Conrad, "your position and gifts will allow you to provide us with much useful information. From your perspective your employer commits waste, fraud, and theft on a grand scale, but all of this is a mask for their *true* purpose: protecting the world, as they see it, by funding our enemies."

"Are you telling me," said Conrad, "that the people you are fighting against are intimately associated with my institution's bosses? *Those* ghoulish corporate suits?"

"That and more. All of their *enhancements, revitalizations,* and *transformations* are designed to finance covert actions meant to banish the Hidden Ones from our world. But this is futile; this is not our world and never has been. Their experiments with shamans defy their puny rationalist account of reality, and they will never approach the abilities of the truly initiated. They see themselves as tragic guardians, secret martyrs, but they are mere children playing at heroism." He wiped the blood from his face.

As if to prove that he was fine, he stood up and walked around the room. Conrad could see the huge hole the blade had made in the back of his jacket. *This isn't possible.* Sophie was leering at them triumphantly.

"So what do you say, gentlemen? Enter my service and fixing your situation tonight is the least I will do for you. You will learn things the likes of which you never suspected. You will achieve enlightenment and discover the wonderful Ways of the Hidden Ones."

Conrad suspected that they might not leave the basement alive if they refused. He shrugged and said, "Winston Churchill reportedly said, 'If Hitler invaded Hell, I would gladly shake hands with the devil himself.'" He shook Abban's hand, then looked over at Aaron.

"We've been banging our heads against the glass for a long time," he said. "Why not see what's outside the goldfish bowl?"

Aaron seemed to come back to life upon accepting the inevitability of it all. "Our lives are going nowhere," he said. "Not much to lose. Fuck people, y'know?" He shook Abban's hand.

"Now comes the initiation," said Abbadi Abban, a look of deranged joy on his face.

———·•·———

Hours later, they stumbled back into Conrad's apartment and walked down the hall to the living room. If there was ever a body there, it had been cleaned up one hundred percent. That and more—the room was spotless. The laundry was even done.

THIS IS WEIRD

David Annandale

I was once told that Winnipeg is unusual because it is, statistically, the Average City. I cannot confirm this statement, but it pleases me to think it is true. There is something agreeable about the paradox: we are the embodiment of an abstract conception of the common, and therefore something that does not exist. This is weird.

We are weird in our nostalgia, still muttering darkly about that damn Panama Canal ruining everything. We have great weirdness in our history, what with the spiritualist scene having been strong enough to draw Arthur Conan Doyle's attention. And we are also weird in our artistic tradition, a tradition that is carried on in this anthology.

But is there truly something inherently weird about the city? Or, more precisely, is there a particular flavour to its weirdness? I am hesitant to claim there is. This is not to say there aren't certain visible trends, or that we could not identify a cluster of works as belonging to, for example, the Prairie Gothic. But we must resist the totalizing impulse too, and be wary of attributing an inherent quality to the imaginative work emerging from a given location. I don't believe Winnipeg's literature of the fantastic can be nailed down or pigeonholed. Nor should it be.

This isn't to say we aren't influenced by our surroundings. Of course we are, and I think that is clear from the stories in this collection. But Winnipeg is not one thing. It is its history, its upheavals, its traumas, its struggles, its sins, its summers, its winters, its mosquitoes. The Average Writer is as mythical as the Average City. Winnipeg's writers are not the products of one collective experience any more than their literary formation consists of a single group of stories.

But again, I am not arguing that Winnipeg hasn't shaped the authors and the stories in this collection. Of course it has. Winnipeg is in the DNA of these stories, even if it is not explicitly mentioned, or necessarily the setting. But which Winnipeg, and how it manifests itself, varies enormously.

What also delights me about this collection, and another reason I am proud to be part of it, is the sheer number of stories here. This is not insignificant. Genre fiction in general, and horror fiction in particular, has had its share of struggles in Canada. And this is doubly true on the Prairies. When I was coming of age as a writer (during the Devonian period, I believe), an established author once exhorted me and my fellow apprentices: "You could write the Great Canadian Novel. Why would you want to write like Stephen King?" I recall enumerating many reasons because in my head. (Not to mention recoiling at the idea of the Great Canadian Novel.) It seems to me that the situation is rather different now. I have been struck in recent years by the growth of genre fiction on the Prairies and in Canada, in terms of both its presence and its range.

This book is, I believe, a reflection of that growth, but also evidence of what those of us who love the field already knew—that the landscape of the dark imagination in Winnipeg is a very fertile and active one. In that respect, I like to think this collection is also a celebration. Thank you, then, to Keith Cadieux and to Dustin Geeraert for throwing the party, and for inviting me to join in.

EDITORS' ACKNOWLEDGEMENTS

The editors would like to thank the staff at McNally Robinson Grant Park and everyone who attended the preview event for this project, "Hell Freezes Over," in darkest February 2015. We would also like to thank Bryan Scott, whose visual documentation of Winnipeg's strange architectural moments in *Winnipeg Love Hate* was inspirational for many contributors. Finally, we would like to thank all of the contributors. The project began as a form of venting, where we would discuss horror literature over pints while the winter winds howled with hostility outside. As we gained participants, it became more like group therapy. It's nice to know that we are not alone. As well, thanks are due to Enfield & Wizenty, for taking a chance on such an odd collection of stories. And thanks also to you, for reading.

David Annandale has racked up a fictional body count in the untold billions in his *Warhammer 40,000* and Horus Heresy novels and short stories for the Black Library. He is also the author of the horror novel *Gethsemane Hall* and the Jen Blaylock thriller series. He is one of the co-hosts of the Hugo-nominated *Skiffy and Fanty Show* and, with his academic hat on, he is a senior instructor in the Department of English, Film and Theatre at the University of Manitoba.

Jonathan Ball holds a PhD in English and is the author of five books. He also directed two short films, edited the journals *dANDelion* and *The Maelstrom* (which he founded), and writes the humour columns "Haiku Horoscopes" and "What Rappers Are Saying." In 2014, he won the John Hirsch Award for Most Promising Manitoba Writer. Visit him online at www.jonathanball.com, where he writes about writing the wrong way.

Eric Bradshaw was born in Pennsylvania in 1990, later spending significant amounts of time in New Jersey, Winnipeg, and Toronto. He is a classicist and avid reader, with a strong familiarity with fantasy and early 20th-century literature.

Keith Cadieux's 2010 novella *Gaze* was listed for a Manitoba Book Award and the ReLit award. His short fiction has most recently appeared in *Prairie Fire*, *Grain*, ELQ, and *The Exile Book of New Canadian Noir*. He lives in Winnipeg.

Nothing is known about **Richard Crow**. Jonathan Ball is the guardian of the Crow archives, which are online at www.TheCrowMurders.com.

Dustin Geeraert was born in Saskatoon, SK in 1983, and has lived in Winnipeg since 2007. He has a love-hate relationship with the prairies. He has studied Creative Writing, English literature and Icelandic literature at the University of Saskatchewan and the University of Manitoba. His Master's Thesis was on H. P. Lovecraft, and he is completing work on a dissertation about modern interpretations of medieval myths and legends.

Joanna Graham was born and raised in Winnipeg. She graduated from the University of Manitoba with a degree in literature and recently completed the Creative Writing MA in Prose Fiction from the University of East Anglia while spending a year living in Norwich, England. She is currently working on her first novel.

Christina Koblun is originally from Thompson, Manitoba (a place even colder and darker than Winnipeg), but moved to Winnipeg when she was 17 for university. She has an MA in English and has worked as an editor for two years. This year, she is at home taking care of her beautiful infant daughter.

Zacharie Montreuil studies literature while cultivating an interest in computer science at the University of Manitoba. He has called Winnipeg his home, to his infinite terror, for the entirety of his life. *The Shadow over Portage and Main* marks his first entry into fiction. His academic interests revolve around cybernetics, new media, and early modern English literature. His non-academic interests include "good" fiction, "bad" movies, "strange" podcasts, and "interesting" people.

Josh Gerard Moore spent his childhood moving all over Canada but has lived in Winnipeg for the last 20 years. He received his Master's degree in English in 2011, which he has since put to good use unloading cargo planes.

Daria Patrie is a delusion, agreed upon by society, that sometimes manifests during the process of reading. If you are reading this right now, you may be under the presumption that Daria exists. You would only be partially wrong. Some say Daria evolved from the leftover pasta sauce forgotten in the back of a second-year Physics student's fridge, emerging fully formed and blinking from the crisper drawer one rainy afternoon. Others say Daria is one of several humans possessed by the long dead and quite angry spirit of a three-legged alley cat named Pickleface. Still others say that long ago, Daria arose from a failed poet's recycle bin, the mountain of crumpled paper having gained sentience through a strange mutation of grammar, and that the fiction attributed to this "author" is in fact a misguided attempt by the abomination to locate its accidental creator.

Born in the Yukon but raised in Winnipeg, **Brock Peters** loves making connections between his Manitoban sensibilities and his multifarious experiences abroad. When not writing, he works in a bookstore, plays the double bass, and enjoys sitting on a bench in Munson Park looking out at the river as people amble past him with their dogs. He aspires to drink astounding quantities of coffee professionally. Find him online at brockpeters.ca.

Dr. Géza A. G. Reilly is originally from London, Ontario, and lived in Winnipeg for 15 years. He now lives in Tampa, Florida, with his wife Andrea and their cat, Mim. Géza completed his PhD dissertation on weird fiction in 2014, and its influence can be seen in his contribution to this volume. That story is his first non-academic publication in many years, and will shortly be followed by a novel-length project. In the interim, Géza works as an adjunct professor of English literature at a Florida university. When not writing or teaching, Géza thinks too much about cyberpunk science fiction, Lovecraftian horror, role-playing games, superheroes, and video games.

John Stintzi—a Winnipeg expatriate—is a writer of poetry, fiction, and book reviews. He's currently working on his MFA in Creative Writing at Stony Brook University in Southampton, New York. He was recently named a finalist for the 2015 William Richey Short Fiction Award (out of *Yemassee Magazine*) as well as *Epiphany Magazine*'s 2015 Chapbook contest for Poetry. His work can be found in *Lemon Hound, The Malahat Review, Los Angeles Review of Books, The Southampton Review, CV2*, and *Geez*. John can also be found ever-prowling and occasionally blogging on johnstintzi.com.

Jeremy R. Strong is a PhD student in the department of English, Film and Theatre at The University of Manitoba, where he studies 20th- and 21st-century literature and film in its intersections with public policy. He recently gave a TEDx talk on the importance of popular apocalyptic films and fiction. He has also published two articles that investigate the zombie as significant cultural artifact and has recently finished work editing an interdisciplinary volume of essays on the apocalyptic. He lives in Winnipeg with his wife Jessie and two children, Samantha and Quin.

Elin Thordarson is a Winnipeg-born writer and translator, working in the Children's Department of the city's largest public library.

Thoughts pretentious, odd and eerie
Haunting snowstorms, bleak and dreary
Echoing through the empty streets
Spirits that hide yet won't retreat
Careening through confused minds
Carelessly finding futile rhymes
In the dumpsters, amidst the dregs
Discarded by denizens of dim Winnipeg